1808: The Road to Corunna

Book 5 in the Napoleonic Horseman Series
By
Griff Hosker

Published by Sword Books Ltd 2014
Copyright © Griff Hosker First Edition

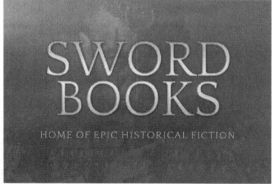

A CIP catalogue record for this title is available from the British Library.

Chapter 1

October 1807

Sergeant Sharp and I had barely landed from the '***Black Prince***' when we were urgently summoned to Whitehall. There was a young ensign waiting for us at the jetty when the sloop edged along the Thames to tie up at Westminster. Even the Captain of the ship, Jonathan Teer, who was used to the cloak and dagger operations of Colonel Selkirk, was surprised.

"I think it is damned unfair Robbie! Your leg has barely had time to heal."

I had been wounded in Denmark. Despite what Jonathan had said it did not bother me overmuch. I had been fighting since 1794 and my body still recovered quickly enough. The Danish war was over and we had secured the Danish fleet but it seemed I was needed once more. "It comes with the uniform Jonathan. Thank you for your hospitality and thank your surgeon once again."

"You are welcome and I dare say we shall meet again." The young captain had taken me on many such forays behind the lines of the French Empire.

Sergeant Sharp hoisted our bags above his shoulders as we made our way down the gangplank to the waiting carriage. We slumped back into the comfortable seats of Colonel Selkirk's coach. Sharp chuckled, "Well sir, we certainly get to see the world, don't we? I wonder where we are off to this time."

"Perhaps the colonel just wants to find out about Denmark."

Sharp actually laughed out loud this time. "No offence, sir, but I will bet a month's pay that we are being sent off again."

"It is hard to see where. Italy is now too far away for us to do anything about and Sir Arthur has dealt with Copenhagen and the Danes quite well."

Sharp looked out of the window and watched the Metropolis as it passed by his window. "I am just saying, sir!"

We had served with Sir Arthur Wellesley in Denmark. At first, he had been sceptical about us. He was a snob and had not liked my way of working at first. However, the results we had obtained for him had proved useful and he now saw the advantage in having a multilingual spy who could also fight. He had almost tolerated my presence which was unusual for the Irish aristocrat.

I had never wanted to be a spy. I served in the French army under Napoleon Bonaparte and it had been he who has used my skills as a spy first. However, I had been forced from France and I had fled to Britain, my mother's home. I had sworn revenge upon Bonaparte for he had abandoned my regiment to its death. Only one remained now, Pierre Boucher. All the rest had died in the sands of Egypt. I now served in the 11th Light Dragoons as a Captain. Colonel Selkirk, however, liked to use me and my contacts to spy on my former countrymen. It still did not sit well. It was not the French I fought but Napoleon whom I believed to be an evil man who would destroy my former country.

Sharp and I were familiar figures in Whitehall and especially in Colonel Selkirk's wing. We were whisked to his presence and our bags remained in the coach. Sharp was right. We were not going back to the regiment.

The dour Scotsman rarely smiled and so when I saw his grin and his outstretched hand, I was suspicious. The Nile crocodile has a similar look just before it ate its victim. "Ah, Robbie and the inestimable Sharp; good to see you. Sit down, sit down."

I knew him well enough to begin to work out where we would be sent. The map on the wall told me all that I needed to know. It was the Iberian Peninsula. I said nothing and waited for his opening.

"What's the matter, laddie? You don't look very happy to be here."

"I had thought to return to my regiment. We have done all that you asked of us and this sudden summons reeks of another foray on foreign shores."

He laughed, "Bright as a new pin! I can't fool you." I exchanged a glance with Sharp. Flattery from the colonel was always a bad sign. "You are right, of course." He stood and pointed to the map.

"Your old friend Bonaparte has decided to take over Spain. Now he might just intend to make the Spanish king his puppet," he shrugged, "I don't know but," he jabbed a finger at Lisbon, "Portugal is another matter. It is an old ally of ours and we have strong trading links. I need to know his intentions."

"I speak neither Spanish nor Portuguese. Surely there must be someone else you could use."

"Not really but you have skills and attributes I can't buy."

"Such as?"

"The Alpini wines." I slumped into my seat. Once again, my Sicilian family would become embroiled in the machinations of Colonel Selkirk. "Oporto is the centre of the wine trade in Portugal. It would arouse no suspicion if you went there to negotiate for some Portuguese wine and to sell some of your family's wine."

That made sense however it was not as easy as it sounded. "But I would need to arrange that with my cousin and we would have to wait for a ship to be here in London."

He smiled again and I thought immediately of the Nile. "Captain Dinsdale is in port and I believe you are a part-owner of his ship are you not? He is due to sail on the morning tide and Oporto is on the way to Sicily."

"Just suppose I did go there, what would you expect of me and how would I get the messages back to you?"

He rubbed his hand. "We are allies of the Portuguese; '*Black Prince*' will call in for some repairs. I am sure she will be damaged in the Bay of Biscay. It should not take you long; perhaps three weeks. Just find out what you can."

"But I would have to go to Spain too?"

"Where they also have wines! It's perfect Robbie."

If I did not know that the colonel put himself in harm's way just as much as he sent us, I might have resented his cheerful attitude.

I looked at Sergeant Sharp who gave a shrug and said, "I have never been to Portugal, sir!"

"There! And you needn't feel you are missing out for your regiment is still down in Kent. There is unlikely to be a need for them until the spring anyway."

That was where we differed. He saw the 11th Light Dragoons as a disguise. I saw it as my home. It was the closest thing I had to a home now. But he was probably right. I had been in action since I was sixteen; I would probably become restless if I was confined to barracks. "Very well then, sir."

He reached into a drawer and pulled out a leather bag which jingled. "I want you to sniff around. We both know that Bonaparte has people in place before he attacks. Seek them out. Find out about the land. When he does attack, we shall need to respond and you have an eye for terrain. Here are some expenses for you. Try to bring some back eh?"

I shot him a look which left him in no doubt what I thought of that. I would need the whole bag and then some more. It was fortunate that I had an income from the Alpini family and my share in Captain Dinsdale's ship also brought in revenue.

"My carriage will take you to the docks. I think His Majesty's Customs are examining the vessel at the moment." He was a devious man and I had no doubt that poor Matthew would have had to wait in port until the colonel decided he could leave. The colonel was a ruthless and single-minded man.

The *'Queen of Sicily'* was a fine vessel. It brought a steady income to me. I knew that it worked well for Matthew too, for he now had a second ship. When the war ended, he would be a wealthy man- if he was still alive. These were parlous times for captains who plied both the Mediterranean and the Atlantic. If Bonaparte captured Iberia then he would be in even greater danger. Bonaparte had introduced a Continental system which forbade trade with England. With Iberia in his pocket, he could slam the back door shut on that lucrative trade.

When we stepped on to the dock we were recognised immediately by the crew. They had recently taken us to Denmark. I saw the exchange of looks between the senior hands. They knew that we would be off again soon. The moment the Customs officers saw the carriage, they saluted Matthew and strode down the gangplank. Matthew shook his head as we stepped aboard.

"I take it Colonel Selkirk arranged the inspection?"

I nodded and held out my hand to shake his, "I am afraid so, sorry."

He shook my hand and shrugged, "Well, as they normally leave us alone, I suppose we should not complain. Our association with you is highly profitable. Where to this time?"

"You may sail back to Sicily if you wish, all we need is to be dropped off in Oporto. It is on your route back to Sicily is it not?"

He nodded, "And picked up?"

"No, Matthew, Colonel Selkirk has made arrangements."

"Well, the tide is about right. I wonder if the Colonel arranged that too? Mr Johnston, prepare for sea. Jenkins, take Captain Matthews' bags down to the guest cabin."

Sharp and I stood to one side. We had sailed with the captain before and we knew he would be fully occupied with the ship until we had left the busy waters of the Thames. As we passed the Royal Naval vessels, I saw Jonathan and I waved. I wondered if he had received his orders yet. I knew that I could rely on my old friend. It was getting dark by the time we began to head south through the Channel. Matthew had time for a pipe and I joined him. Sergeant Sharp was below deck, unpacking our bags.

"How long to get to Oporto?"

"It depends upon the weather but I expect a week, possibly more. The Navy has the French bottled up fairly tightly but I like to give the coast plenty of sea room."

"What can you tell me about the wine trade in Portugal?"

He looked at me in surprise. "You are actually doing business there then?"

"Possibly. I will need a case of wine as a cover."

He nodded. "There are a couple in my cabin. I find it helps to grease our way through customs." He tapped his pipe out and let the ash fall astern. "They produce some fine wines but not as good as the Alpini ones. They tend to fortify them with brandy. It preserves them and makes them very popular in Britain. They have a Madeira too which comes from one of their islands. But Oporto is the centre of their Port trade." He gave me a shrewd look, "You will find that many people understand English there."

"Good. And Spanish wines?"

"Not quite as good but they also fortify one, down in the south at Xerez." He was a clever man; he had survived blockades and the vagaries of many governments. "You are going to Spain too?"

"I may be."

"Then watch out. I heard a rumour that the French are casting greedy eyes over it." I gave him a questioning look and he shrugged, "We captains have an eye and ear not only for the weather but political changes too. Sea captains talk. Now that Boney has most of Italy under his heel it makes sense that he is looking west too."

"Thank you for that, Captain Dinsdale. I always keep a weather eye out for the French!"

Chapter 2

The voyage took just over ten days for the winds were against us. We prudently left our uniforms with Matthew when we went ashore at Oporto. I had spares back in England. I saw that the Colonel had been correct; our arrival was seen as not worthy of note. The Portuguese customs gave us a cursory inspection. The wine samples were viewed as necessary. No one gave us a second look. We were just a wine merchant and his servant landing from a Neapolitan ship. We both wore swords but our pistols were in our bags. We did not look out of place.

Once ashore I spoke Italian as part of my cover. We took rooms at a large hotel close to the town square. The gold from the colonel helped the illusion that I was a businessman. As I stood looking out over the harbour, I saw Captain Dinsdale as he conned his ship south. I was now trapped here until Jonathan Teer came for me. We would have to survive on our wits.

I quickly discovered that English was widely spoken in Oporto, especially by the wine merchants who had been dealing with the English for years. I affected an accent whilst speaking English. They saw nothing unusual in an Italian trying to buy and sell wines; especially a Neapolitan who were known to have close links with the English. The Colonel had planned well again and I learned a great deal. On that first full day in Oporto, I actually did some business. I arranged to buy some port from one of the older port houses and paid a deposit. It would not be ready until the following year; it needed more maturity than many of the Alpini wines. I would arrange for Matthew to pick it up. The Alpini wines themselves went down well, as I knew they would, and I took many orders for the wines. I promised that I would have the wine for them by the New Year. All of this meant that we were free, as November arrived, to explore the land closer to the Spanish border.

I had got on well with Charles who was the eldest son of one of the winemakers in Oporto. When I mentioned travelling east, he took me down to the river to counsel me where we would not be overheard.

"I have to tell you, Roberto, that it would be exceedingly dangerous to travel to Spain. The French are there and they have no love for you Neapolitans." He had lowered his voice as though there were French spies all around us, "I have heard that there is a French army heading this way. Perhaps you should take ship while you may."

I had laughed it off. I was playing the young Neapolitan who cared not a jot for danger. "I promise you, Charles, that I merely wish to see a little more of the country so, pray tell me, what is the best way to travel west?"

He had resigned himself to giving me the information I desired. "The river is the best way. We have some good roads close to Lisbon but up here," he pointed to the mountains which appeared to be precariously close, "there are only tracks." He pointed to some wine barges which were unloading their wares. "I will see if I can get you a passage on one of those when they return up the Douro."

"You are most kind."

Sergeant Sharp managed to buy two horses for I did not want to be tied to a barge for our whole time in Portugal and we boarded the next morning and travelled up the Douro towards the Spanish border. Conversation on the barge was limited. I had but a handful of words in Portuguese and they were mainly to do with eating, drinking as well as the usual *'please'* and *'thank you'*. We passed a ferry a few miles north of the port and that appeared to be the last crossing of the river until we reached the handful of bridges further upstream. The trip took two days and I saw few roads on either side of the river. The gorge rose high on both sides of the river. Charles had been right. When we reached Peso da Régua we had to leave the barge for that was as far as he went. After thanking him we headed into the town to find some accommodation for it was too late in the day to travel any further on.

It was the only inn which actually had a room and a stable and so we had little choice but to stay at the tiny bodega on the edge of town. It turned out to be a wise decision. This was partly because of the food, which was excellent and also because the owner, Jose, spoke passable English having been a sailor before becoming an innkeeper. Sailors learned to be multilingual.

After we had eaten, he wandered over, "The food, it was good?"

"It was excellent. Tell me, Jose, what are the roads to Spain like?"

He said, "May I sit? My bones are old."

"Of course."

He took out a clay pipe and lit it. "I would not recommend the road. Peso da Régua is a nice little place. Stay here and enjoy the country. Beyond are the mountains and the, how do you say, bandits?"

We had dealt with bandits before in Italy. I knew how dangerous they could be. "I need to find out if the route into Spain is a road we could use. We have wines I wish to sell."

He laughed, "You wish to sell Italian wine to Spaniards and Portuguese? I think we have lakes of wine here."

"Alan, go and bring a bottle for Jose. Let him taste the quality." When Sharp disappeared upstairs, I tapped my sword. "We can look after ourselves, Jose."

"You look like a soldier."

"I was a soldier, once."

He nodded, "And I was a sailor. We both miss our old professions, I think."

I smiled my agreement to that sentiment. "Well, have you a map?"

"No, but I can draw you one which might help you."

Just then Sharp reappeared with a bottle of white wine. "Here Jose, open this and tell me what you think. I would that you were honest with me for if you do not like it then there will be little point in wasting my time trying to sell it."

He poured himself a beaker of the wine. I was not certain that the pot would do the wine justice but glasses were rare in this type of establishment. His eyes opened when he tasted. "This is a good wine. It is not as full-bodied as our reds but it tastes much better than our whites and the Spanish ones are like vinegar by comparison. You will sell it but why go to Spain? The roads are dirt tracks you will break more than you will sell."

"You may be right but I am obligated to go to Ciudad Rodrigo."

His face darkened. "The French are there, my friend. Beware."

I discussed our future with Sharp when we retired to our room. "Well sir, we have the information Colonel Selkirk wanted. The French are coming. Everyone seems to know that. We just head back to Oporto and wait for the '*Black Prince*'."

"As much as I would like to that is just half the job, Alan. We need to know his intentions towards Portugal and that means looking at the troops who are at Ciudad."

"Type of troops, sir?"

"If there are assault troops there then it means they intend to invade. If they have just garrisoned the fort then they are just protecting the borders."

He nodded, "It looks like I will have to brush up on my French then."

"It does indeed. We will only talk in French from tomorrow onwards. That should help you get back into the language."

Jose had a crudely drawn map for us but, having been a sailor, he had made it functional. I could see where the towns were and what passed for roads. As we set off towards Ciudad Rodrigo, I began to feel more hopeful. I had thought that the roads in Italy were bad enough but these would take days for artillery to cross. Bonaparte would struggle to use these roads for an invasion.

Jose had also marked the places where the bandits made a nuisance of themselves. We had brought holsters for the horses and we each had a brace to hand. We also had a third tucked in our belts. We had learned the power of three pistols. The first few hours passed quickly as we chatted in French. The road twisted and turned as it climbed the mountains towards the south. It was a perfect ambush country. If I had had the Light Dragoons with me, we could have held up the French for days and slowed an invasion down to a crawl. As it was, I knew that soon after the next town, Moimenta da Beira, we would be in bandit country.

Jose had just put a circle for the towns with no idea of the size of the place. They all looked to be the same. Moimenta da Beira was just a large village and, as we rode through, we saw no-one. We were not trying to hide and the villagers would have seen us coming from some way off. Perhaps they feared strangers. It was peculiar to be this close to people and not to see them. The village had a threatening air about it but our horses needed a rest. We stopped at the water trough and watered the tired beasts. It was eerie knowing that everyone was hiding behind closed doors, just watching us. I kept my hand on my pistol.

When we mounted and rode up the road which climbed south and east, I felt a sense of relief. The village had made me wary. I could see many places as the road climbed up to a col where we could be ambushed. This was a dangerous country. I now worried that we might be the ones who were ambushed. We dismounted. These were not the best of horses and we needed to care for them. As the crest of the road hid the other side, I thought this might be the most prudent course to take to avoid being seen in this bandit country. It proved to be another wise decision.

We were a few yards from the top when I heard a woman's scream and immediately drew my pistol. I handed my reins to Sharp and made my way up through the scrubby undergrowth and rocks which lined the rough mountain road. When I reached the top, I crouched behind a large rock. I saw a coach surrounded by seven bandits. There were three dead men lying on the road their blood already puddling. There was a well-dressed woman who was crying. She looked to be of an age with my mother. She looked to be in her late forties. She was trying to edge back into the carriage. She looked terrified. The men were searching her bags, discarding shoes and dresses while one was pawing at her. It was most distressing. I took the scene in and then descended.

I told Sharp what I had seen. "We have a choice, Alan, we can find another route and leave a woman to be... well, we could leave a woman or we could do something about it and risk our lives."

He smiled, "I know what you want to do, Captain, and I am not the sort of chap to leave a woman to suffer at the hands of bandits. What do we do?"

I grinned, "Use surprise. We gallop over the top. I think I know who the leader is. We use our three pistols and then our swords. You look after the woman."

"Righto, sir." He said it in such a matter of fact tone that one would have thought he did this sort of thing every day of the week.

We mounted. After we had primed and cocked all three weapons I turned to Sharp. "Let's do this!" I rode on the right of the track and Sharp on the left. I knew they would hear the hooves but we were so close to the top of the road that they would have little time to react for the coach was not far down the other side. I had noted that they did not have their weapons in their hands. We had a few moments' advantage and we had to use them well.

As we burst over the top, I saw them look around in surprise. At thirty yards I was deadly accurate with a pistol and I fired at the bandit leader. The huge ball made his face unrecognisable. I took out a second pistol and fired at the bandit who was raising his musket in my direction. The ball hit him in the chest and threw him to the ground. I holstered it and drew the third. I pulled the trigger at a bandit who was running at me with an axe. The pistol misfired. I dropped it and drew my sword. He swung the axe at my horse's head. I jerked the reins to one side and slashed down with the razor-sharp blade. It sliced his head open like a ripe plum.

I heard Sharp's pistol fire and I turned my horse to see where the others were. Two of them were running away. I could not allow them to escape. Who knew if there were more bandits close by? I urged my horse on. It was not as fast as Badger, my own horse, but it was game and it was faster than the two men.

As I thundered up behind them one turned and raised his musket. I saw him sight at my head. I leaned forward and down. The flash of the musket was just five feet from where my head would have been. I skewered him with the Austrian cavalry sword. I suddenly heard Sharp shout, "Look out sir!"

The last man had turned and was pointing two pistols at me. I threw myself from the horse and rolled to the side. He fired one pistol at me and I felt the ball tug at my sleeve. I was on my feet in an instant and I lunged at him as he brought the pistol up. My blade went into his throat and I felt the barrel of his pistol touch my chest. He rolled backwards and his dying hand lifted the pistol vertically and his finger spasmed on the trigger and the ball sailed into the sky.

The horse, wide-eyed and panting, stood just behind me. "Good boy!" I grabbed the reins and stroked his mane while speaking close to his ear. "Good boy, well done." I did not try to mount him. I led him back to the carriage. I could see that Sharp had disposed of the bodies by pushing them into the ditch which ran next to the rough road. The woman looked to have regained her composure. She had recovered her coat and donned it. I could see that she must have been a handsome woman in her youth. I could see that she was both well dressed and expensively dressed. I knew why the bandits had targeted the coach.

I gave a slight bow. She spoke to me in English. "Thank you, sir. I owe you my life."

She had a slight accent and I knew she was not English. How had she known that we were? "You are welcome. I am just sorry we could not save your people. I am Roberto d'Alpini."

"And I am Donna Maria d'Alvarez." She held out her hand for me to kiss. "And what is an Englishman with an Italian name doing here in this out of the way place?"

"We can talk about that later. Sharp, tie your horse to the back of the carriage and you drive." I turned to the lady. "Others may come. There is a village just down the hill."

She shook her head. "That is the village of the bandits. They were about to take me there. I would not have risked the journey save that we saw French troops on the Spanish border and I had to inform the authorities."

That was a double problem. There were Frenchmen behind us and bandits before us. "Sharp, when we get close to the village whip the horses along and have your pistol ready."

"Right sir. I had better reload them."

"Sir, could I have one?"

I looked at the old lady. "You can fire a pistol?"

She smiled, "Do not be taken in by these grey hairs. I can handle a pistol. Had I had one handy earlier then they would not have taken us quite so easily." She reached into the coach and pulled out a tiny lady's pistol. "I was trying to reach this. At close range, it can kill. I am also an accomplished swordswoman too." I gave her a sceptical look, "Oh do not be fooled by my earlier tears. I wished to play the weak woman for later I would then have used it to my advantage when their guard was down."

I handed her a reloaded pistol. "I will put the bodies of your people on the roof."

"Thank you. They died well and I would that they were buried equally well."

When we had manhandled the bodies on to the roof, I mounted my horse. "Ready, Alan?"

"As ready as I will ever be!"

"Then ride. Keep it steady until we are at the edge of the village and then whip the horses."

"The road is a little rough, sir."

"I know. Just do your best." As we rode down the hill, I reflected that you could make the best plans in the world but it only took one tiny event to change them. The mission would be a failure. I had no idea if there was a garrison in Spain or an invading army. I just knew that there were Frenchmen and they were on the border.

Now that we knew the village was the home of the bandits then the atmosphere earlier became clearer. They would expect their men to be bringing the loot back for distribution and I did not think that they would allow us to pass unhindered. I rode next to Sharp. The hill was becoming gentler and I felt that we could risk galloping.

"Ready Sharp?"

"I was born ready sir!"

"Then ride like the wind." I slapped the hindquarters of the leading horse as Alan cracked his whip. They took off. Their earlier fright had made them nervous and we used it to our advantage. Sharp had to have two hands to control the careering carriage. I drew a pistol.

A large man stepped out of a hut with an old blunderbuss. As he raised it, I fired and he was flung backwards.

"Watch out!" Donna Maria d'Alvarez shouted and fired her pistol. I turned around and saw the body of a woman with a wicked-looking meat cleaver lying dead in the road.

I drew my sword and saluted my saviour. More of the villagers were now rushing from their places of concealment. Had I had a better mount I might have used him aggressively but I dared not risk a fancy manoeuvre with the hired horse. Instead, I used my long reach and my sword to keep them at bay. It takes a brave man to approach a whirling sword wielded from the back of a horse. As we neared the northern edge of the village, I heard a crack from behind me as Donna Maria d'Alvarez fired her pistol again. I saw a man drop his musket and clutch his arm.

I remembered this part of the road from our ascent and I knew that it twisted behind some rocks. I dropped back, sheathed my sword and drew my last loaded pistol. As the villagers hurtled after us, I fired into them and they all ducked into cover. I whipped my horse's head around and followed the coach as it disappeared behind the rocks.

Sharp did not stop them for a mile or more. By then they were lathered and needed to slow down. "Well done Alan, best to walk them for a while and I will see how our guest is faring." I looked back up the road and the pursuit appeared to have halted. I saw no one.

I dropped back to the coach and saw that Donna Maria d'Alvarez had a pistol ready. I smiled, "I think we have lost them. Thank you for the shot."

"I told you that I could shoot." She put the pistol on the seat next to her. I rode next to the open window so that I could speak with her. "You are a soldier." She said it in a matter of fact way that allowed for no denial.

"I was. Now I deal in wine."

She laughed, "And I am a prima ballerina at the Lisbon Opera House! I may be old but I recognise a soldier and I know when orders are being given by an officer." I did not answer. She smiled, "If it makes it easier for you, I am happy that you are a soldier for if that is true then we have a greater chance of escaping."

"Escaping?" I frowned, "The villagers will not pursue us."

"I am not worried about the villagers, it is the French I worry about."

"The French?" I tried to keep the alarm out of my voice. I had thought she said they were just on the border.

She nodded, "I would not be risking a journey through bandit country if the matter were not urgent." She pointed behind her. "My husband and I were staying with friends high in the mountains when the French cavalry came." For the first time since the attack, I saw the emotion on her face. "They killed my husband. Shot him down like a dog. I have no idea what they would have done to me but I think they thought I was a harmless old woman." She laughed, "The poisoned guards will have told them that I was not. I think they were the vanguard of an army."

"They will follow you?"

"I believe so especially if they are the advanced guard of an invasion force. We discovered that before they shot my husband." She shrugged, "He had been a senior officer in the Portuguese army and knew such things."

"Sharp, we will have some Chasseurs on our tail soon enough. Better get the speed up."

"But, sir, the horses!" Like me, Sharp was a horseman and did not like to abuse such fine animals.

"Don't kill them but keep them moving."

I rode back to the window. "When did you leave?"

"This morning before dawn." I nodded. We had some time then. "Where are we headed to, Englishman?"

"We took a wine barge up from Oporto. I was going to see if we could get one back."

"I know many people in Peso da Régua. My husband has a wine warehouse there but there is no garrison."

"Then I will have to think of something else before we get there."

I knew how quickly Chasseurs could move. They could be less than an hour behind us. It would take us at least another two to three hours to get the slow-moving carriage and weary horses across the Douro.

A thought suddenly occurred to me. "My lady, what of the garrison at the border?"

"I fear they were either killed or they were captured. Either way, the French are in Portugal.

"Then we will be the first with the news?"

She nodded, "I would assume so."

"This is your country. If you were invading would you attack along the Douro?"

The same thought must have arrived in the resourceful lady's mind. "The Tagus would be their route and then directly to Lisbon."

"Exactly and I believe the royal family are there." I saw the worry appear on her face.

"I hope there is a ship in Oporto harbour else the French will take our Regent, Prince John and our Queen Maria. She is a dear friend of mine although I have not seen her since her husband died."

I nodded, "There were a couple in the harbour when we left but that was two days ago. Who knows what may have happened since then?" I hoped that Jonathan was there already if not then my mission would end in failure. I now had a double mission: send the news to England and warn the Braganza royal family.

Chapter 3

The carriage made it to within four miles of the bridge before the rigours of the journey and road destroyed it. The axle broke along with a wheel. Had we had time we could have repaired it but time was a luxury we could ill afford. I dismounted, "My lady, can you ride?"

"I can."

"Then mount this one, please. Sharp unhitch the horses. I will ride bareback."

"Sir... I"

"There is no argument Alan, I am the better rider." Donna Maria d'Alvarez looked comfortable upon the horse. Her voluminous dress had made it easier for her to sit astride the horse and maintain her dignity. I glanced up at the bodies on the carriage roof. "Your men..."

"I know. They will have to rest here if we are to save the royal family."

Just them I heard hooves in the distance. "The French!" Sharp led a horse to me and I threw my leg over. "Sharp, take the other horses we can use them in case these tire. Now ride!"

The horses needed nursing and we did not gallop. I kept glancing over my shoulder as we descended to the Douro below. If there had been a garrison, we might have held them at the bridge. As it was, we had to pray that there was a barge in port and Donna Maria d'Alvarez had enough authority to make it move as soon as we arrived. The road twisted and turned. I hoped that we would keep disappearing from the view of the pursuing French. Once they passed the carriage they would hurry.

I saw the bridge. It was a mile or so ahead. The road had flattened somewhat and I risked looking around again. To my horror, I saw the green Chasseurs less than a mile away. They had spread out along the road and it was just the three scouts who were behind us. With the lady for us to protect, they would be enough. I had one pistol with me and it was loaded. A second was with my horse in the holster. Sharp had three and they would be loaded. I rode next to Donna Maria d'Alvarez. "We will try to hold them up. There is a loaded pistol in the holster in case you need it. Try to get a barge and we will join you."

She nodded. "You are brave men. Do not throw your lives away."

"Don't worry, we will not. Sharp, let the spare horses go and join me."

The horses carried on down the road following the lady. The road had turned a bend and I could no longer see the Chasseurs. "Daw your pistols, Alan. When they come around the bend then shoot them. I have one pistol and my sword."

"How many are there, sir?"

"Three scouts. I just need to buy the lady some time."

As he cocked his guns he said. "She is a game 'un sir."

"She is that and she has done our job for us. We know that there are probably two armies invading Portugal. They are French armies! The country is lost."

Just then the three troopers galloped around the corner. They were so intent on catching our party that they had no weapons drawn. I fired my pistol and the leading trooper clutched his shoulder and fell to the ground. Sharp's ball took a trooper in the head but his second pistol misfired. I drew my sword and galloped up to the last trooper, a Brigadier. He had the waxed moustache so beloved of the light cavalry and he had the scarred face of a veteran. He drew his sword as he charged me.

I was at a disadvantage. I had neither saddle nor stirrups and he had a cavalry mount. He swept his sabre at head height. I leaned back and hacked at his sword. Sparks flew. He reined around and his well-trained horse began to push against mine. It was no contest and I felt my beast start to tumble. The Brigadier saw his chance and he hacked down with his blade. I tumbled from the back of the carriage horse and the sabre sliced down through the horse's head. The dying beast saved me for the Chasseur could not reach me across its dying body. I used it to my advantage and I sprang on to the dying beast and leapt in the air. The Brigadier was not expecting the move and, as I descended, I brought my sword down on to his neck. It sliced through his collar and when I saw the spurting blood, I knew that it was a mortal wound. Even as his body fell from the horse, I grabbed the reins and straddled the saddle.

"Ride, Sharp!"

It was much easier for me to ride with stirrups and it was a fine horse. I glanced down and saw that the dead Brigadier had had two horse pistols. They would be handy if his comrades caught up with me. The wooden bridge was a more than welcome sight. I turned my head and saw that the Chasseurs were less than half a mile away now.

"Sir, I can see the lady. She is on a barge and waving."

"Sharp, get on that barge and tell them to set sail. If they don't the Chasseurs will be all over us and we won't be able to sail. Give me a loaded pistol. Now go!"

"But sir!"

"Sergeant!"

He handed me a pistol, saluted and headed down to the barge some four hundred yards along the river. I rode to the end of the bridge nearest to the town and I turned. The bridge was about eighty yards from bank to bank and just wide enough for a carriage. I drew one of the Chasseur's pistols and checked that it was loaded. I had two pistols aimed at the far side of the bridge. I resisted the temptation to see if Sharp had reached the water. The whole wooden structure shook as the thirty men thundered across. They saw me and the leading riders drew their pistols to fire. They might as have well have spat at me for all the good that it would do. The balls didn't even come close enough to buzz!

I levelled both pistols and when they reached the middle I fired. I didn't wait to see the effect of my shots. I whipped my horse's head around and dug my heels in. As I galloped along the stone jetty I looked to my right and saw that I had brought down one horse and rider. The rest were trying to get past them. I had bought moments only. I leaned forward and began to speak to the horse in

French. I used the same words I had used when I had ridden Killer and they had the same effect. He surged forward.

Sharp had persuaded the bargemen to leave and I saw a visible gap opening between the shore and the barge. It would be close and it would depend upon the ability of my mount but I intended to leap the gap and land on the moving barge. I yelled as I approached, "Out of the way!" I would have no control over my landing. The gap was twelve or thirteen feet. I lifted the reins as I dug in my heels and the valiant beast soared. I would either clatter across the barge's wooden deck or I would end up in the Douro. His front hooves struck the deck and he pulled his hind legs to slither and slide along the deck like an ice skater. We clattered into a barrel. I was winded, as was, I suspected, the horse. But we were safe.

The Chasseurs tried to ride along the road firing as us. The current had begun to take us, and the bargemen, who were being urged by Donna Maria d'Alvarez, were poling for their lives. The musket balls hit the wooden hull. Sharp had his pistols out and he fired back at them. After a few more shots the Chasseurs decided that they would not catch us and they waved their fists in frustration. I stroked the wide-eyed horse's mane. "Bon cheval! Bon Cheval!" I reached into my pocket for the apple I was saving for my original horse. I gave it to the beast which munched it happily.

"I'll put him with the other two, sir." He began to lead the horse to the bows. "He's a fine horse, sir."

The Portuguese lady came down the deck and threw her arms around me. "You are not only a soldier, but you are also a horseman. My husband would have loved to meet you. What courage! What a magnificent leap!"

There was little to say in reply to that and I merely nodded, "You persuaded them then?"

"It did not take much. I told them that the French were coming and would confiscate their wine. They moved happily enough once they knew that."

I looked back at the sleepy little town. How would Jose, the innkeeper, cope, I wondered? I knew the French. They could be cruel masters. I had seen that in Italy when they had butchered and raped whole villages. They liked to live off the land and this was not a rich country. As we watched the river banks slide back I asked a question which had been on my mind since we had met Donna Maria d'Alvarez. "Your English is perfect, Donna Maria d'Alvarez. Did you study in England?"

"No, I was brought up at the Royal Court in Lisbon. My mother was a lady in waiting for the old Queen. I learned my English from Rodolpho, my husband. His mother was English; the daughter of a wine exporter. She lived with us after Rodolpho's father died." She laughed, "She never mastered Portuguese and it was easier to converse in English." She smiled, "As soon as I heard you shout to Alan, I knew that you were English."

I hesitated before I asked my next question. "You seem to be taking the death of your husband better than I would have thought."

She nodded and linked me. She led me towards the front of the barge. "My husband was a cavalry officer when I met him. He was very dashing. When he left, he became a wine merchant but he always yearned for a life of action. We had no children, God did not bless us that way, but we were happy. When he was killed, he was fighting for his country. He died in my arms and he died well. He was happy. I shall miss him but I would not take away his last moments. We had a good life together and I can dedicate the rest of my life to fighting his killers, the French."

I felt a shiver down my spine. My father had been guillotined but he had died well. I, too, would not take that away from him. I could understand this gracious lady.

The bargemen had a cabin for Donna Maria d'Alvarez. It seems her husband had been a good customer of the men who plied the river. In addition, the couple seemed to have been very popular with the people of the Upper Douro. As she went to go to her crude cabin she said, "We should reach Oporto by morning. I pray that there is a ship to take us to Lisbon and that we are in time."

Sharp and I took it in turns to watch. While he slept, I examined the Brigadier's horse. From my time in the Chasseurs, I knew that any orders, maps and important documents were kept in a small pouch just beneath the holsters. In one I found some coins, which I pocketed, and some maps. In the other were requisitions for fodder for the horses. I recognised the name; it was Colonel Guy Laroche and he was the Quartermaster for Marshal Junot. I vaguely remembered him from Italy. This was important intelligence and I slipped the documents into my jacket. I went back on watch. I trusted the bargemen but I trusted us more. We were now in great danger from the French and I did not want to lose this intelligence because we slept. I was grateful when it was time for Sharp to watch.

He woke me before dawn. He handed me a jug of warmed wine. "Here you are, sir. Not what we are used to but, when in Rome."

It was sweet and it was spicy. More importantly, it was warming. "How is her ladyship?"

"She is the one who made this sir. She has made breakfast for the crew. She is different from the other ladies we have met on our travels." He chuckled, "Certainly not like the English ladies I have met."

"No, she seems like a unique character." I stared ahead. I was desperate to see the masts of a Royal Navy ship. As dawn broke behind us and the light flooded the river, I saw an empty harbour. There were no ships at all.

Donna Maria joined Sharp and me. "God is not smiling on us today eh?"

"No. It does it look that way."

"I have a villa by the sea. The three of us need a change of clothes and I must speak with the Prefeito. Perhaps he can send a message by road to Lisbon but it is many miles hence. I fear he would be too late."

"Are there any troops in Oporto?"

"Not enough to fight French regulars. I am afraid we have been caught unawares. We are more used to border disputes with Spain. We have some of our best troops in Brazil and that is a voyage of some weeks. We are resigned to being invaded by France." She gripped my arm a little tighter, "But the French have bitten off more than they can chew. We Portuguese will fight; not in ranks of brown or red but with a knife in the night!"

The indomitable lady was quite happy to ride my horse to her home. "I am anxious to change from these clothes; especially if I am to meet the Prefeito."

It was almost a palace we reached rather than a home. There were large imposing gates and, whilst there were no armed guards the men who were working in the gardens and who opened the doors looked to be more than capable of handling themselves.

She rattled off some Portuguese and then said, "I have asked Antonio to take you to my husband's wardrobe and give you some of his clothes. I will have these laundered for you"

"Shouldn't we hurry? The French may be here soon."

She put her hand on my arm. "There is no ship to carry a message yet and it will take the French a day of hard riding to reach here; even their much-vaunted Chasseurs. We have time to bathe, change and eat some decent food and then we shall worry!"

The house was wonderfully cool and still. Antonio, who looked like he had been a soldier too, led us up the stairs to a pair of enormous rooms. One whole wall had mirrored doors and behind it were fine clothes. Antonio gestured to the wardrobe. Sharp and I chose the plainest set of clothes we could. We did not want to stand out and I was worried that we might damage some of the beautiful suits. I made sure I transferred the maps and the documents to my new suit. Other servants appeared with buckets of hot water and Antonio opened another door to reveal a bath. Sharp said, "After you sir!"

When we both descended having bathed, shaved and changed I felt like a new man. Donna Maria looked resplendent in black as she greeted us. "I have sent a message to the Prefeito and he will come here so you need not worry about our message getting through." She had a twinkle in her eye as she said, "You seem to have a great deal of interest in the military matters of our country; for a businessman that is."

"War makes for bad business; that is all."

"An assured and practised answer my English friend. Come, I have had food prepared. One cannot think on an empty stomach."

The Prefeito arrived during the meal but our hostess asked him to wait. When he was admitted she was gracious yet commanding. This was a woman with power. We understood not a word of Portuguese but the Prefeito kept nodding and he left after twenty-minute bowing his way out.

"He will call out the militia but I fear they will do little. Still, it may delay the French however briefly. He is also trying to acquire us a ship."

"Donna Maria, I am a little concerned by this lack of shipping. When we arrived a few days ago the port was heaving with ships."

She nodded, "Astute, Roberto; I too have noticed the same thing. I wonder if the captains of the ships had wind of this." She shrugged, "Not that it matters, we can do little about it anyway. I have a man watching the entrance to the harbour for any sign of a sail." She picked up her glass of port. The wines we had supped had been the finest I had ever enjoyed and that included the Alpini wines. "We shall go to the terrace and watch the sea. Perhaps we can conjure one."

While we enjoyed our wines, she told me more about her husband and his wine trade. I had the impression that she had made up for her lack of children by helping her husband with his business. She had also kept up with European politics and knew all about Napoleon Bonaparte. "It is a pity the army has been allowed to degenerate. We could have stopped the French at the passes. Our country is like a fortress but if you do not defend it then any fortress can be breached."

Just then Antonio burst in and gabbled away in Portuguese. Donna Maria d'Alvarez's face lit up in a huge smile. "It seems our prayers are answered. A Royal Navy ship has just entered the harbour. I have asked Antonio to prepare my carriage. Shall we go down and see if we can beg a berth?" Once again there was a knowing twinkle in her eye.

25

The ship had docked when we reached the harbour. I was not surprised to see it was the *'Black Prince'*. Any pretence I might have maintained about being a businessman was ruined by the waves and greetings from the crew. The bosun looked askance at Donna Maria. "She is with me."

He knuckled his head, "Captain!"

As she went ahead of me up the gangplank she whispered, "I knew you were a soldier and now I know your rank."

Jonathan looked perplexed when he saw the lady. "Jonathan, we need to go to your cabin. We have the most important news."

He waved a hand and I led Donna Maria to his tiny cabin. He had worked for Colonel Selkirk longer than I had and he was not easily surprised. Once inside Donna Maria took the only chair while I explained to Jonathan about the French invasion. He nodded while I spoke and then glanced at Donna Maria. I saw the question on his face.

"Donna Maria d'Alvarez needs to get to Lisbon. The French are also advancing down the Tagus and the Portuguese Royal Family is in danger."

Jonathan Teer was a quick-thinking and decisive captain. He nodded, "I am afraid the accommodation is restricted to this cabin but I shall endeavour to reach Lisbon as quickly as my little ship can manage it." He gave a small bow, "And now if you will excuse me, I shall go and order us to sea. Your carriage?"

"Will already be heading back to my home. If you could ask one of your sailors to collect my bags from the bottom of the gangplank, I will be grateful."

Sharp grinned, "I will get them."

I nodded, "And I will come with you Captain Teer and find out what prompted this early rescue."

When we reached the quarterdeck, I waited until he had given his orders and Sharp had disappeared below decks with the bags before I spoke.

"Did you suddenly get the second sight?"

He laughed, "No. We were patrolling south-west France as the colonel had ordered us when we saw many ships fleeing

Portuguese waters. I was suspicious. We caught a Genoese ship which I am certain was smuggling and the captain told me, after a little persuasion, that there would be trouble in Portugal soon and he wanted to be away from such trouble. He seemed to think it would be the French and he wanted to get his cargo back to a market. Captains are like merchants. They know the market. All of them will make more profit. We headed down here as soon as we could."

"And thank you for that. It was timely."

He nodded in the direction of his cabin. "She is a force of nature. She looks like my aunt."

"Well, I doubt that your aunt can load and shoot a pistol as well as ride horseback in a dress. She is formidable but she has connections to the Portuguese royal family so I do not doubt that we are obeying Colonel Selkirk's orders." He nodded, "Portugal is lost. They have virtually no army and the French have sent good quality troops. They mean business. I think that this means Napoleon can finally have his Continental Blockade of Britain."

The First Lieutenant saluted, "All ready, sir."

"Good then cast off and lay a course for Lisbon."

"Do we avoid the coast, sir?"

"No, Mr Bulley, we get there as fast as we can. Tonight, we race the French! Let us see if our little ship can do what her namesake did!"

"Aye, aye, sir." The fast little sloop was soon under full canvas and hurtling south.

Chapter 4

The *'Black Prince'* did, indeed, do us proud. She flew to Lisbon and we saw the Portuguese capital just after dawn. It was with some relief that we saw the masts and cross trees of British battleships. The fleet had arrived.

Donna Maria d'Alvarez was especially pleased. "The royal family is safe! My country has been saved."

It had been during the voyage south, for neither of us had slept, that she told me more of the royal family. Her friend, Queen Maria had been ill since 1786 when her husband, the king had died. Her son Prince Regent João, who would soon be named King John VI, was Regent and ruled in her name.

Donna Maria had shown great concern for her friend. I know what it is like to lose a husband but I think the Queen had rarely left the palace. It is easy to see plots and danger in such a place. Perhaps I can help her now."

I had come to see, in the short time that I had known her, that Donna Maria was not only a clever and powerful woman but a kind one. They were a rare combination anywhere.

Donna Maria thanked Jonathan when we tied up. "Thank you for your help, young man. You and Roberto here give me hope that our two countries can fight this greedy Frenchman." She turned to me. "Roberto, would you and Alan accompany me to the palace at Queluz? It is the last task I ask of you but it may be safer for me if I am escorted. Who knows what spies and assassins are in our streets? And then you can go about your... er business"

"Of course." I turned to Jonathan. "Will you report to the Admiral?" We had both seen the flag of an Admiral on the 'Marlborough'.

"Of course, but I dare say he will have questions for you."

"Then I will answer them when I have returned from the palace. Sharp, bring our pistols, we may need them."

Donna Maria took my arm as we descended the gangplank. Sharp went ahead of us. He had brought a marlinspike from the ship in case anyone needed persuading to move. It was early and the people who were about were those going to work, business or trade. The robbers and cutpurses would be out later.

We made our way to the palace at Queluz. It was a huge pink palace. It looked as though it was an iced cake in a bakery. The sergeant there looked at us suspiciously. Donna Maria's arrival with just two servants and neither horse nor carriage was not usual. I heard a torrent of Portuguese from Donna Maria and the sergeant quailed. The gates were opened and we were allowed in. As we were taken inside, she snorted, "Normally sergeants are the backbone of an army but that one is a fool! Did he think we would arrive to murder the Queen dressed like this?"

Two officials raced down the stairs to greet us. From the looks on their faces, I saw that they recognised Donna Maria. Even in Portuguese, I recognised their words as abject apologies. We were taken to an antechamber. Food and drink were brought and a chair for Donna Maria. Sharp and I were considered bodyguards at best.

The Prince Regent arrived and Donna Maria curtsied. We bowed. He was older than I had expected. The term prince implies someone younger. The man was forty and going grey already. He and Donna Maria spoke rapidly. There were glances in our direction. There were soldiers with the king and they viewed Sharp and me with a mixture of suspicion and interest in equal measure.

Eventually, they stopped talking and the Prince turned to us. His English was good but more accented than that of Donna Maria.

"It seems, Captain, that our country owes you a great deal. Thank you for rescuing my mother's cousin." That came as a shock. I had been with royalty if we had but known it. "Your timely news and the presence of your ships are fortuitous."

I was not certain if there was a hint of suspicion in his voice which mirrored that of his soldiers. Sharp and I must have seemed like shadowy characters at best.

Just then a courtier entered and bowed. He spoke with the Prince. Donna Maria turned to me, "It seems your admiral craves an audience." He smiled, "When he arrives, we might actually find out who you really are?"

I had met Sir Sidney Smith before and I nodded my recognition when he entered. I saw that as well as his Flag Lieutenant he had brought Jonathan who shrugged when he saw me.

"Your Royal Highness, Captain Teer has informed me of the invasion of your country. I am here to place the resources of Great Britain at your disposal."

The Regent smiled, "And you have an army on your floating wooden fortresses?"

Sir Sidney had the good grace to smile and shake his head, "No, Your Highness, but our presence may deter the French and I can send Commander Teer here back to England for reinforcements."

"Very laudable but the voyage would take time. The army would have to be prepared and by that time my country would be captured and we would be prisoners."

"We could take your family to Great Britain. You would be safe there until we could raise an army."

Donna Maria snapped, "You would abandon our country?"

The Regent put his hand on her arm "I am afraid that we have little choice. Our army was defeated by the Spanish last year. The best troops, as you know, are in Brazil." He rubbed his cheek thoughtfully, "We have the *'Principe Real'* in port. If Sir Sidney will provide an escort then we will sail to Brazil and rule from there." He smiled at the Admiral, "And hopefully Great Britain will send soldiers to free my country."

Sir Sidney bowed, "Of course, Your Royal Highness."

"Then we will sail this afternoon. Every moment we waste in talking allows the French to close with us. Donna Maria, will you accompany us?"

She shook her head defiantly. "I am too angry to travel halfway around the world while my country is invaded. I will stay here and fight."

"I urge you to come with us. You would be of invaluable comfort to my mother." She shook her head. "If you stay you may die."

"We all die Your Royal Highness. It is the manner which is important. I shall stay."

I could see that he was unhappy about leaving this patriot to the French. "How will you get back to Oporto?"

I coughed, "Perhaps Captain Teer could return her?" Jonathan nodded but I saw an irritated look flicker across the face of the Admiral.

The Regent turned to me. "Ah, the resourceful Captain er... what is your name?"

I sighed, "Captain Matthews of the 11th Light Dragoons."

For some reason, that fact seemed to please the Regent. "Excellent. I do prefer openness. If that suits the Admiral?"

"Of course, Your Royal Highness."

"Good, and, Captain Matthews, as a reward for rescuing Donna Maria d'Alvarez I appoint you a Colonel in the Alcatrana regiment of cavalry." He nodded to an official who scurried off. "It is the least we can do but if what Donna Maria d'Alvarez tells me is true then I have high hopes for you." He inclined his head and strode off.

Donna Maria turned to me, "Thank you, Roberto, I shall enjoy travelling with you and Alan one last time. I shall just go and say goodbye to the Queen. I fear I shall never see her again."

The British officers were now alone in the room and Sir Sidney turned to me. He was irritated more than angry. "I think you should allow the Royal Navy to offer passage, Captain! You take much upon yourself."

"I am sorry Sir Sidney. I didn't think."

"Quite. Still working for Colonel Selkirk?"

"Yes, sir."

"And what did you discover?"

"Just what we told the Regent. There are two French armies and they are led by Marshal Junot. One is heading along the Tagus and the other, the Douro. They will be in both cities within a few days at the most."

"How do you know?"

Like a magician, I pulled the maps and requisitions from my pocket. He glanced at them, nodded, and returned them to me.

"You had better take these back to the Colonel. When Captain Teer has taken the lady home he can sail, post-haste, to England. Wheels need to be put into motion." He turned to his flag lieutenant, "Ellis go and tell the captain to prepare for sea. Have the marines deployed. When the Portuguese discover their Queen and Regent are fleeing then it might turn ugly."

After Ellis had gone, he turned to me, "The title you were awarded may come in handy although there will be no money attached to it; you know that?"

"Yes, sir."

"Good, just so long as you know."

The official returned and handed me a document with a seal upon it. His English was heavily accented. "Here you are, Colonel." Behind him, a servant hovered with an all-white uniform, a cocked hat and a sword. "And this is your uniform, sir. It may not fit." He shrugged. "The last owner was somewhat larger than you are." They left and Sharp took charge of the uniform.

Sir Sidney allowed himself the hint of a smile. "Well done Matthews. You are a resourceful chap. You and Teer here make a good team." He went over to a desk where there were pen and paper. He scribbled away for ten minutes. He applied his seal and handed the document to Jonathan. "Deliver this to the Admiralty in Whitehall."

Jonathan and I took Donna Maria directly to the ship. We had to get her back as soon as possible. I was also concerned to be away before the news broke. Like Sir Sidney, I feared the Lisbon mob.

Donna Maria stood at the stern as we headed out to sea. I joined her and she took my arm, "This may be the last time I see the city in which I was born Roberto." I heard the catch in her voice and saw the tears as they trickled down her cheeks.

"You do not know. You may return."

"I am not certain that I wish to but at least I can use my husband's money to fight the French!" The tears were gone and defiance returned to her voice. She said, "Come, take me to my cabin I am tired. I am not used to this much excitement and I am no longer, what was it my mother in law used to say? Ah yes, a spring chicken."

I returned to the quarter-deck having left Sharp to watch over our guest. Jonathan said, "A colonel eh?"

"Honorary only."

"Still…" He looked up at the masthead. "It will be the middle of the night when we arrive in Oporto."

"And the French will be there. You will not be able to use the port itself."

"That is a blow but you are right. Where exactly is the old dear's villa?"

"Ssh! She might hear you." Donna Maria was no 'old dear'.

He laughed, "I doubt it. Go on. Is it close to the town?"

"No, it is on the coast west of Oporto. There is a path from the house and a small beach."

"Then we can take the longboat in and drop her at the beach."

I shook my head. "We must escort her to her home."

He snorted in exasperation, "But for Heaven's sake why? It is her country. She will be safe enough!"

"If it had not been for her and her intervention with the barge then Sharp and I would be dead or prisoners. We owe it to her."

He laughed, "You are a knight in shining armour. Very well! But you shall pay for every hole in my ship."

We saw few ships whilst sailing north. We knew that there were hardly any French in the Atlantic but there were privateers who might risk the wrath of the navy by attacking a ship even one as small as '**Black Prince**'.

Our passenger rose during the afternoon. The Bosun, Jack Harsker, made a real fuss of her and brought a chair out for her on the deck. He gave her some cocoa with rum in it. I know that it was not what she expected but it was the sort of thing the crew enjoyed. She was touched by the gesture.

"This is delicious, Bosun. You must tell me how you make it." The delighted old sailor knuckled his head and back away as though she was the Queen of Portugal. "You have a fine crew Captain Teer."

"Thank you."

"I know I am causing you trouble. You can always drop me at the cove close to my home. I can make my own way from there."

Jonathan gave me an '*I told you so*' look but he said, "That is not a problem, my lady."

"Besides," I added, "There are some things we need to do at your villa."

They both looked at me, and Sharp, too, had a puzzled expression on his face."

"What do we need to do?"

"We have a horse to dispose of and a saddle. If the French find them, and they do search efficiently, believe me, then you will be in trouble. I shall take the saddle and drop it in the sea."

"And the horse?"

I took a deep breath. I was not happy about what I was going to say but it was the only solution to the problem. "If we release the animal it will hang around the villa and the French will deduce what happened to their Brigadier. We will have to shoot the horse. It is for the best."

Like me Sharp loved horses. He exploded, "You can't do that sir!"

Even Jonathan was shocked, "I say, Robbie, that is a bit harsh is it not? Is there no other solution?"

Only Donna Maria d'Alvarez seemed unmoved. "You have steel in you, Captain Matthews. It is the one thing you do not wish to do and yet you will do it to save someone you barely know. You were born out of your time."

"We can take it back to England, sir. You said yourself it was a fine horse."

"And how in God's name would you get it aboard? It would sink the longboat!"

"I will swim it out, sir! Please do not kill a dumb animal whose only crime is that it saved your life!"

That was as near to insolence as Sharp ever got. Jonathan smiled, "I'll tell you what, Sergeant Sharp. If you can get it alongside the ship, I will have it hoisted aboard in a sling. How's that?"

He grinned, "That'll do me sir and I promise I will make her swim." He looked at me, "Sorry for speaking out of turn, sir."

I relented, "I fully understand, Sharp."

It was after dark when we edged north past the mouth of the Douro; we were just sailing under reefed topsails. There were fires burning at the entrance to the harbour and Jonathan saw, through his telescope, that the Tricolour was flying. As we had suspected the French had arrived.

We headed closer to the coast. Lookouts watched for the small beach which would mark our destination. Instead of using shouts, they whistled. We had the sails down in a flash as soon as it was spotted and the anchor half-lowered in case, we had to make a quick getaway.

While the longboat was lowered Donna Maria said goodbye to the captain and the crew.

"I doubt that I shall see any of you again but you have given me hope that the French monster can be defeated." She kissed Jonathan on the cheek, "But find a good woman, Captain Teer and marry!"

The shore party, led by Jack Harsker, were already aboard the boat as Donna Maria was lowered in the Bosun's Chair. Sharp and I used the tumblehome. The sound of the oars was muffled by the surf on the small beach. Two men leapt ashore and pulled the longboat a foot or so onto the beach. Two others stood guard with muskets. Jack Harsker came with Sharp and I as we took the lady up the path to the darkened villa.

We all had pistols and they were cocked although Donna Maria did not seem worried. She did frown when the door was locked and she rapped sharply upon it. The door opened and a worried-looking Antonio appeared. We hurried inside and they spoke in Portuguese.

"You must hurry. Antonio had news from Oporto that the French are moving from house to house. I think they are looking for arms and soldiers."

"Sharp, take Jack and get the horse and the saddle." They disappeared. "It is not too late to come with us. We can take your people."

"You are more than kind Roberto, you are honourable. This is my land and all of those who live here are my people. We shall stay and, when you return, I hope you find me here still." She pulled my face down so that she could kiss me on both cheeks. We heard the horse whinny. "Now go for you put me in more danger by staying here."

Jack had the saddle while Alan led the horse. I covered them from behind with my pistol and sword. I could hear shouts from the houses closer to Oporto as the French troops began to search. They were probably searching for treasure but they would question everyone. That was their way. It would not be easy to reach the beach unnoticed.

"Farewell and stay safe, Donna Maria d'Alvarez."

I followed the other two. I had just slipped down the path when I heard the clatter of hooves as the Chasseurs rode up to Donna Maria's villa. I prayed that Sharp's horse would not whinny and alert them.

When I reached the beach, Sharp had slipped off his boots and trousers. I picked them up. He led the horse towards the water. I clambered into the boat with Sharp's clothes. Jack and the crew began to pull away from the beach. The horse walked in as far as its hocks and then stopped. Sharp began to urge the horse on, into the water but it refused to move. I knew that the Chasseurs would investigate the path. "Come on Alan, talk to her... in French."

"My French is awful, sir!"

"She's not bothered by the accent. Speak to her. Give her a name."

He walked in front of her and put his face close to hers. "Allez, s'il vous plais... Maria!"

Amazingly she began to walk into the water. Sharp slid across her back and urged her on. I held out my hand and clicked her on. She began to swim and follow the boat. "Keep her close lads." I began to call her name and encourage her. Sharp had his face close to her ears and he too encouraged her. I felt the longboat bump into the side of the ship and we were there. We had to rig the sling to lift her and I hoped that she would be compliant. The last thing we needed was a whinnying and thrashing animal to attract the attention of the French.

"Sharp, give me the reins and get up the tumblehome. If she hears your voice and sees your face, she will be less nervous."

Jack edged the boat so that the horse was between us and the ship. The sling was lowered down. The Bosun looked at me. "Sir, if I hold the reins can you rig the sling underneath her? I am a sailor, not a jockey."

I gave him the reins and I manhandled the sling under her middle. I made sure that the fastenings were tight and then said, "You can haul away, Bosun."

He gave a whistle and I heard, from the deck, "Heave!"

Gradually the horse began to move. I could hear Sharp as he encouraged the horse.

"Right sir, get on board and we'll get the boat back aboard."

An hour after we had landed, we were heading north. Our mission was completed and Sergeant Sharp had a new mount, Maria!

Chapter 5

The voyage home seemed never-ending. The weather was against us; there were adverse winds and early December rains. Poor Sharp had to virtually spend every waking moment with his new horse Maria. All of us were glad when the Thames hove into view.

Sharp appeared to be the most relieved of all. The French saddle came in handy and he rode Maria up and down the docks to regain her confidence and to get her land legs back. I left Sharp to his horse and Jonathan and I hurried to Whitehall; he to the Admiralty and me to meet with Colonel Selkirk.

Colonel Selkirk actually smiled, "You have done well Robbie. It was not necessarily what I intended for you to do but it has worked out better than I might have hoped. And you say Captain Teer has gone to the Admiralty?"

"Yes, sir."

He stood and rubbed his hands. "Then no-one in this building knows of the fall of Portugal! Excellent!" He almost propelled me to the door. "Well done, Robbie." He held out his hand. "Show me the warrant from Prince João."

I gave him the document with the royal seal at the bottom. "It is only honorary, sir. A gesture, nothing more."

He shook his head, "My Portuguese is a little rudimentary but this is an official appointment. I should learn Portuguese if I were you."

"Why sir?"

"Come on laddie you are a bright young man! We will be sending soldiers over to Portugal soon. We need boots on the ground. Hopefully, we won't make a mess of it this time like we did in the Low Countries. You will be over there again, either with or without your regiment. A colonelcy is useful."

"I don't see how."

"You get to command the Portuguese and, when this is recognised by Horse Guards, then you become a major. More pay laddie! Leave this with me and I will show it our lords and masters. Don't worry I'll see you get it back. This is most fortuitous."

"Sir."

"You can go back to your regiment now!"

It was the fastest exit I had ever had. As I made my way back to the ship, I worked out why. Knowledge was power. By telling his lords and masters his news his status improved and his influence widened. I shook my head. There were politics in every army. I was just glad that most of my time would now be spent with troop. I suddenly stopped and turned around. I headed to Piccadilly. I, too, could use this knowledge to my advantage. If there was to be war in Portugal then my regiment would be sent there. I went to see Mr Fortnum and order goods which might be useful to me in a hot clime and I decided to order another uniform. I had no doubt that the rigours of Portugal would soon wear one out and besides one was on board my ship heading for Sicily.

I had forgotten the extent of the trade in wine. Mr Fortnum became quite concerned when he heard of the fall of Portugal. I was not giving away anything which would not become common knowledge soon enough.

"You have done me a huge favour, Captain Matthews. There will be a shortage of port and fine wines soon enough. Prices will rise and a wise businessman will hang on to his goods until the prices rise."

I realised that I was benefitting from the power of knowledge for my bill was discounted by a grateful merchant.

I reached the ship at noon. Jonathan had returned too. His experience was much the same as mine and his star was also rising higher. "I fear I shall have to relinquish the '**Black Prince**'. Their lordships wish me to have a brand new thirty-gun frigate. They have been pushing for some time but I had resisted. I think that Colonel Selkirk will need a new messenger boy."

"How does that work, Jonathan? Will you lose your crew?"

"Not necessarily. When I transfer to my new ship, I will take my officers and skilled sailors such as the top men. The rest can choose to come with me."

I smiled. I knew how popular he was. His crew contained at least ten different nationalities and they were all totally loyal to Jonathan. They were a polyglot bunch of pirates but they were Jonathan's pirates. "Then the new ship will have the old crew. And now we must leave you and get back to the regiment." I had sent Sharp to hire two horses; one for me and one for our luggage. I was anxious to get back to the regiment. I knew that I would be arriving back at the quietest of times. Most of the officers would choose to be on leave over Christmas with their families. I had no family, not in England, at least. I would enjoy the peace of the barracks.

We waved goodbye to Jonathan and set off towards our barracks. There was little chance we could reach it in one journey and we decided to break it at a coaching inn on the way.

We rode up to the barracks at the start of the second week in December. It was the first time we had been home since well before the summer. It all looked the same but it was what went on below the surface which counted. I recognised the trooper and sergeant who stepped out from the guardhouse.

"Captain Matthews! You are a sight for sore eyes. I dare say you have some exciting stories to tell."

"A few, Sergeant Harrison. Is the Colonel around?"

"No, sir. It is just the Major and Lieutenant Stafford. The rest have taken Christmas leave, sir."

"Thank you, sergeant." We rode to the offices and I handed the reins of my horse to Sharp. "See to the horses and then start unpacking."

"Sir!"

"Sergeant Major Jack Jones was poring over papers. He looked up, ready to snarl if I had been a trooper. As it was his face broke into a grin. "Captain Matthews! Good to have you back, sir. It is dull here without you and your adventures to enliven the evenings. Where was it this time, sir?"

I tapped the side of my nose, "I shouldn't really say Sarn't Major but Denmark and Portugal."

"You do get about. And are you back for a while sir?"

"Hopefully. Is the major in?"

"Yes, sir and he will be glad to see you too. He had hoped for a leave himself."

"I am back now and I can pull my weight again."

Major Lucian Hyde-Smith was also poring over lists. "I'm back, sir!"

"The best news I have heard in a long time!"

"And if you want to go on leave sir, I am more than happy to hold the fort."

His face brightened then fell, "That's dashed good of you Robbie but it should really be a senior officer who stays. A major or a colonel."

I smiled, "It is funny you should say that sir." I went on to give him a sanitized version of my trip to Portugal and my appointment. I told him what Colonel Selkirk had said. "So, you see sir, technically, I am both."

He laughed, "I know that what you told me isn't the whole truth just the parts you could tell me but it is damned good news." He went to the cupboard and pulled out a bottle of whisky. "Let's celebrate!" He poured two generous glasses. "Colonel Matthews!"

"Cheers sir. And I think it means we might have regimental action next year."

"Portugal?"

"I am guessing so but if it is true then we will lose many horses. The roads are little more than tracks."

"So long as we have action. The men are becoming indolent."

"And now I shall pack."

"Er sir, Sharp and I hired two horses. If you wish you could use them to return to London. They are paid for."

"I will take you up on that. I hate taking Arthur into London. They have no damned respect for horses there." He stood and shouted, "Sarn't Major Jones."

Jack's head appeared around the door, "Sir?"

"I am going on leave and Captain Matthews will be in command. You will let him know his duties eh?"

"Of course, sir."

That evening there was just myself and Lieutenant Stafford in the mess. Everyone else, the doctor and vet included, were all on leave. William was a keen Lieutenant. He came from a family of moderate means and would not have the money to buy himself a promotion. He had served in another regiment and was quite experienced. I had no doubt that he had volunteered to stay in the barracks to better himself and to save a little money.

I quite enjoyed the silence of the empty mess. The life of the regiment was always one I enjoyed for it was the one place I could be myself without worrying about a knife in the night or being discovered. I knew that my fellow officers knew of some of my activities but not the true extent of them. Certainly, my French father was still my secret as was the fact that I was the illegitimate heir to a French estate.

After the meal was over, we retired to the lounge for brandy and cigars. I noticed, when I opened the box, that we were down to just ten. I had meant to buy some when in Portugal but I had not managed to do so. It gave me something to do the next day. It would cost more but I would buy some in the town.

Before I left, I checked in with Sergeant Major Jones. "How many men do we have on roll this year?"

"Just four hundred. A number of men have retired and a couple ran."

That surprised me. "Really?"

"A bit bored, I think sir. I heard that two of them fancied going to the Americas. There is more action over there."

I nodded, "And is Christmas organised?"

"Yes, sir but if you are expecting anything grand then I am afraid you will be disappointed."

"I take it the Sergeants' Mess will have a fine celebration?"

He grinned, "Oh yes sir!"

"Then I shall take Sharp with me to town and see if I can make it special for Mr Stafford and myself."

"Do you need any funds, sir? The Major left me some petty cash."

I remembered the largely unused bag of coins I had received from Colonel Selkirk. He had not asked for its return and I would put some of it to good use. "No, Sergeant Major, I will take care of that."

I went to the stables. As I expected Sharp was there with his new horse. "Sir, do I have to dock her tail?"

"It is your mount, Sharp. Do as you please but I have not docked Badger's."

That was the way I had been brought up. French cavalry did not dock tails. For some reason, the British army thought it was neater. It was however cruel as, in hot climates, the poor animal could not swish the flies away. "Anyway, mount up and we'll have a ride into Canterbury. We need to buy some supplies for Christmas."

As soon as we set off, I knew that it was not a good day for a ride. The wind whistled from the east and it was below freezing. Badger, however, did not mind. He enjoyed being ridden again. He had been exercised during my time away but it was not the same as being ridden. Partly because of the cold and partly because the horses enjoyed it, we galloped for part of the way. Maria was a good horse. The French Brigadier who had ridden her had trained her well. Both horses managed to build up a healthy sweat by the time we reached the ancient city of Canterbury.

There were other places we could have shopped but Canterbury had the widest range of shops and I liked the old place. We dismounted and led our horses through the streets. As we passed close to the Cathedral, I saw some beggars. The majority would be ex-soldiers and sailors. The navy and the army had little use for those crippled by war and abandoned them as soon as possible.

There were three of them. Two of them wore the faded rusty uniforms of the infantry. One was a one-legged man and the other had lost an arm. However, it was the third man who intrigued me the most. He was dressed in rags and had an olive complexion. He, too, had lost his left hand and his left eye.

I reached into my bag of coins. I handed over a shilling to each of them. Their eyes widened. The soldiers had been given a shilling to join up and it was the equivalent of a day's pay for a soldier. I had given them more than they would beg in a week.

They chorused, "Thankee, sir." The delight on their faces was more than enough reward for me. It was a better use of the Colonel's money than he had intended.

I was about to walk on when the beggar with the olive complexion knuckled his forehead. He was a sailor. "Thank you for your kindness, captain."

The two soldiers gave me a salute and the two of them headed off for the nearest inn. I think I had just given them drink money for a day or so. I did not blame them. I was interested in this man who did not look English and yet spoke like one.

"Are you a sailor?"

"I was sir."

He had a slight accent. "Which ship?"

"The '*Royal Sovereign*', sir. Admiral Collingwood and Captain Rotherham. I got these at Trafalgar." He tapped his stump and his eye patch.

"I met Admiral Nelson once. I liked him, he was a fine man."

He rolled up the sleeve of his right arm with his stump. There was a crude tattoo, '*Our Nel*' with hearts around it. "He was the best officer I ever knew and he only had one eye and a stump."

There was pride in his voice which made me smile. "What is your name?"

"I was born Jorge but my messmates couldn't pronounce that and I answer to Georgie now."

"You aren't English, are you?"

"I was born Portuguese sir but I was pressed when I was fourteen years old, sir and I served in the Navy for twenty years. I feel English."

I turned to leave but paused, "Where do you sleep, Georgie?"

He pointed behind him with his stump. "In the cathedral, if the priests are in a good mood."

I reached into the bag of money and pulled out another shilling. "Buy yourself some decent clothes and replace those rags."

"Thank you, sir. You are a gentleman."

As we continued into Canterbury Sharp said, "He'll spend that money on ale, sir. It's a waste."

"Not him, Sharp. The other two headed directly for the pub but he did not. He intrigues me and I have an idea in my head. If he is still there when we leave then Fate has put him in our way for a purpose."

We purchased some cigars and I ordered food for Christmas day. I ordered a goose, good cheese and some fine claret. We had some Alpini wine but I enjoyed claret especially with goose. The rest of the Christmas feast would be provided by the mess. I knew that they made plum puddings. There would be but two of us for Christmas dinner.

We rode along the icy streets. I saw women with fur coats and muffs and men wrapped in thick woollen coats. They contrasted with the rags worn by the beggars. Georgie still huddled close to the Cathedral and was still dressed in his rags.

We halted. "Why did you not buy yourself some warm clothes, Georgie?"

"I will sir but there are still people coming by. Look." He held out his hand and I saw my two shillings and an additional six copper coins.

I made my mind up. I would use my temporary position as Commanding Officer to do some good. It was Christmas in six days and I would do a Christian act in an unchristian world. I put my hand down. "Jump up behind, Georgie. I will get you some clothes, a hot meal and you shall be warm. At least for tonight." He hesitated, "Come on man! You have served this country well and I am repaying a debt which should have been paid by others."

He took my arm and I pulled him behind. I need not have worried about Badger. The man was all skin and bones. As we rode back to the barracks I asked, "What did you do on the Sovereign?"

"Topman, sir."

That explained his small stature. Top men had to scurry up the ratlines to the highest part of the mast. They were also amongst the most skilled. It was, however, a dangerous job. A top man could be pitched to his death in a storm.

When we reached the gate, we dismounted. "This chap is with me."

The sergeant saluted but I saw him sniff at the man's smell. He was pungent but he was still a man and had his dignity. "Sergeant Sharp, take Georgie to my quarters and let him bathe. Let him have the suit of clothes I took to Portugal. I know they will not fit him but we can have them tailored."

"Sir."

The poor sailor looked mystified. I needed to see the Sergeant Major. I wanted more than one meal for the Portuguese sailor.

"Back already sir? I thought you and Sharpie would be in a boozer for the day!"

"Don't judge us all by your standards, Jack." He grinned. "Now tell me, Sergeant Major, do we have civilians who work in the barracks?"

"Yes, sir. We have laundrymen and women; dishwashers. In the summer we have gardeners. That's about it." I could see that his curiosity was piqued. "Why sir? What is on your mind?"

"Do any of them stay at the barracks?"

He shook his head. "No sir, most of them come from the villages around here. One or two are soldiers' wives and they live close by too."

That decided me. "I have found a one-armed, one-eyed sailor and I want to give him a job. I also want him to be able to sleep in the stables. It is warm there."

He did not seem surprised. "But why sir? I know that you are in charge and you can make the decision but I am interested."

"I know you can keep your mouth shut, Sergeant Major and that what I am to tell you will go no further." He nodded, "We will probably be sent to Portugal in the next six months. The sailor was pressed in Portugal almost twenty years ago. I intend to have him teach me Portuguese."

He began to laugh, "You are, sir, the most complicated officer I have ever met. You are always looking at things differently. I think that is a clever idea. Heaven knows we can all do with the skill to speak to the natives. But can you trust him? He comes from Portugal and you know what these foreigners are like."

It was my turn to laugh. "He was wounded at Trafalgar and he served in the Navy for almost twenty years. What do you think? Besides, it is Christmas and I think that this act is as Christian an act since the baby Jesus was born in a stable."

The reference to the baby Jesus did it. "I think you are right, sir. If you bring him along, I will get the paperwork done. We might as well do this properly."

I went to find Lieutenant Stafford. He was on the parade ground with some of the sergeants drilling the troops. I watched for a while. Soon I would have to get back into the swing of training but, for the moment, I had other matters on my mind.

"Lieutenant, a word please."

The earnest lieutenant was always keen to please and he looked worried at my words. "Have I done something wrong, sir?" I could see him running through his mind all of his recent actions.

"No, William. I am going to learn Portuguese. It might come in handy. Would you like to have a go too?"

"Why yes sir. It sounds grand. Have we hired a tutor?"

"You could say that, lieutenant."

Chapter 6

By the time the other officers returned from their Christmas leave, Georgie had settled in remarkably well. Every tar was naturally hardworking and Georgie seemed especially determined to prove that I had been right to extend a charitable hand to him. He worked in the kitchens as a dishwasher and proved to be a good asset, despite the one hand. Some of the troopers seemed to get on well with him and they built him a lean-to close to the stables. He seemed happy enough there. The cooks made sure he was well fed and he began to put on some weight to cover his bones. The biggest difference was that three of us began to learn how to speak Portuguese. Sharp and I were the most accomplished as we both spoke other languages but even Stafford had made strides.

Surprisingly, the one who had gained the most in all of this was Georgie himself. He was needed once more and had a purpose in his life. He was not receiving charity, he was earning his money. I ensured that he received money for his tutoring. I hoped that one day, he would be able to live a relatively normal life. He was frugal and he did not waste his money. I knew that he was saving and that was a good thing.

Colonel Fenton was a little bemused by my actions but as he said to me, "Nothing about you surprises me anymore. I am just pleased to have you back."

The next few months had more urgency about them as we sent recruiting parties out to secure more men. We did pay better than the infantry but the recent debacles in the Low Countries and in Sweden had made the army less attractive. The Navy was far more popular. Trafalgar and Nelson had ensured that.

Percy Austen and I worked hard with our troop. I had been away too long from them and I knew that we needed to be at the peak of our training if we were to fight in the upcoming conflict. Some of the troopers took a shine to Georgie. I think it is the British love of an underdog. When they heard how the Navy had treated him, they took him under their wing and made him one of their own.

Sergeant Joe Seymour took a special interest in the Portuguese. One of Joe's brothers had died at Trafalgar and, for some reason, it made them closer. Joe also began the Portuguese lessons. He had no idea why he was doing so but he seemed to enjoy it.

By the time May came, we had extra horses and most of the troops were up to their full complement. We just heard rumours from the Continent. I had wondered why I had not been summoned by Colonel Selkirk. I was not unhappy about the fact that I had been overlooked but I was curious. Finally, in the first week of June, Colonel Fenton and myself were summoned to Whitehall. I took heart from the fact that the colonel was with me. It seemed unlikely that I would be sent spying again. That suited me.

We left early to make the journey in one day. "We will stay at my club."

I glanced around at Sharp, "But sir, Sergeant Sharp."

"They have rooms for servants, don't worry Robbie." He chuckled, "The major tells me we now have two colonels in the regiment!"

"I do not think so, sir."

"It may prove useful to you. I know you have a private income but you are a born soldier. The troopers and the officers admire you and you are damned lucky. That is a fearsome combination. Do not shun the talents that God has given you."

"It will be a long war anyway colonel. I shall be happy just to survive."

"You are right there." He threw away the stub of the cigar he had smoked since leaving the barracks. "Portugal, Robbie, what do you make of it?"

"It is not cavalry country; lots of narrow passes and raging rivers. From what I heard Spain is better but we would have to take Portugal first."

"I hope they have a decent general. The Duke of York was a fine fellow but he didn't know his arse from his elbow when it came to tactics. Pardon my French!"

"Sir Arthur Wellesley has his head screwed on. He is not a particularly nice man but then again neither is Bonaparte. I think he can do a fine job if he is given the chance."

"That's the trouble with us, English Robbie. We want everyone to be a nice chap."

I smiled. I was half French and half Scottish. There was not a drop of English blood in my veins.

When we reached Whitehall, Sharp waited with the horses and we joined Colonel Selkirk. He was effusive in his praise for me. This was unusual and had me worried. "Their lordships were more than happy with your intelligence Robbie. You did a grand job."

The colonel and I waited. Colonel Selkirk continued, "Obviously we will be sending troops out there." He addressed Colonel Fenton, "As Robbie may have told you it is not cavalry country but we want you to have a squadron ready to go to Portugal at a moment's notice."

Colonel Fenton nodded, "And you would want Captain Matthews to command I take it?"

"Well, that would make sense. He could combine his work as an intelligence officer with his cavalry duties." Colonel Selkirk frowned. "Is there a problem, Colonel?"

"You seem to be putting a great deal of unnecessary pressure on my officer. You expect him to do your work and run a squadron. It is not satisfactory at all."

I saw Colonel Selkirk reach for the whisky bottle. I smiled. If he thought he could sweet-talk Colonel Fenton with whisky then he was wrong. Colonel Fenton was old school.

"Have a whisky. I am sure we can come to some agreement here."

As he sipped the whisky Colonel Fenton smiled, "Oh I am sure we can but I fear it will cost the war department."

I saw Colonel Selkirk's shoulders droop in resignation. "What would you like?"

Colonel Selkirk smiled, "If you are going to have my officer here running around the country doing your nefarious work then I need a captain to command the squadron."

"That is simple, transfer one of your other captains."

Colonel Felton snorted as he downed his whisky, "Which shows how much you know about serving in a cavalry regiment! Esprit de Corps. My officers are vital to their troops and squadrons."

"Very well then I suppose you wish my department to purchase a captaincy for one of your officers?"

"Of course, Lieutenant Stafford. A fine chap."

"Very well. And then we are happy?

"Of course, there is seniority. We really need a major to command such an expedition."

"That is preposterous! I cannot pay for a majority too."

Colonel Felton smiled, "But you do not have to. Captain Matthews is already a colonel in the Portuguese Army. I understood that such a promotion automatically bestowed a majority on the recipient."

Colonel Selkirk clapped his hands, "Well done, Colonel and remind me never to play chess with you. A clever gambit. Very well, Robbie, you will be made up to a major."

"Thank you, sir."

"Actually, it suits me for it gives you a little more power with the other officers. Now let us get down to the important issues. I do not know who will be in overall command, probably some general who has not fought for fifty years. But I do know who will be commanding the soldiers. It will either be Sir Arthur Wellesley or Sir John Moore. Now Sir Arthur is preparing to take an expedition to South America but Sir John Moore is at Shorncliffe. Robbie, er Major Matthews, I would like you to go to Shorncliffe and brief the general on what you know of Portugal and the problems he will be likely to encounter. He will need to prepare himself for the expedition." As I rose, he took something from his drawer and handed it to me. "Here is your commission from the Prince Regent. Horse Guards has a copy and it will be gazetted." We spent some time with the Colonel making sure that we had all the necessary information and intelligence.

I wondered just how much Colonel Selkirk had been manipulated by Colonel Fenton. I suspected that he had always intended to make a major but the devious man always liked to use cunning.

We stayed with Colonel Fenton at his club. I felt both underdressed and out of place amongst the senior officers there but Colonel Fenton put me at my ease. "You are now a major and I can see greater things ahead for you. Just ignore any of the looks you receive. Many of the officers you see here have never drawn a weapon in anger! In fact, some of them have never drawn a weapon. I can guarantee that none of them have seen as much action as you."

"I forgot to thank you for the majority sir."

"It cost me nothing and if I am brutally honest it was for Stafford. His people do not have the means to purchase him a captaincy and he seems to me the sort of earnest chap who might try to get one on a battlefield and do something reckless."

"You think the buying of commissions works then?"

"In most cases, I would say so." He smiled, "There are exceptions Robbie. You are one and Stafford is another but my family have been fighting for this country in one form or other since the days of Henry II. It is in the blood. I believe that some men are born to lead."

I supposed, in one way, that I believed him. My father for all his cruelty had been a fine leader. However, the army of France was made up of those who were not titled and had shown their skill as leaders before being promoted. I knew that if I had been with the Chasseurs still, I would be a colonel at the least and possibly a general. Bonaparte's wars brought rapid promotion. It would be interesting to fight against my former countrymen. This would not be a skirmish and then a return home. When we got to Portugal we would stay there. How would the officers who had bought their commissions fare against those who had earned them?

We rode back together the next day. Shorncliffe was close to Folkestone and we would pass our barracks before we reached Sir John Moore's headquarters. We left at six o'clock to make Shorncliffe before dark.

It was a huge army camp and had been built by Sir John some years earlier. I guessed that most of those in the camp would be the regiments sent to Portugal. I noted some of the regiments as they drilled and marched: the Northumbrian and Norfolk Foot were there as well as the 29th Foot, the Worcester regiment. I also saw some green-jacketed soldiers whom I did not recognise but I recognised their weapons. They were the Rifle Brigade. The one arm I did not see was the cavalry.

I was still in my captain's uniform. I had ordered my new uniforms in London and I hoped they would be ready upon my return to our barracks. As we had passed through the town, I had taken the opportunity of reserving a couple of rooms. I was not certain how long the general would require me. I did not relish a journey back to our own barracks late at night.

Sir John Moore's aide was a very young lieutenant. I suspected he was appointed because he was a relative. I had encountered such appointments in Sicily. Sometimes they worked and sometimes they caused more problems than enough. This young man appeared to be the former.

"Captain Matthews?" I nodded; it seemed churlish to point out my new rank. The uniform would serve to tell the world of my promotion and I would wait until I donned it. "I am the general's aide; Lieutenant Henry Stanhope. The general is with the Light Division. He likes to train with the troops each day. He is a great man!"

"I have heard that. Is it right that when he built this camp, he made the builders wait until the soldiers had walked around before ordering where the paths should be?"

Lieutenant Stanhope's face lit up, "He did indeed. He is a great believer in the welfare of the men. They adore him."

I nodded, without committing my approval. Sir Arthur's men did not have the same opinion of that particular general but they trusted him and that was sometimes more important. "Does he have many light troops in the Light Division?"

"Only four at the moment but he has them trained really well."

"They will have to if they are to defeat the Voltigeurs and Tirailleurs of the French."

"You have fought them?"

I smiled I had fought with them and against them. "I have seen them in action. We fought them at Maida."

"Then my uncle... the General will be delighted to meet with you. He likes to prepare well when he faces an enemy."

"Perhaps we could go to meet him?"

"That would be a good idea. I shall just get my horse." As we passed the outer office he said, "Mr Colborne we will just go and see the general."

"Yes, sir."

I asked the lieutenant when had left the building, "Who was that?"

"My uncle's military secretary."

We soon left the roads and headed across the rolling Kentish hills. I heard the pop of blanks and the flash of red in the distance. The troops were engaged in manoeuvres. The route we took gave us a panoramic view of the skirmish. One regiment was in line while riflemen and light infantrymen operated in pairs. One fired while the other ran. It was effective and mirrored the Tirailleurs I had seen. This general knew his business.

We watched until they had finished. I saw General Moore talking with the two colonels. We rode down to meet him. Upon seeing us he turned his horse and met us halfway.

He held out his hand. "You must be Matthews." I saw his eyes widen. "I remember you! Good God, you are still alive!" he laughed, "I confess I am happier now than I was."

I had remembered him. He was an astute man and a good soldier. He also had a very gentle way of speaking. I could not help but contrast him with Sir Arthur who was brusque to the point of rudeness. "Yes, sir and this is Sergeant Sharp."

"Come, we will ride back to the office while we talk." It was getting on for four o'clock. That in itself was unusual for senior officers. They liked a short day and long meal times. "Tell me then of Portugal."

"Very poor roads. There are steep passes and rocky gorges. It will be an easy place to defend but not to attack." I gestured back to the skirmish. "Those are the best troops to take."

"Any good for cavalry?"

"Light cavalry would be needed for skirmishing and scouting but that is all. It is not cavalry country."

"Artillery?"

"Mountain pieces or horse artillery would be the best."

"I will, of course, ask you to commit this to paper for me to read in my own time. I merely wish to get a flavour."

"When do you think the army shall go?"

"That depends upon their lordships. I suspect they will wish to see the viability of such an offensive. I would hope to be there by August. If it is much later then we might be stuck in the middle of an Iberian winter. If what you say is true then such poor roads would become impassable in winter."

"They will be for the rivers are mighty rivers. They flow through steep gorges."

He gave me a searching look as we reined in at the main building. "You were spying for Colonel Selkirk?"

"I prefer the term scouting."

He laughed as he dismounted, "And yet you were not in uniform and would have been shot as a spy if you had been captured."

It was my turn to laugh, "Sergeant Sharp and I are quite good at talking our way out of situations."

We strode into his office. He led the way and Lieutenant Stanhope scurried behind. "You can speak languages then?"

"A few."

"Please, sit. Er, your sergeant can go to the mess if he wishes. We will be some time. Henry, show the sergeant to the mess."

"Sir, the horses?"

"Er yes, General will we be staying this evening? If so then Sharp can see to the horses."

"No, that will not be necessary. An hour at most and you can write your report at your own barracks." The two of them left. "I like a man who looks after his equipment."

"I am a horseman sir and I know the value of a good mount. I have had my life saved before now by a gallant steed."

"Now these languages?"

"French, Italian, a little German and Swedish and I am in the process of learning Portuguese. Sergeant Sharp is too."

Captain, you are unique! How on earth did you come to learn Portuguese? Have you a tutor?"

I told him the story of Georgie and when I had finished, he nodded. "It pains me, too, the way that this country uses soldiers and sailors and then discards them. It is grossly unfair and lacks any honour." He began to scribble something on a piece of paper. "I am not certain if your regiment will be accompanying us to Portugal but I want you and your sergeant on my staff. You would be invaluable." My face must have fallen. "You do not wish to serve me?"

"No sir, it is not that but I am a blunt soldier and a man of action. I do not fit in well with fine uniforms and cultured conversation. No offence, sir."

He laughed, "None taken. I take it you mean my nephew?" I nodded. "He is desperate to serve. However, I do like to surround myself with soldiers. If you serve me you shall see action, Captain and you will command. Have no doubts about that."

"I am a soldier, sir, and I obey orders."

"And I prefer to have officers about me who choose to be with me."

There was something about his honesty that I liked. "Then I will serve on your staff, sir."

"Good. I will let you know when I need you but you are just along the road in any case."

We chatted for some time about his officers and his methods. He asked for clarification on some of the issues arising from my Portuguese visit. He pulled out the maps I had captured. "You did well to bring these. The French have good cartographers. I will have copies made." He stood. "I shall see you within the month and keep up with the Portuguese lessons. They may prove to be the difference between success and failure."

In the event, Sharp and I had a mere two weeks for the Iberian Peninsula was proving to be a fast-moving theatre of operations. On July 1st I received a note from Colonel Selkirk advising me that Sharp and I would be embarking for Portugal. Sir John's note followed the next day confirming my appointment to his staff. It also told me that the army would be embarking from Portsmouth which was better equipped to load large numbers.

Colonel Fenton and I were hard pushed to prepare the men in time. The squadron which would be sailing had to head down to Portsmouth under the command of Major Lucian Hyde-Smith. He would oversee their embarkation. I had expected to do that but Colonel Selkirk himself rode down to see me, Colonel Felton and Major Hyde-Smith.

"Robbie. Needs must you have to sail tomorrow for Portugal. You are to board the sloop '*Crocodile*'."

"What about our mounts?"

"They will need to go with the regiment."

"Don't worry Robbie, I shall ensure that they are safely embarked."

"Thank you, Lucian." Badger was the least of my problems. I had hoped to have longer to prepare. "But why the haste? Sir John will not be embarking until the end of the month."

"We are sending Sir Arthur Wellesley and an advance party. It is the division we intended to send to South America. Their transports were already in Cork. They left Ireland a few days ago. '*Crocodile*' will rendezvous with him. It is a fast ship and will enable you to reach Portugal sooner. Sit Arthur will command until Sir John lands. Your local knowledge and your language skills make you eminently qualified. Sir Arthur needs to be brought up to date with the situation as soon as possible. Your first-hand intelligence is vital."

"But I thought I was on Sir John's staff?"

"Don't sound so petulant, Robbie, it does not become you. You are on Sir John's staff as is Sir Arthur."

I was not keen on Sir Arthur. I thought him a snob. Sir John was more of my kind of soldier. However, I would obey orders. It was in my blood. "Very well sir."

With barely enough time to collect our weapons, bags and spare uniforms Sharp and I were whisked into the Colonel's coach to Dover where *'Crocodile'* awaited us. It was another frenetic ride. We were off to war again.

Chapter 7

The sloop was what was known as a fast cruiser. Accommodation would be tight and I suspected that once Sir Arthur joined us, I would be bunking with the officers whilst poor Sharp would have to endure the rigours of a hammock! As I watched, a detachment of ten marines under the command of a gruff sergeant boarded.

"The colonel has sent some lobsters as protection!" He pointed to the departing soldiers. The young captain reminded me of Jonathan. I discovered, during the voyage, that he had heard of him. I nodded. The Royal Marines might prove useful. "We shall have to hurry, Major, if we are to rendezvous with Sir Arthur. I have heard that he is an impatient taskmaster."

I nodded. "He is that." I had my written orders from Colonel Selkirk, there was no reason to wait. Lieutenant Commander Peter Delaney wasted no time in putting to sea. I had thought that *'Black Prince'* was fast but she was as a sluggard compared to the sloop which fairly flew across the sea. I kept my new uniforms in my chest and wore my old one which had the crown in place of the pips. Salt air would do it no good anyway. Most of my luggage would travel with the squadron. They would be on a large transport.

We headed west to rendezvous with the transports carrying Sir Arthur and his troops from Ireland. There were nine thousand of them. Colonel Selkirk had also told me of the five thousand troops already in the area under the command of Sir Brent Spencer. When I had asked what the French were doing to allow British troops that close to Lisbon he had laughed. "They are being murdered by Spanish and Portuguese who ambush them and make their lives a misery. And, of course, the Spanish armies are doing better now. They have defeated a French army at Bailen so your old friend is not having it all his own way."

I took some comfort from that. I had served Napoleon Bonaparte for some years and I had never seen him bested. Since then he had defeated everyone whom he met. I knew that he had not commanded at Bailen but it was a crack and Sir John was just the man to exploit it.

The fleet hove into view on the 13th of July. I did not envy Sir Arthur and his staff transferring to such a small ship. We lowered our sails and Lieutenant Commander Delaney sent a longboat for the general. There were just four people with him. He had a servant, John, a Military Secretary Mr Taylor and two young lieutenants who, I suspected, would be Sir Arthur's dogsbodies.

The moment he clambered aboard he took charge. "Come on get this ship moving! I need to be in Portugal as soon as possible!"

"Sir!"

The young commander quickly organised the ship and we were under sail far faster than I had ever seen. I was impressed. Sir Arthur saw Sharp and snapped, "You, sergeant, help my man get my bags taken to my cabin." Even though he had no idea where that was the resourceful Sharp saluted and headed below decks with the bags. Sir Arthur peered at me. "Do I know you, sir?"

"Yes, Sir Arthur, I met you in Denmark."

"Ah, the cloak and dagger chap. Matthews isn't it?"

"Yes sir, Major Matthews of the 11th Light Dragoons. On temporary duty with Sir John Moore."

His face clouded for a moment and he held out his hand. I took my orders and handed them to him. He read them and gave them back to me. "Walk around the deck with me I find it helps to clear the mind." As the deck was pitching and tossing alarmingly, I hoped he had his sea legs. "Until Sir John arrives, I will be in command so that makes you my aide." He glowered at me inviting a response.

"Yes, sir. I shall be delighted." I used a neutral tone to avoid giving offence.

"Good. You know the way I work so do not expect an easy voyage. I shall run you and your sergeant chappie ragged!"

"Yes, sir."

"Good. Just so long as you know." He suddenly stopped. "You are a strange choice as an aide. I mean you have neither breeding nor manners; why were you chosen?"

It was fortunate that I knew it was just his blunt manner and he had not intended to insult me or else I might have been upset. I told him of my mission to Portugal and my discoveries. He seemed impressed. "Of course, if you can speak Portuguese then I might actually believe that you could be useful." He nodded to the cabin door. On the other side were the lieutenants. "Those two are still wet behind the ears. I haven't got time to teach them what to do. That will be your job."

"Yes, sir. Actually, Sir Arthur, I can speak Portuguese as can my sergeant."

For the first time he smiled, "Good fellow then I may have misjudged you. Now all I have to do is defeat Johnny Frenchman before Sir John arrives and our names and reputations should be made!"

Sir Arthur never changed. I served with him, off and on for the next seven years. He was always rude, self-centred and ambitious. He was the easiest man in the world to dislike and yet, like Napoleon Bonaparte a great general. I had not liked Bonaparte either!

True to his word he had the two of us working every hour in the day. The poor lieutenants, Smith and Brown became glorified servants. Even Sharp was given more respect than they were. To be fair he worked just as hard as we did and I was reminded of Bonaparte who would exist on just an hour or so of sleep a day. Sir Arthur slept a little more; that was the only difference. The maps I had acquired and my knowledge of the Douro valley were crucial.

In the odd moment where we just chatted, he confided his plans to me. "We need to gain a quick victory so that we can establish lines of communication and put pressure on the French." He had looked carefully at my face as he asked me, "I will need you as a scout, Major Matthews once we reach Portugal. I know from Selkirk that you have some talents in that area. Now I realise that may be beneath a major but I need someone who has a military mind and eye. You, I think have both. Battles are won by good soldiers who obey orders but a successful general uses the land to defeat his enemies. Your linguistic skills and your clever mind will be crucial to me."

It was as near to a compliment as he had ever come. "I am flattered Sir Arthur and I will do all that I can to assist both you and Sir John."

He laughed, "Diplomatically put. You are well aware, as I am, of the chain of command. However, I am certain that Sir John will not wish your obvious talents to be wasted."

As the Portuguese coast appeared on our port side Sir Arthur conferred more with the young commander of the sloop.

"I think we shall approach Oporto." It was not a question it was a command.

"And if the French are there Sir Arthur?"

"Then we shall find a safer anchorage but we have Major Matthews with us and I believe he knows the port."

I nodded, "If I might suggest, Sir Arthur?"

"Go ahead."

"There is a beach just outside the port. I could land there and find out if there are French in the town."

He smiled, "There Commander Delaney, a solution presents itself and your little boat will be safe."

I am not certain if Peter appreciated his ship being called a little boat but he nodded gratefully at me and I gave him the directions to the beach close to the villa.

As we neared the beach, I dreaded what I might find. When I had left, before Christmas, there had been fighting close by. I hoped that the redoubtable lady, Donna Maria d'Alvarez had survived. Sharp and I took our pistols as we headed up the path. The villa looked deserted. I saw holes in the walls from musket fire and I began to fear the worst. I cocked my pistol as we entered. There appeared to be no-one there.

Suddenly a frightened voice shouted, in Portuguese, "Who is there? I am armed."

I did not recognise the voice but I took a chance. It was not a Frenchman. "I am Major Matthews and I am a friend of Donna Maria d'Alvarez."

A man stepped from the shadows. I recognised him as one of Donna Maria's servants. When recognition filled his face, he dropped to his knees. "You have come to save us."

"Where is your mistress?"

"They came three weeks ago and took her to Lisbon as a hostage. They did not see me for I was hiding." He stood a little taller. "I am here to protect my lady's home."

"And you are doing a fine job. Do not worry the British are here now and we will drive the French hence. Tell me, are the French in Oporto still?"

He shook his head. "Their army moved south when they took my mistress."

"How is she?"

He smiled, "You know her, senor, and she is strong."

"We have to go to Oporto now. Do you wish to come with us?"

"No, sir. I will now clean and tidy the house for if the British are here then my mistress will return soon." He put his hand on my arm. "You will save her sir?"

"I will do my best."

Sir Arthur seemed relieved with the news and we headed into the port. There were no tricolours flying but that did not mean that there were no French sympathisers in the town. Sir Arthur and I went to find the Prefeito. He remembered me and I had to smile at his shock when I spoke to him in his own language. He confirmed all that I had learned at the villa.

We reprovisioned and retired on board. We sat at the table and pored over the map. Sir Arthur jabbed his finger at Lisbon. "We are too far here from Lisbon. I do not want to spend weeks marching south. I want to bring them to battle as soon as I can."

I traced a line north from Lisbon. "Here sir, close to Leiria. It looks to be near enough to march."

"But where can we land?"

Sir Arthur's servant brought our food.

As he picked up his knife and fork, he said to his servant, "Send Major Matthews' sergeant to us." After he had left, he said, "Is he reliable your fellow?"

I could have taken umbrage but I knew it was just his manner. "Completely."

"And he speaks the language?"

"Yes, sir." His Portuguese was not as good as mine but he understood and could speak the language.

When he arrived Sir, Arthur jabbed a knife in his direction. "Sergeant go and ask some of the captains of the other ships in port of somewhere we can land close to Leiria or Coimbra."

Sergeant Sharp's face did not change as he said, "Yes, Sir Arthur." He saluted and left.

"Seems reliable. Has he been with you long?"

"Quite some time sir."

"Rum sort of thing the two of you do. Sneaking around behind the backs of the enemy."

I smiled, "Generals require intelligence and it is the easiest way to collect it."

"Quite. I can see your point still, rum sort of thing."

We had finished the meal and were enjoying a bottle of port given to us by a grateful Prefeito. When Sergeant Sharp returned Sir Arthur sat back as though expecting a show. Sharp took the map and held it so that the General could see. "They all reckon that the best place is here. A place called Mondego Bay; near the Mondego River. There is a beach there."

"Any French?"

"One of the captains said that there was a fort at Coimbra but that is eight or ten miles from the coast and he says he didn't see any French there. Certainly, he saw no French flags."

"You have done well, sergeant. Go and have your food now."

"Sir." The wry shake of his head told me that Sharp had been halfway through his meal when he had been summoned.

"Come, let us find the captain."

Commander Delaney was supervising the loading of fresh water when we arrived. "Captain, I want to sail on the morning tide to a place south of here, Mondego Bay."

"Sir."

"Now I need a reliable officer to remain here to tell the fleet where we have gone. Whom do you suggest?"

"Mr Pennock is my middy. I'll leave him with a couple of hands."

"Good."

As he turned to go, I grabbed his arm, "Er Peter, send him to me, will you?"

Sir Arthur looked at me. "Why, Major Matthews?"

"Sir, we do not know when the fleet will reach us and Mr Pennock could be here for some days." I saw a blank look on Sir Arthur's face. "He will need somewhere to sleep and money for food and drink."

"Really?"

Richard Pennock was no more than sixteen but he was a keen young officer. I recognised the delight at being chosen. "Mr Pennock I am going to give you a few lessons in Portuguese for you will be here until the fleet comes."

"Yes, sir."

I took out a small leather bag. It contained some of the money I had taken from the dead Brigadier. It was all Portuguese. "Here is money for you and your men. I will take you ashore now and arrange some accommodation for you."

He took it gratefully. Sir Arthur took the map. "Now when they arrive you will tell the admiral that he is to meet us here." He jabbed a finger at Montego Bay. Can you do that Midshipman?"

"Yes, sir."

"Good now go with Major Matthews here. And listen to him! He appears to know what he is doing!"

As I strode along the streets with young Richard close by, I gave him a few phrases in Portuguese. I knew that he would need them if he was to complete the task Sir Arthur had given him. I found a small inn and entered. There were half a dozen sailors drinking there. I went up to the man I took to be the owner. As soon as I spoke Portuguese, he showed surprise and then smiled. Poor Richard just watched as I began to gabble away in a foreign tongue.

"I am a friend of Donna Maria d'Alvarez."

He looked suitably impressed, "She is a fine lady." he suddenly seemed to recall something. "Are you the man who rescued her?"

"I am and you are right she is a fine lady. I hope to find her again soon." I pointed at the midshipman. "I require rooms for this man and two sailors. They will need the rooms tomorrow and until the British fleet arrives."

"The British are coming?"

"We are. Now Mr Pennock here only speaks a few words of Portuguese but I want you to look after him. As a favour to me and Donna Maria."

"I shall do so."

I took out a gold Louis which Colonel Selkirk had given to me. "This will pay for the accommodation and food. You will give the balance to my friend." I saw his eyes widen when he saw the coin and his hand reached greedily for it. "I am going to be in Portugal, my friend, for some time and I will be back."

"Of course, sir and you can trust me."

I turned to Richard. "I have arranged for rooms and food for you from tomorrow. He will look after you and I have paid for the rooms. Now tell him goodbye in Portuguese."

He did so and the owner nodded his thanks.

As we walked back to the ship I continued with my lessons. "Practice the words all night. If you have the chance then speak with my sergeant, he can speak Portuguese too. I know Commander Delaney will pick good men for you but watch them and do not let them drink too much."

"No, sir."

Once back on-board Sir Arthur and I went over the maps to familiarise ourselves with the terrain.

The next morning while Mr Pennock strode off with two of the biggest sailors from the sloop, we headed south for Mondego Bay.

Mondego Bay had nowhere for us to dock. It was a river and a beach. We could see, on the hillside a couple of miles away, a fort. We knew that it would be the one the sailors in Oporto had identified. It confirmed the intelligence as being accurate. "Commander Delaney, be so good as to send a man up to the masthead with a telescope. I want to know what the flag is."

The young commander leapt up the shrouds himself.

"'Pon my soul! I didn't expect him to do that!"

I laughed, "In my experience captains of ships such as this like to do things themselves."

We watched as he reached the top of the mast. His voice came down clearly, "It isn't the tricolour." There was a pause. "It is the flag of Portugal."

"Excellent, then we can land. Hopefully, your Portuguese will come in handy Major."

The journey ashore was exhilarating. The Atlantic surf took us in at a prodigious rate. Sharp and I went first with the marines. Sir Arthur would come with his servant and the others when we had secured the beachhead. It was fortunate there was no opposition for there were just thirteen of us. "Sergeant Bridges spread the men out and we will head to that fort on the hill. Leave four of them here to guard Sir Arthur when he lands."

"Shouldn't we wait here, Major. I mean we don't know who is up there."

"We know that they are Portuguese and that is all that matters."

The fort proved to be further away than I had thought but, fortunately, some of those from within met us. They were all young men and none of them were in uniform. They cheered us when they saw us round a bend some four miles from the fort.

"Are you the men from the fort?"

They were surprised that I could speak their language. "Yes, I am Jose Borge and I lead the students who captured the fort."

"Are there any French?"

He nodded, "There were but they are dead."

"Excellent. We need three horses. Did the French leave any?"

"There is one. It belonged to the officer."

"Sharp, go with him and fetch it. Have a look at the fort too." I turned to the student. "An army will be landing here soon. My sergeant will go with you and bring me the horse."

He frowned, "And why should I take orders from an Englishman? This is Portugal!"

I sighed and pulled my Portuguese commission as a colonel from my coat, "Perhaps because I am also a colonel in the Portuguese cavalry?"

He read the document and saluted. "I did not know. We will obey you." He was very earnest and I deduced that the French they had killed had not been very good if he and his fellows were able to capture the fort.

I made my way back to the beach. "You speak the language then sir?"

"Yes, sergeant."

"That's handy." He spat. "Takes me all my time to speak English!"

"A little tip, sergeant, learn a few words. It will make life easier."

"No need to, sir. We'll be back on a ship as soon as the rest of the army gets here."

His attitude typified most soldiers. Sergeant Sharp was the exception. Sir Arthur was waiting for us. Some of the crew, the lieutenants and the servant were helping the marines to put up tents. The military secretary was busy organising the document cases he had brought ashore. "Well?"

"They are Portuguese students, sir. They have killed the garrison and they say there are no French nearby."

"But do we believe them?"

"I have Sergeant Sharp getting a horse for me, sir and when he returns, I shall scout the immediate area."

"Surely your sergeant could do that?"

"Of course, he could, sir, but you want more than just the numbers of French do you not? You need to know the best way to go to get to Lisbon. The line of least resistance. You need someone to make a decision about what is valuable information and what is not."

He smiled, "I have obviously made my needs clear to you Major. Carry on." He turned to the men erecting the tents. "Get a move on or do you expect me to boil in this sun?"

In truth, it was not very hot at all but then I had served in Egypt where it was really hot all of the time.

Sharp returned an hour later with a fine-looking animal. He dismounted, "Sir, there were twenty or so Frogs. They are all dead. I saw no signs of any others. They were the 65th regiment, sir."

"Good. I will have a little look around. Don't wait food for me."

I paused as Sir Arthur looked up at me. "Be careful, Major."

I smiled. This sounded like concern. "Always, Sir Arthur."

I headed south along the beach. I had studied the maps and knew that Lisbon was some hundred miles to the south. Sir John's light infantry could do that in three days but the rest of the army would take four or five days. I needed to see where the French were and find a good site for Sir Arthur to fight. I rode hard and passed through a quiet Leiria. The locals hid as I galloped through its streets but there were no blue uniforms. My mount was tiring when I neared a tiny village, I later found out was called Roliça. It was fortuitous. I had to turn back but I had found a good place for Sir Arthur to defend should the French attack. It would take the army two days to reach it but the light infantry could make it in one day. I turned my horse and headed north.

I saw the fires on the beach as I led my weary horse the last mile or so. I had ridden further than I ought to have done. I am a horseman through and through and I felt guilty about abusing the captured animal. I noticed that the tents were all perfectly laid out in straight lines. The Marines always did things properly. I saw a pair of sentries. They did not see me until I was lit by the firelight. Had I been a Frenchman I could have killed them before they had known I was there.

"Halt, who goes there?"

"Major Matthews."

"Advance and be recognised."

Sir Arthur and Sergeant Sharp came out of their respective tents. Sir Arthur did not look happy. He flapped his hand at the insects.

"Should have stayed aboard the sloop. Damned flies. Well, Matthews? Found anything?"

"There are no French within a day's ride of us, sir. This will make a good landing site."

"Good. Well, goodnight, Matthews, and well done."

As he turned to enter his tent Sharp said, "I've saved you some food, sir."

Sir Arthur turned as Sharp spoke as though he had suddenly realised that I had not eaten since we had landed. For Sir Arthur, such considerations did not even merit a thought.

Chapter 8

The fleet reached us on the 31st of July. It was too late to land the men but the senior officers and some marines managed to get ashore before the light went completely. As soon as they did so it was as though I had vanished. Sir Arthur totally ignored me. I did not mind for I had been at his beck and call for the better part of two weeks and his abrasive rudeness had begun to get to me.

The next morning, we began the job of landing soldiers, supplies and most importantly, as far as I was concerned, the horses. My job was to help find the French and I needed Sergeant Sharp and another horse to enable me to do so. The captured French horse was not of the best quality. It was no Maria that was for sure.

I hovered close to the tent where Sir Arthur was conferring with his senior officers. I watched as the sailors began to row the soldiers ashore. It was a disaster! Half-naked sailors had to lunge into the foaming surf to rescue soldiers flung from overturned longboats. The soldiers were not used to the violence of the sea and many were lost before they had even set foot in Portugal. For once I could not help.

Midshipman Pennock came ashore from the '*Crocodile*' with some of the supplies we had left aboard. He strode up to me confidently and handed me some coins. "Here you are, sir. Francisco said he kept his word."

"Francisco?"

"The owner of the bar sir. He was a nice chap."

"And you spoke with him?"

"A little sir. Between his English and my Portuguese, we understood each other. Will it be worth continuing my lessons, sir?"

"I think we will be here for some time to come, Middy so yes."

He nodded, "Then I will continue." There was a sudden shout from behind us as another longboat overturned pitching ten red-coated soldiers into the sea. "This isn't good sir. Is this usual?"

"It is the first landing I have seen and I am just grateful that the French are not here!"

The senior officers seemed oblivious to the disaster just yards away from their tent. I wondered just how long it would take. "Middy, which ship has the horses on?"

"That one there I think sir."

"Right, take me out to her if you please. Sharp!"

"Sir!"

"Come with me."

We rowed to the ship and I saw that the horses were waiting to be unloaded. The troopers were watching, nervously from the rail. I climbed up the tumblehome. As soon as they saw my uniform, they all saluted. The captain came over to me, "Yes sir? Who are you?"

"I am Major Matthews the aide to Sir Arthur Wellesley."

He seemed satisfied and some of his annoyance at the uninvited guest disappeared. "How can I be of service?"

"I take it you wish to be rid of these horses?" I knew from Captain Dinsdale that sailors like their ships clean.

"If I had my way, I would hurl the stinking animals from the side but their officers do not think it right."

I nodded, "Sergeant Sharp go and find the senior officer and ask him if he will come over for a moment."

"You have something in mind?"

"If we try to load the horses into longboats the boats will be overturned and the crews may well be injured. Even worse, so far as I am concerned, we would lose valuable horses which we cannot replace."

"What else can we do?"

"Sir?"

I turned and saw a captain and a lieutenant of the 20th Light Dragoons. I wondered if their blue uniforms might cause a problem.

"I am Major Matthews, 11th Light Dragoons and Sir Arthur's aide. You are?"

"I am Captain Harold Goodwin and this is Lieutenant St. John Hart."

"How many men do you have?"

"Forty troopers from 1st Troop A squadron sir."

"I was just explaining to the captain here that the horses may react badly to a longboat."

"That they will, sir."

"Captain, how close can you take your ship in?"

"Our draught means I can get to about a hundred yards or so from the beach; if I put a man with a lead in the bows."

"If you do that, we can swim the horses in."

Captain Goodwin said, "Sir! That is madness! They will drown."

"I can assure you they will not." I turned back to the ship's captain. "What do you say, Captain?"

"We'll give it a go. First Lieutenant, prepare to hoist anchor and signal the flagship to tell him we are moving station."

I leaned over the tumblehome. "Mr Pennock, we are going to move and then swim the horses ashore. Would you be so good as to stand by in case I get into difficulties?"

"Aye, aye sir!"

Lieutenant Hart said, "Sir? You are going to swim ashore?"

"I am Mr Hart."

"But you are a major!"

I laughed, "And majors can get just as wet as Lieutenants. Sergeant Sharp, get your boots off we are going swimming."

"Righto, sir."

By the time we were in position, we were stripped down to our shirts and overalls. "Captain Goodwin, if you send a dozen of your troopers ashore, they can watch the horses after we land them."

I think the poor officer was too bemused to argue and he ordered his troopers into the longboats.

As soon as the first horse was in the sling I stood on the tumblehome. "You have the next one sergeant. Er Captain Goodwin, what is the name of this horse?"

He did not know but his troop sergeant shook his head and said, "Blackie sir."

"Thank you, sergeant …?"

"Smith sir and I can swim. Can I help?"

"Of course, you can. The more the merrier. Just watch Sharp and me. We have done this before. Well, here I go!"

I jumped from the side and disappeared beneath the Atlantic which seemed like ice after the warm air of the land. It was colder than I had expected. I bobbed to the surface, spluttering, and waved to the crew. "Lower away!"

The horse came slowly down. The sailors were being as thoughtful as they could be. As soon as it was in the water, I swam next to it. I stroked its muzzle, "There Blackie. There's a good horse." I kept talking as I grasped the reins in my left hand and undid the knots on the sling with my right. The Royal Navy knew how to tie good knots. That meant they could be untied. The sling fell free. I pulled Blackie's head around and lay flat along his back with my feet over his rump. "Go on old chap." I kicked both sides of his rump with my bare feet and he began to swim to shore. The waves and the tide made it easy. I should not like to do this in reverse but it was not so hard going with the tide. The waves did not strike his head and he could see the shore.

Pennock and his men stroked next to us. "Are you alright sir?" I saw the concern on his face.

"I am indeed, Mr Pennock. We will be fine. Be so good as to go back and wait for the sergeant. Sergeant Sharp will manage but Sergeant Smith may find it difficult."

I saw the troopers ashore as they shouted encouragement. One of them was up to the waist in the foam and he was shouting to Blackie. The horse swam harder. The trooper grabbed the bit and said, "Thank you, sir. I didn't think he would do it."

"Your horse, trooper?"

"Yes, sir. I can't swim else I would have done it."

"He's a good horse and he will not be afraid of water anymore." I gave him the reins and stepped out of the sea. The air felt much warmer. I turned and saw Sharp halfway across and Smith about to jump in. I looked around for another boat to take me back out but there were none. I would have to wait until Midshipman Pennock returned. Sergeant Smith was finding it more difficult than Sergeant Sharp who was almost at the shore. Then, to my amazement, I saw another trooper stripped and preparing to jump into the sea.

When the Midshipman arrived, with Sergeant Smith, four of the troopers who were close by came up to me. "Sir, our horses are still on board and we can swim. Can we bring them in?"

"Of course, you can. I would leave your clothes here though."

And so, Sergeant Sharp and I did not need to bring ashore any more horses. The two officers did not bring any across but the troopers seemed to enjoy the experience and by late afternoon we had all their mounts and the five remounts safely landed.

I had just dressed when Sir Arthur walked up to me. "Just when I think I know all there is to know about you then you surprise me again. I must admit you have helped considerably. We now have scouts."

"They will need a day or two to get their legs, sir." I pointed to the soldiers who had just landed. They were staggering around like drunken men. "And the horses too."

"Annoyingly, you are correct again. As soon as you can I want you to lead a patrol south and find the French. Oh, and I want you to brief the senior officers in the morning." He waved an irritated hand towards the ships and boats still coming ashore. "God knows how long it will take us to land everyone. If Johnny Frenchman had a bit more about them, we would have been attacked already!"

When Captain Goodwin and his lieutenant arrived ashore, I took them to one side. "I am afraid you will not have long to adjust to life ashore. We have just two days to have the horses ready for a patrol."

"We sir? I thought you were the general's aide."

Obviously, Captain Goodwin did not relish taking orders from an officer from another regiment. There was no time for such niceties. "Until you hear differently, Captain, then you will take orders from me. This troop is the only cavalry we have and, as such, we are the eyes and ears of the whole army. We have nine thousand men coming ashore. Junot has more than three times that number available to him. Until Sir John Moore lands and General Spencer reaches us from Gibraltar then we have to do the job of a Light Brigade."

I could see that he was chastened and I had not made a friend. I had enough friends. I needed men who would obey my orders. I was happier with the men. My actions in swimming Blackie across appeared to have impressed them. Sergeant Sharp and the troop sergeants had bunked in together and I knew he would be singing my praises. The officers could be as awkward as they liked so long as the troopers obeyed me.

The next morning, I made sure that my uniform was as clean as I could make it. I knew that I would be judged on my performance. There were General Hill, General Ferguson, General Nightingale, General Bowes, General Crauford, and General Fane seated in the tent with a couple of colonels. They all listened intently to all that I said but Colonel Lake looked to be bubbling with excitement. He could barely keep his seat. It was disconcerting to watch him. Some of the generals kept flashing him irritated looks. When the General asked for any questions it was Colonel Lake who bombarded me with questions. He was desperate to get to grips with the French. Eventually, General Wellesley had had enough. "Colonel Lake we will find the French eventually and Major Matthews will find them for you but we are still unloading the damned ships. I am just glad that Major Matthews was able to get the horses ashore safely."

Colonel Lake subsided. General Hill asked, "Can we expect any Portuguese help? It is their country, after all."

"Colonel Trant is somewhere south of us with two thousand men and I hope that Major Matthews can find them tomorrow."

When the briefing was over, I asked, "Who is Colonel Trant sir?"

"He is like you, Matthews. He is a British major who has been appointed a Colonel in the Portuguese army. You two should get on. He commands a brigade of Portuguese troops. They are somewhere north of here."

"I thought you wanted me to scout south, sir?"

"I do and when you have found the French then you can find our allies." Sir Arthur set high standards for everyone.

In the event, we did not need to find Colonel Trant. Even as we headed south his weary brigade marched into the camp to swell our numbers.

I took my new command south to Leiria. I had seen no French there on my solo scouting expedition but who knew if they would have arrived in the intervening days. As we rode into the village, I ordered skirmishers out. "Captain Goodwin, skirmishers."

Sharp and I rode up to the largest building in the town. I rapped smartly on the door. I was lucky. I had found the Prefeito. Once again, my use of the Portuguese language made us welcome. And I discovered that the nearest French were either in Lisbon or closer to the Spanish border. We were in no immediate danger.

I pushed on more confidently now and we made good time. We camped in the hills above Torres Vedras. I saw a French flag flying from the top of a tower. I summoned the officers and sergeants of the troop. "We have found the French. There is a tricolour above the fort." They looked at me expectantly. "Sergeant Sharp and I will go down for a closer look. Captain Goodwin, you will hold the troop here. I should be back before dark but I may be delayed."

"What happens if you are not back by the morning sir?"

"Then you will return to the General and tell him that we have found the French."

"Then why don't we just go back now sir and tell him that?"

"Because the men and horses are tired and we need them to rest but, more importantly, the general needs the numbers of the French and that is what we will do."

"My men could do it, sir."

"Unless they speak French and Portuguese as well as knowing how to identify the French units I think not. The sergeant and I have done this before." I turned to Sergeant Smith, "Make sure you have pickets out and no fires. It will be cold rations."

"Sir." I could rely on Smith. He reminded me of my own troop sergeants.

We made our way along the track which led through the woods. As soon as the woods thinned out a little, we entered them. It soon became obvious that there were soldiers camped in the vicinity. We could smell the wood fires. I found a dell and dismounted. We took off our Tarleton helmets and left them on the saddles. If we were seen our tunics might be mistaken for French blue n the fading light. I led Sharp up the slope. I did not envy the French soldiers. The ground was not level and they would have had a hard job to erect tents. I suspected, as it was now summer, that many of them had not bothered with tents.

The darkness which had descended aided us. I knew that there would be cavalry pickets out as well as infantry. It was another reason for leaving our horses behind. A strange horse could alert the vedettes. I saw a glow as we neared the first of their camps. The trees and the undulating land made it difficult to ascertain numbers but we had their position. The tricolour had told that the town was occupied. The camp told us that it was a French army.

I gestured right and we moved along the edge of the darkened forest. I counted on our blue tunics and grey overalls hiding us in the forest. I could see that the camp was a mixture of light and regular infantry. We kept moving around the edge to see if we could identify regiments. A whiff of horse manure reached me. We were close to horses. That meant there were cavalry too. The tree line was further from this camp and I saw the horse lines. The horses were a clue as to the regiments but the saddle clothes confirmed it. They were Chasseurs à Cheval and Dragoons. I had seen enough. If there were cavalry and infantry then there would be artillery. Napoleon Bonaparte loved his cannon and he would not send an army to Portugal without artillery support.

We had almost made it back to our starting point when I voice shouted, "Halt."

I mimed for Sharp to drop his overalls and squat.

The question was repeated.

As the question had been asked in French I answered in French, "We are cavalry! My companion has the shits!"

Two infantrymen emerged from the direction of the camp. They
had bayonets on their muskets and they were pointed at us. "What
are you doing out of camp?"

"Jean here has a taste for mushrooms and we were about to look
for some when he needed to crap. I blame the cook."

They both laughed at that. Then one of them said, suspiciously,
"Where are your mushrooms?"

"I told you we didn't have time yet to find any."

Sharp moaned and then began to pull up his overalls.

"Where are your shakos? What regiment are you?"

I could see that they were not taken in. I knew it was not my
accent. They must have noticed that our uniforms did not look like
theirs. They had, however, made the mistake of closing with us.
Their muskets were barely three feet from us and close enough for
me to see that they had not cocked their weapons. That made
sense. Sentries rarely walked around with a cocked musket; if you
tripped and fired it would bring down the wrath of the duty
sergeant upon you. I gave the slightest of movements with my
head.

I half bent over and groaned. It allowed me to reach the stiletto in
my boot. "What's the matter?"

"Now I have the shits!"

Sharp played his part and moved towards me his left hand held
out as though to aid me. The two sentries were still suspicious and
came closer. I grabbed the musket with my left hand and pulled the
sentry to me. I ripped my stiletto across his throat and he died
silently. Even as his companion watched, Sharp had taken his own
knife and plunged it into the heart of the other.

"Grab their bodies and we'll dump them. Hopefully, they will
think the locals have done it." I slung the body over my shoulder
and we trudged down the hill. When we reached the horses, I
emptied the pockets of the soldier to make it look like theft and
took his musket. Once mounted, we headed back to our camp.

"Who goes there?"

"Major Matthews."

We dismounted and led our horses into the camp. I dropped the musket down on the floor. Captain Goodwin walked over. "Is that French?"

I nodded and took the piece of bread Sergeant Smith proffered. "A couple of sentries disturbed us."

"We heard no shots."

I pulled out my stiletto. "I used this."

Goodwin looked shocked, "It is a dagger!"

I laughed, "And it is quiet. An Italian bandit once tried to use it to emasculate me. He died." The captain walked off, offended, I think by the crudeness of the weapon.

Sergeant Smith said, "Could I have a look at that sir?"

"Of course, you can Sergeant."

He balanced it in his hand and then drew it down his cheek. He looked at the hairs in his hand, "By Christ sir, but that is sharp."

"A blunt weapon is of no use to anyone." He handed it back and I slipped it inside my boot.

"That's very handy. I shall have to get one."

I pointed to the musket with the bayonet. "If you take the bayonet then the blacksmith can make it shorter and thinner. It will then fit inside your boot."

"Thank you, sir." He took the bayonet and then nodded to Sharp who had finished feeding and watering the horses. "Sharpie said you weren't like most officers. He was right." He cast a dark glance in the direction of his own officers. I noted that. It was not good. My men would never have dreamt of implying such criticism at me.

The next day, as we headed east, Lieutenant Hart noticed my jacket. "Sir, there is blood on your tunic."

I nodded, "It was the sentry I killed." He had a look of horror and revulsion on his face. "Lieutenant, have you been on active service yet?"

"Yes, sir, I was in South America two years ago."

"And did you see much action."

"Action sir?"

"Yes, fighting. Have you used your carbine or your sabre against someone who was trying to kill you?"

"No, sir, but I know what to do."

I pulled out my sword. "I took this from the dead hands of a man who had been trying to kill me almost fifteen years ago. Let me tell you that there is a difference between knowing what to do and actually doing it. When you have fought your first Frenchman come and talk to me about it."

Chapter 9

We arrived back at the beach two days later. We had seen no other French troops. To my relief, most of the troops and supplies appeared to be ashore. "Captain, see to the men and make sure they rub-down the horses. They need looking after in this country."

I received a peremptory, "Sir" and a look of disbelief. I do not think the young captain liked me. He did not need to. He just had to follow orders.

Colonel Lake accosted me before I could report to the general, "Well, Major, did you find the French?"

"Yes, sir."

"Well, where are they then?"

"With respect sir, my orders were to report to Sir Arthur. You may ask him once I have reported."

"For God's sake, Matthews, we are all on the same side!"

"Yes, sir."

I strode past him and approached the sentry. The marines had returned to the sloop and been replaced by the Northumberland Foot. "Tell Sir Arthur that Major Matthews has returned."

"Sir!"

His accent reminded me of Geordie my seafaring friend from Newcastle upon Tyne and I smiled. I heard Sir Arthur say, "Come in, Matthews!" He was poised over the map and asked, eagerly, "Well?"

"We found their main camp at Torres Vedras. We swept to the east and saw nothing."

"Any sign of their scouts?"

"No, sir but that doesn't mean they aren't out there." He gave me a quizzical look. "The troops you have here sir, well the cavalry we rode with at least, are not experienced in this type of warfare. They will take time to gain the skills. Sharp and I have the experience necessary but not the 20th. Not yet anyway."

He nodded, "And your 11th is with Sir John Moore on their way to Lisbon."

The news pleased me, "They have left England?"

"Yes, which means we have to get to Lisbon and secure the port so that the rest of the troops can land."

"We will leave tomorrow and head for Leiria. I intend to march down the coast."

"The roads might be easier sir."

"We only have eighteen guns and two wagon trains. We need support from the fleet until we reach Lisbon."

I understood his dilemma. "The men will find the march hot and hard sir."

"Perhaps but it will allow them to build up their land legs again." He seemed to notice my bloody uniform. "Been in action already?"

"Sharp and I had to kill two sentries." I saw the look of alarm on his face, "Oh don't worry sir we made it look like the work of the partisans."

He shook his head, "The Spanish are calling them guerrillas. It is an ugly war between them and the French. It may come back to haunt Bonaparte. You had better be off and get yourself cleaned up."

"Oh, by the way, sir, Colonel Lake wanted to know what I had discovered."

"You didn't tell him, did you?"

"Of course, not sir but I wanted you to know as he did not look happy."

Major, I do not give a fig for my officer's happiness; just so long as they follow my orders."

As I headed towards my tent, I saw a uniform I didn't recognise. It was an all blue uniform which looked vaguely French. The officer held out his hand, "I take it you are the infamous Major Matthews. I am Nicholas Trant, Colonel of the Portuguese troops."

I shook his hand. "Pleased to meet with you."

"Come to my tent and we'll have a drink. "

I could smell the alcohol on his breath. I later discovered he liked a drink. Sir Arthur once said of him, "*A very good officer, but a drunken dog as ever lived.*"

I was keen to talk to someone who commanded the Portuguese, "Of course so long as you don't mind someone in a bloody uniform."

He put his arm around my shoulder, "Unlike most of these officers it shows you are a soldier who knows how to fight." In his tent, he poured me a healthy goblet of wine. "Cheers!"

"Cheers!"

He nodded at the tent walls, "Most of these look down on me. They think a Portuguese Colonel is the lowest of the low." He smiled at me, "But you are a Portuguese Colonel too, I hear."

"Purely honorary and I doubt that I will ever get to used it."

"Do not be too certain about that. You speak Portuguese and I have heard that they are appointing Viscount Beresford as a Marshal of Portugal. It might be worth taking up the appointment full time."

I shook my head, "I think I will stay with the 11th."

"Your loss, still at least I have someone to drink with here."

"I think we will be moving soon and heading south."

"Good, my lads are itching for a fight. Listen, I understand from his lordship that you have led cavalry in engagements before."

"I have."

"Sir Arthur seems to think it might be a good idea to brigade your Light Dragoons with my cavalry. There are only two hundred and fifty of them but your knowledge of Portuguese might come in handy."

"Quite happy to but I am not certain how Sir Arthur wants them used."

He shrugged, "We will all find out soon enough how he works won't we?"

We saw the bad-tempered side of Sir Arthur the next day as it took a whole day to cover twelve miles. The three hundred cavalry which were under my command were spread out in a thin screen before the army and I did not see his angry outbursts. I heard the reports of them that evening. I knew why he was so anxious. When Sir John Moore arrived, he would be subordinate and Sir John was on his way. However, at least Sir John Moore was a soldier like himself. The other two commanders who were on their way, Generals Burrard and Dalrymple, had not fought for over twenty years. Sir Arthur wanted a victory before they arrived.

That evening I was invited to dine with Sir Arthur. "This is going to take forever, Matthews. I want you to take the cavalry tomorrow and keep pushing ahead of us. I want to know where the French are and we must bring them to battle."

"Yes, Sir Arthur." Something had been playing on my mind. "Sir Arthur, the lady I told you about, Donna Maria d'Alvarez is being held in Lisbon. She is a friend of the Queen of Portugal. I would like permission to take some men and try to rescue her."

He peered down his beak-like nose, "I can see it is important but you are too valuable to the army. Until we get Paget here with the cavalry, I need you as a cavalry commander. Once they arrive with Sir John then you have my permission but until then I want you to be the eyes and ears of my army. If the French twitch I want you to know first. Understand?"

"Yes, sir."

"You are a good fellow, Matthews, but you need to get your priorities in perspective."

As I led off the three and a half squadrons the next day, I reflected that I had never led such a large force before. As Colonel Trant had predicted the Portuguese were impressed with my language skills. In addition, the story of my killing of a sentry had been circulated and exaggerated. The Portuguese are always impressed by someone who can handle a knife is held in great esteem and I had their respect. Sadly, I did not have the respect of the two officers of the 20th. They viewed me as some sort of assassin. I hoped combat would change their opinion.

Behind us, we had the support of two companies of the 95th Rifles. They were reassuring in their green uniforms with their Baker rifles slung over their shoulders. I was not certain if the carbines of the 20th had ever been fired. The Portuguese did not even own a carbine. Unless we met cavalry, we would have to run.

It was on the second day out to Leiria that we met our first Frenchmen. I was with Captain Luis Moreno of the 6th line regiment when we saw a flash of blue in the woods ahead. The Portuguese knew of my honour from their Regent and the captain said, "Colonel, my men say there are blue uniforms ahead."

"Sharp, my compliments to Captain Kincaid of the 95th and tell him there are French ahead and we may need him and his rifles."

"Sir!"

"Captain, have your men form a skirmish line and follow me. Be ready to retreat if I so order it."

We trotted forward. I had no telescope with me. That was with my carbine and the rest of the luggage with the squadron but I saw that they were light infantry and they were in the woods. French light infantrymen were not afraid of cavalry if they were in woods. They knew we were helpless. I hoped that our presence would drive them back but the crack of a flurry of muskets told me that I was wrong. One of the Portuguese troopers clutched his arm. "Captain, order your men to fall back."

He did so, albeit reluctantly. Captain Kincaid and his riflemen appeared behind me. I dismounted. There was little point in giving the enemy target practice. "Sharp, hold my horse. They are in the woods, captain. Light infantry."

He shielded his eyes from the sun. "About two hundred yards. Let's see if we can shift them then eh sir?" he turned to his men. "Right lads, use the cover we have here and let's see how many Frogs we can knock off."

The captain took his rifle and used the back of my saddle to rest it. He squeezed off a shot. The horse barely moved. It had been trained well. I saw a blue figure fall to the floor.

"Good shot, captain."

"It's unfair really. These Bakers are accurate up to three hundred yards and my lads are better than I am."

The rifles cracked away irregularly and I saw more and more figures fall. Some of them began to move back.

"Right, Captain Moreno. Get your men up here. Let's see how they handle their swords." When they formed up behind me, I said, "Forward."

There was a hollow below the woods and we dropped into it. I drew my sword. The rifles were able to continue to fire as we approached the wood. I turned to the bugler. "You stay close and captain when I order recall, I want your men to stop. Is that clear?" He nodded. "Good. Sound the charge!"

The eighty troopers all screamed their own war cry as we hurtled towards the woods. They were spindly woods which would not hinder us and the French were fleeing. The hardest job we had was avoiding the tree roots which threatened to trip unwary horsemen. I did not ride the strange horse too hard. Badger was surefooted in woods; this one I did not know. I saw a musket suddenly appear behind a tree some twenty yards away. He could not miss. I lay flat against the horse's mane and felt the ball as it creased the crest on my helmet. Unless he has time and is calm a man firing a musket will always shoot slightly high. That knowledge had just saved my life. He tried to spear me with his bayonet but I flicked it aside and plunged my sword into his throat.

We had come far enough. "Sound recall!"

The bugler had stayed close to me and the notes rang out.

Captain Kincaid appeared next to me. "Well, that is unusual."

"What is?"

"Cavalry actually stopping when they are ordered to."

I laughed, "I know. Thank God these are Portuguese and scared witless of what I might say if they disobey me!"

It did wonders for the Portuguese morale. Colonel Trant was delighted when we returned to camp with the news that we had found the French. "They think you are a lucky charm, Major. The first victory and it has fallen to the Portuguese."

I didn't like to spoil his party but it had been the rifles which had driven off the enemy and ten dead Frenchmen hardly made a victory. But there was an exultant mood in the camp that night. Colonel Trant was always ready to celebrate and he involved all of the others. The officers of the 20th felt snubbed and they wondered why I had not been with them. I could not wait for Paget to come and take them off my hands.

We continued to harry the French as they retreated south. Sir Arthur was frustrated for he wished to bring them to battle. When I reported their numbers at the end of the second day of chasing, he became even more excited. "There are less than five thousand you say? By God sir, I can have them. Tell me Matthews are there any hills close by?"

"Yes sir, close to the tiny village of Roliça." I pointed to the map. "There are four gullies leading up to it. There are plenty of woods in the surrounding hills." I anticipated his next question. "The woods are too thick for artillery but horses and men can pass easily through them."

He smiled and patted my back, "Good fellow! You know my mind." He thumped the map. "Go and bring in the senior officers. I have my plan!" They were all enjoying a cigar and wine in the cool of the early evening.

Sir Arthur Wellesley had the quickest mind of any man I have ever met save for Bonaparte. He could gauge the way the land would aid or hinder him and use it accordingly. His one weakness appeared to be when working with troops and officers he did not know. This would prove to be crucial the following day.

I brought them in and Sir Arthur started without any preamble. "Gentlemen tomorrow we rid ourselves of this little force which is holding us up until Marshal Junot can reach us. There is a hill here," he jabbed his finger at Roliça, "close to the village. It controls the roads to Lisbon and our French opponent will try to hold it." Such was the power of the general that no one asked where he had gained his knowledge.

"Colonel Trant you will take your Portuguese, the 20th under Major Matthews and a company of the 95th and you will advance to the west of the hill. Generals Ferguson and Bowes, you will advance along the east. Take a couple of the lighter guns with you. We will outflank them. We have superior numbers and better troops. The rest of the army and the guns will hold their attention to the front to enable us to outflank them. Questions?"

The only question came from Colonel Lake. "Sir, might I be allowed to accompany General Ferguson and his brigade?"

Sir Arthur looked down his hook-like nose at the Colonel. Sir, you are part of General Nightingale's Brigade and I need your 29th in the centre. Do not try to interfere with my dispositions. Any further questions?" The rebuke had silenced them all. "Good, then study the map and the attack begins at nine in the morning."

Nicholas put his arm around me as we left the tent. "We shall have the honour of beginning this attack. My fellows will be pleased that their lucky charm is with them."

"Have you fought the French before, Colonel?"

"Not in a large battle, why?"

"I have and Bonaparte does not appoint bad generals. All of those who lead the French began at the bottom and worked their way up. They know their men and they know how to fight. I do not doubt that we shall win but unless we fight carefully, we will lose men. The courage of the men you lead is frail." I held up my hand. "I have spoken with those who know. They were soundly beaten by the Spanish and the French just walked into their country. You saw yourself how hard it is to land men from the sea. The French can come by land. If we lose men, we cannot just send to England for them, can we?"

"God but you are a misery, sir! I thought you would have been ready to lead a glorious charge tomorrow!"

I laughed, "I do not think Sir Arthur likes such charges. Cavalry have a habit of continuing to charge long after the objective has been achieved."

"But not you."

"No, sir, not me. I have been fighting since 1794 and I do not see this war ending any time soon. One day I hope to retire to my family estate in Sicily. You will not see any attempt at glory from me."

I finished the wine and Nicholas refilled it. Sharp brought my sword. "Here you are, sir, I have put a nice little edge on it for you."

"Thank you Sharp, now get some rest, tomorrow promises to be a busy day."

"Sir."

"Do you mind?"

I handed the sword over.

"A fine weapon. Austrian isn't it?"

I nodded and sipped my wine. It was a pleasant evening. There was a breeze from the west which made the flies less voracious. Tomorrow would be as hot as Hades.

"I thought the Austrians were our allies. How did you capture such an expensive blade?"

I smiled enigmatically, "The fortunes of war Nicholas. I keep my eyes open! I advise you to do the same."

Chapter 10

We were in position by eight o'clock. I gathered the troop
commanders around me. I had to translate my words for Captain
Goodwin but it was important that they all knew both my mind and
the orders of Sir Arthur. This would be the first battle where
British and Portuguese had fought alongside each other. It would
not bode well if it went badly.

"We are to support Colonel Trant and attack the French left
flank. The Portuguese Cacadores and the 95th will be responsible
for the actual attack. Our job is to keep the French from escaping.
If they have cavalry then we will neutralise them. If the
opportunity presents itself then we will pursue them. That will only
be when I give the command. We have too few cavalry to throw
them away. I will personally punish any officer who disobeys my
orders." The Portuguese officers seemed to accept the threat but
Captain Goodwin looked offended. I decided to keep him close to
me.

Colonel Trant sent his scouts towards the French at half-past
eight and they reported that the French had their guns in the centre
and their cavalry on the left flank facing us. The French cavalry
outnumbered us and were better than the Portuguese I had with me.
My men were brave enough but I knew that the French were better
mounted, equipped and trained. Had I had my own regiment then
things might have been different. I did not know how the
Portuguese would react under battle conditions. I had seen both
Austrians and Italians fleeing the superior French cavalry.

The battle began with a barrage from the handful of guns which
both sides possessed. They were of small calibre and did little
damage but they did cause a mist of smoke which disguised
positions. The whole field was covered in a masking of pungent
grey. Colonel Trant ordered his Portuguese forward and I led the
small force of cavalry at my command to guard the right flank of
the attack. The French commander was wily. He could see he was

outnumbered and he ordered his Chasseurs forward to cover his men while they fell back to better positions.

"Sir! Let us charge them! We can chase them away easily!"

"Captain Goodwin, wait until you are given orders. They are Chasseurs and they are well trained. You may not have noticed but they outnumber us! Back in line, sir!"

Once the infantry had reached their new positions the cavalry withdrew a safe distance to be away from the rifles which had already claimed four or five victims. The cannons were set up again and we moved forward. I could see that the French General was heading for the top of the hill. It would enable him to fire down at the advancing British. I could see how clever Wellesley had been. Our flank attack would work for he did not have enough guns to cover three sides.

Once again, he ordered his cavalry forward to cover the retreat of his men. "Cavalry! We will advance and, on my command, discharge our weapons!" The Portuguese cavalry had a single pistol but the 20th had carbines. The French musketoon did not have the range of our carbines and I hoped to make them move early.

We trotted forward in one line and the French advanced too. When we were a hundred yards apart, I shouted, "Fire!"

The French were not expecting the volley and few had their musketoons out. The Portuguese pistols did little damage but two Chasseurs were hit by carbines. "Fire!"

The second volley was more ragged and the French replied with their weapons but two more Chasseurs were hit before a wall of smoke descended between us. I heard the bugle sound the French recall but one Chasseur took it upon himself to charge towards me with his sabre held before him. I took out my pistol and aimed at him. As he approached, I could see that he was young. Yet he had the pigtails and the waxed moustache. He could have been me ten years earlier. At twenty yards I pulled the trigger and he fell backwards over the rump of his horse. Sharp grabbed the reins of the frightened beast as it stopped at the wall of horses before it. He began to talk to it in French and it started to become calmer.

I nudged my horse forward and dismounted over the body of the Chasseur. His face had disappeared and he was obviously dead. He was a lieutenant. His commanding officer would be berating the others and ordering them not to try such foolishness again. The days of single combat were a thing of the past.

As I rode back into line, I could see from their expressions that the Captain and Lieutenant of the 20th did not approve of my actions. I did not care.

This time the French retreat had halted at the hill. They could go no further. Nicholas waved me over. "I shall start my Cacadores working their way up the hill. Take the cavalry and cover the end of their line in case they try to flee."

"Yes, Colonel."

"Good shot by the way and very cool. My lads approve of such things."

I led the squadrons to a small rise which afforded us a good view of the hill and yet allowed us to move freely. I heard the crack of the guns as Sir Arthur softened up the French centre. In contrast, the crack of the rifles and the Cacadores muskets was erratic and irregular as they duelled with the French light infantry. The French Tirailleurs and Voltigeurs were superb and had defeated Austrians, Prussians and Russians. However, the Baker Rifle negated their effect. Quite simply the 95th could fire with impunity and the French were being steadily driven back.

I liked the way Sir Arthur fought. It was not glorious but it was effective and saved men's lives. So far as I could see we had barely lost a man and yet there were blood-stained blue uniforms littering the land before us. It was, quite simply, a matter of time and Sir Arthur would have his first victory over the French.

Suddenly I saw the standard of the 29th, Lake's battalion. The bugle sounded the charge and I saw the flag head up a defile towards the crown of the hill. I knew that it had not been ordered by Sir Arthur. Colonel Lake was making his bid for glory. The cacophony of noise from the muskets and the cannon told its own story and I did not need to be there to know what was happening.

The 29th were bleeding to death and Sir Arthur's battle plans were now in tatters.

Colonel Trant waved me over. "That's upset the apple cart. Take your chaps around their flank. We need to draw men away from the centre or none of the 29th will survive."

"Yes, sir." Colonel Lake's attack meant that we would now not be able to pursue them when they broke. We would be needed to apply pressure to their flanks and their rear. "Follow me!"

I led them on a parallel course to the French. It looked as though we were moving away but I had remembered a dry valley which would allow us to approach Roliça from behind their centre.

"Sir, we are moving away from the battle!" Captain Goodwin broke formation and rode over to me gesticulating wildly as he did so.

I had had enough of Captain Goodwin. I put my face close to his and said quietly but forcefully, "If you question me one more time, Captain Goodwin, I shall bring charges and send you back to England. Is that clear?"

He recoiled at my words and my anger, "Yes sir!"

"Sergeant Sharp, take a couple of the Portuguese and scout ahead of us. I want to know where the French are before they see us."

"Right sir." I heard him detail off two troopers and they rode off.

"Reload your weapons!"

It was not easy whilst riding but it could be done. I wanted to be ready if we came upon either blue or green uniforms. I could hear the gunfire to our left as it intensified. Sir Arthur had been forced to commit more men to the main attack. Colonel Lake was in serious trouble. He would learn that it did not pay to cross Sir Arthur Wellesley.

Sergeant Sharp and the two troopers appeared from the woods to our left. "Sir, there are French infantry ahead and a gun."

"Is it dug in?"

"No sir, but it is well protected by rocks and it is on a steep slope. We can't use horses; they would be cut down. We can go through those woods and it will bring us out level with them. There is a

94

little valley and their gun is facing the main attack so we should be able to flank them."

"Captain Goodwin, have your troop form a skirmish line over there. Protect our flank in case the French attack. I will take the Portuguese and we will try to attack them on foot."

"Yes, sir." I think he was pleased that he would not be required to fight on foot.

"Your job is to guard our flank. Do not let me down. I will have the Portuguese support me but no matter what happens you stay here and hold the line."

"Yes, sir."

I caught the eye of Sergeant Smith who nodded.

"Captain Moreno. Have your troop dismount. We are going to attack on foot. Make sure they all have a gun as well as their swords." I turned to the other captains. "Stay here. If you hear me sound the charge then come as quickly as you can."

With horse holders assigned I led the sixty men towards the woods. I had taken my two-horse pistols and I had one in my belt. I could fire three shots. I hoped it would be enough. Sergeant Sharp was close behind me with a French musket he had saved from our reconnaissance. I should have had the wit to keep one too.

I held my hand up when we reached the edge of the woods. I could see the gun. It looked to be a little four-pounder. There were twenty or so infantry below and in front of the gun. I looked to my left and saw smoke in the distance but no British soldiers. We had managed to get around the extreme flank of the French. I turned to Captain Moreno. We move across this valley. I want neither noise nor firing until we are seen. I will give the command to fire." He nodded. "We could capture a gun today and win the battle for the general."

"My men will not let you down, Colonel!"

"Sharp, take out the officer as soon as the firing starts."

The gun crew and the light infantry were totally focussed on the ground before them. My men dropped unseen down to the valley and then we began to climb up the slope towards the gun. We reached to within fifty yards before we were seen. One of the gunners turned to spit and saw us. Even as he started to shout Sharp's musket barked and the officer commanding the gun fell. I fired one pistol and then began to run up the hill. It was not easy. The gun sergeant began to shout orders and I fired at him. The ball hit his shoulder and he spun around. I jammed my spent pistols in my belt and drew my last pistol and then my sword. There were more infantry descending from the hill above the gun and I fired blindly into them and then I clambered over the rocks and rested behind the gun.

I heard musket balls whizz above my head. Thankfully it was not a volley and they were ineffective. "Take cover. Bugler, sound the charge!" Another ragged rattle of muskets sounded and I saw a couple of the Portuguese troopers clutch at wounds.

I hoped that the Portuguese would hear the bugle and join us. The men who had followed me now had no loaded weapons. The French began to advance down the hill. They had fired their muskets and were reloading. I raised my sword. "Captain Moreno, at them. Give them the blade!"

The French musket and bayonet is a fearsome weapon but they require both hands. I had a sword and a free hand. I led them into the fray. The first Frenchman I met thought that he had me at his mercy. As he plunged his bayonet at me, I flicked the point away with my sword and then whipped the edge backhand across his face. It ripped through his eyes. He dropped the musket and fell screaming at my feet. I had no time to despatch him for a second soldier thrust his bayonet at me. I half turned my body and grabbed the barrel. It was hot and it burned but I held on and stabbed the soldier through the side.

Behind me, I heard hooves as the Portuguese came to our aid. We now outnumbered the French who fell back. The steady retreat became a rout as the Portuguese discharged their pistols over our heads.

"After them! We have them!"

I heard a roar from my left and saw Colonel Trant leading the rest of the Portuguese up the hill. The whole of the French army was now in full retreat. We reached the top of the hill and I stopped to get my breath. As I looked at the road south, I saw, to my horror, Captain Goodwin leading the 20th at the Chasseurs. He was charging the Chasseurs and he was outnumbered by more than two to one.

"Bugler, sound recall!"

The Portuguese bugler did as he was ordered and I saw half of the troopers halt and then make their way back to me. A knot of troopers carried on until they were surrounded by the Chasseurs and they were hacked down. I saw eight riders emerge from the melee and they followed the others back towards us.

I was annoyed but I could not let it show. The Portuguese had fought well and obeyed their orders. It was the British horsemen who had let me down! I would have Goodwin's hide for this!

That would come later. The Portuguese were ecstatic. Captain Moreno rushed over to me, "Magnificent! We have shown these Frenchmen that we are warriors and we can fight. With you leading us we can defeat them all!"

I smiled, "Your men did well. We had better see to the wounded and put a guard around the prisoners." I looked around and saw that fewer of the Portuguese had fallen than I had expected. There were just three men who looked as though they had perished.

"Sharp, get a horse and fetch the remnants of the 20th here."

"Sir."

Nicholas rode up to me. "Well done old chap. Captured a gun too. That should please old Nosey!"

I shook my head. "Nicholas, he might hear you."

"Oh, he is miles away yet. If we had more cavalry, we could have pursued them."

"If Captain Goodwin had not disobeyed orders, we might still have been able to do that. Your boys did well and they obeyed their orders. There are twenty prisoners over there. I think we might go and interrogate them."

"I'll join you."

The light infantrymen were looking dispirited. A couple of them were wounded. I turned to a Portuguese sergeant, "Bind their wounds for them, sergeant." He looked at me as though I had taken leave of my senses. "We need information and this will make them give it to us." He smiled and shouted for his men to find some dressings.

I saw that there were the remnants of two regiments; the 2nd and the 4th. I watched a lieutenant being bandaged by an ancient sergeant. I wandered over to them. The sergeant looked at me and said to the officer, in French. "It is the Roast Beef who led the charge and killed Jacques."

"What is he doing leading these bandits?"

"Those bandits are soldiers for the country you have invaded lieutenant."

They looked at me in shock. "You are French!"

"No, I am Scottish but I speak French. Who was your general?" They looked at each other and then defiantly back at me. "Come, it cannot hurt to tell us. Either his body will lie on the field or he will be back at Torres Vedras with Marshal Junot."

I had surprised them with my knowledge. "General Delaborde."

I had heard of him. He had risen from the ranks having been a private. "He fought well today. You all fought well."

The young officer shook his head, "Not well enough. We were beaten by Portuguese!"

Luckily, he said it in French. Had Captain Moreno heard it then the prisoners would all have been slaughtered. I told Colonel Trant the information. I heard hooves behind me and turned to see Sergeant Sharp and the survivors of the 20th.

I saw neither officer. Sergeant Smith had a cut to his face. I just looked at him without saying a word. "Sorry sir, I tried to stop Captain Goodwin but he was adamant and he made us charge. I brought the lads back as soon as I heard the recall. Sorry, sir."

"It is not your fault, Sergeant Smith. You were obeying orders and you did well to bring so many back."

I turned to Alan, "Where are the officers and how many men did, we lose?"

"Captain Goodwin is dead and I sent Lieutenant Hart back to the surgeon with the rest of the wounded. He had a bad cut to his arm. Eight dead, sir and as many wounded."

I nodded, "Thank you, Sergeant Smith. That is not as bad as it could have been. Until we join the rest of your regiment you will command the troop."

"Yes, sir."

"Captain Moreno, take a troop of your men and pursue the French. I want to know where they go."

He grinned, "Yes Colonel!"

"You do not fight. You watch." I saw the disappointment on his face. "There will be many more battles and you and your men will have the chance for glory."

He brightened, "With you and Colonel Trant to lead us I know so."

Sir Arthur brought the rest of the camp up to the village. I set vedettes to watch for a sneak attack. When I reported to the general you would have thought we had been defeated rather than winning the battle. "Give me some good news, Matthews. I am in dire need of it."

"We captured a gun. The Portuguese fought well and General Delaborde and the survivors are now racing back to Torres Vedras."

He grunted, "What happened to the 20th?"

"I had them watching the flanks with strict orders not to charge. They did."

"I'll have Goodwin court-martialled."

"He's dead sir and Hart will lose an arm. He will have to be sent back to England."

"It was the same with Lake! Damned fool lost over half his men and his own life when he went for glory. Dammit, we could have won this battle with just a handful of casualties and captured the entire French force but for that damned fool."

"Yes, sir. Still, it is the first battle and we did win."

"Glass half full eh Matthews? By the way, you did well today." He chuckled. "Our allies have been singing your praises to Colonel Trant all evening."

"Any orders for tomorrow sir?"

"We have reinforcements coming from Gibraltar and the rest of the 20th." He smiled. "You will be able to relinquish that particular command. We are to rendezvous at Maceira Bay. Take the 20th tomorrow morning and secure the beach for us. I will follow with this behemoth of an army!"

Chapter 11

We left before dawn. I knew that Torres Vedras was not far from the bay and there was a good chance that we would encounter the French on our patrol I had not spoken to Lieutenant Hart before I had left. Had I done so I might have spoken rather too freely. He had just followed his superior and he had paid for it with his arm. His military career was over.

Sergeant Smith was happy to be away from him. "Well sergeant, your regiment will be landing in force soon. You will have your own officers."

"To be honest sir I am quite happy serving with you. I reckon I would have more chance of surviving this war."

"I think it just takes time to adjust to this type of war, sergeant. I have been fighting for a long time. It is just experience and your officers will gain that when they find their feet.

The River Maceira flowed past a small village of the same name. Two miles away was Vimeiro Hill. It would make a good defensive site for Sir Arthur. We had no idea how many men Junot had with him. We could easily be outnumbered. The prisoners were reluctant to tell us anything. Although I was not certain that the ones we had knew the numbers. They had been sent to shadow and slow us down while Junot gathered his forces. It would be a formidable force. Napoleon would want the British throwing back into the sea before they had a toe hold.

We made camp on the 18th of August. Sharp went into the village to buy some fresh supplies. We still had money and the troopers deserved it. The villagers were happy to sell us a couple of sheep and chickens for coins. They knew that soldiers would tend to take without payment. We ate well that night.

The first ship arrived the next morning. It was a sloop. A young lieutenant rowed ashore and saluted. "Sir, do you know where Sir Arthur Wellesley is?"

"He is north of here but he should arrive today."

He nodded. "Good sir. The new commander Sir Harry Burrard will arrive this evening with the transports and troops from Gibraltar."

"Good, for the General should be here by then."

The lieutenant looked behind me at the hill. "Are there French close by sir?"

"I do not think so. We defeated their advance guard the other day but I dare say they will be along soon."

He looked at the river. "Is that drinkable sir." He pointed to the barrels in the boat. "We need fresh water."

"Just go half a mile upstream. We had the men and the horses using the sea but it pays to be careful."

"Right sir!"

He looked up at the hill, nervously as though he expected blue uniforms to come flooding down. "Sergeant Smith, take a couple of troopers and watch the watering party."

"Righto, sir."

The young lieutenant looked relieved.

When the sergeant returned from his water protection detail I said, "Mount up and we will see what is in the vicinity. We will need ten men no more."

"Right sir."

"Sergeant Sharp, take care of the camp. I suspect there will be many more soldiers arriving soon so get us a decent billet for the night eh?" I was leaving Sharp for he was organised and he spoke Portuguese. It might come in handy.

"Yes, sir."

We headed east. Sergeant Smith asked, "Sir, do you mind me asking you a question? I don't want to be impertinent."

"Sergeant, I served as a corporal before I was even a sergeant. If you are impertinent, believe me, I will let you know!"

Hs smiled, "Sharpie reckons you are rich, sir. You own a half share in a ship and you have an estate in Sicily."

I had not thought about it but I supposed they were right. "Yes, I suppose I am well off. Not that I think about the money."

"Then why are you here sir? I mean if I had a half share in a ship, I would be sat on my arse all day drinking myself stupid."

"It is not in my nature. I was made to work hard from an early age and I cannot sit around doing nothing."

"Well, you could work on your estate. Sharpie says it is in Sicily and it is a beautiful part of the world."

"It is. But I suppose the real reason is Bonaparte. I think he is dangerous and needs stopping. When he is no longer a threat to Britain and the rest of the world then I will retire and enjoy myself."

Smith considered this for a while. Both of us were constantly scanning the road ahead and the ground around us for signs of the French but so far, we had seen nothing.

"Sharpie says you have met Bonaparte."

I nodded, "I have."

"What's he like?"

"Physically he is small and neat. As a general then imagine Sir Arthur with a French accent. They have much in common."

"Do you reckon Sir Arthur can beat him?"

"I do, Sergeant Smith, but I also believe that the British Army with any good commander is capable of beating Boney. We did it at Roliça and we will do it again. You know that the lads are stubborn. The British soldier would as soon spit in your eye as say you were a better soldier."

He laughed. "Aye, you are right, sir." I suddenly reined in. "What's up, sir?"

I looked around and ignored the sergeant. There was something wrong and I could not put my finger on it. Then I realised what it was; the birds which had been roosting in the small copse ahead had suddenly taken flight and we were surrounded by the sound of silence. It felt unnatural. There was an ambush ahead.

I turned to Smith. "There is an ambush ahead. I hope your men have loaded pistols and carbines."

"They do, sir."

I dismounted and began to examine my horse's hoof. I spoke loudly enough for the eleven-man patrol to hear me. "When I mount up, we are going to charge in two columns. I will take one file to the right of the woods and Sergeant Smith to the left. Use your pistols and carbines to shoot the Frenchmen who are hiding there. Then go in with sabres."

"Sir, how do…."

"Just do it Sergeant and I will explain later. Now when I get on my horse all of you laugh as though I have told you the funniest joke ever. We walk until you see me whip my horse and then we ride like the wind."

I mounted and they all laughed. I led them forward. When we were just forty yards from the woods I yelled, "Now!" drew my pistol and kicked my horse hard. I had to trust that five men were following me or this could turn out to be a disaster. I entered the wood some thirty yards from the road. In single file, the troopers could just follow me and it was up to me to choose the best line.

I caught a glimpse of green. They were Chasseurs. I headed towards the road. A surprised trooper turned with his musketoon. The ball from my pistol hit him in the middle and at such close range that it threw him from his horse. I holstered the pistol and drew my sword. I saw a Chasseur trying to mount his horse and I slashed at him blindly. I felt the edge grate against his forehead as I took the top of his skull from his head.

The handful of Chasseurs took to their horses and headed south. "Sergeant Smith, after them!"

I burst out into the road. Ahead I saw a Chasseur grab his musketoon and aim it across his saddle. I grabbed a pistol with my left hand and rode with my knees. I fired at the horse. The ball hit the saddle and the horse reared and ran off to the west. The trooper tried to lower his musketoon to hit me. I leaned forward and my sword took him in the chest. I flicked his dying body to one side as I galloped after the other five riders who were heading for Torres Vedras.

If I had had Badger, I would have caught them but the horse I rode was not the swiftest. I slowed to conserve her strength and to allow the others to catch me. Smith appeared next to me. I glanced at him. "Did we lose any?"

"Danny West caught one and Larry Lamb was wounded."

The French did not extend their lead. They kept glancing nervously over their shoulders and we kept following. I knew where they were going and I just wanted to see the size of the army we faced.

As we neared Torres Vedras, I saw all the signs of a French camp. There was smoke in the distance and I caught glimpses of blue and green. It was Junot. I reined in and stood in my stirrups. I saw a vast cavalry camp. The one-arm we lacked Junot had in abundance. I estimated more than fifteen hundred cavalrymen were with Junot. Sir Arthur would have his hands full.

"Right sergeant, we have seen enough. Let's go home."

We wheeled our mounts around and headed north. "Sir, how did you know about the ambush?"

"The birds moved and it was just the sort of place I would use as an ambush. And, "I shrugged, "it just didn't feel right."

When we reached our camp more ships were arriving but they were too far out to sea to identify them. "Alan, ride and find the general tell him that the reinforcements are here and," I added quietly, "I think the new general is here too."

"That should please him!"

It was dark by the time that Sir Arthur and Sergeant Sharp arrived at the camp. Captain Moreno and a squadron of Portuguese were their escort. The general dismounted and peered out at the gathering fleet. Their lights bobbed about the bay. He shook his head.

"I had hoped to defeat Junot before he arrived. Is he coming ashore?"

"He won't be able to tonight Sir Arthur. It is too dangerous."

"Well, the army will be here by the morrow. Any sign of the French?"

They are just north of Torres Vedras. I should warn you, sir, that they have over fifteen hundred cavalry."

He waved an airy hand. "Cavalry are overrated." He peered into the eastern darkness. "That hill there looks useful."

I nodded. "There is a village on the top and it is a long ridge. It would be a good defensive position."

"If God gives me the chance, I shall line up our battalions on its top and even old Bonaparte could not shift me." He turned his view to the west. "Of course, it all depends upon Sir Harry!"

Sir Harry, it seemed, was not willing to land without an army there to protect him. We were summoned out to his ship while Sir Brent Spencer landed his men. Sir Brent's boat landed while we were boarding. Sir Arthur said, "Be so good as to make your camp close to the village of Vimeiro eh Sir Brent."

"But Sir Harry has not made his dispositions yet, Sir Arthur."

"Better camping up there and there is water. This place is too sandy and full of flies."

"Ah, good idea."

As we were rowed out to the flagship Sir Arthur chuckled, "Well we have our defensive position come what may. Now I just need to get Sir Harry to allow me to command."

I was not so certain. I had heard of Sir Harry. His men called him Betty because of his lack of aggression. I had seen him in Copenhagen with Lord Cathcart and he seemed fairly ineffectual to me. Why he had been appointed, I could not see.

He was, however, an affable chap. "Ah good to see you again, Arthur."

I knew that Sir Arthur hated informality and would not like the address but he had to grin and bear it. "And you, sir. "This is Major Matthews, my aide."

"I have heard much about you. Now then, Arthur, Sir John will be here by the end of the week and when we have all of our troops we shall begin to think about an offensive."

Sir Arthur gave me a weary look. "Sir, we have already beaten one French force at Roliça and there is another one close by. I can drive the French from Portugal with one battle."

"Fought already? But you have only just landed. No, no, we will wait for Sir John. Sir Hew Dalrymple is also on his way. Let us be patient eh?"

"But sir…"

"Now then let you and I sit down and plan this campaign properly. We'll have a decent dinner. If you like I can arrange for a cabin for you aboard the flagship. It will be better than a tent."

A sudden look of cunning flashed across Sir Arthur's face. "No sir, I will sleep ashore and, if you don't mind, I'll just send Matthews here to sort out my tent for me. I shan't be a moment."

Once outside the cabin, he said, "I want you to make sure that Sir Brent makes a defensive position. As the troops arrive, put them on the ridges facing south and east. That is where the French will attack."

"Yes sir, but what if Sir Brent asks for written orders?"

"Just tell him I ordered it on Sir Harry's advice."

"But what if he asks Sir Harry?"

"Trust me he won't. Come on Major, you are a soldier and you know that we can win. You are just following orders eh?"

"Yes, sir."

Once at the camp I sought Sharp. "When the army arrives, direct them to the village."

"Yes, sir. Have you eaten yet?"

"I'll grab something later. I am under Sir Arthur's orders."

I rode up to the village. I had to put on a show. I went into the manner I adopted when I was behind enemy lines. I exuded confidence. "Ah Sir Brent, the generals sent me to see if everything was going well and you were aligning your men on the ridges facing south and east."

"Whatever for?"

"Well there are twenty thousand Frenchmen out there and if they head north that is the direction they will take."

"Dear me. And Sir Harry knows this?"

"Sir Arthur has informed him of the danger. Those dispositions make sense." I saw the hesitation and doubt on his face. "The rest of our army will be here by tomorrow. Sir Arthur is finalising details with Sir Harry now and I dare say he will brief you later this evening."

"I believe you old chap it's just that Sir Harry gave me the impression that he wanted to wait until Sir John Moore arrived before engaging the French."

"Ah, but the French are closer than anyone knew. This is merely a case of being careful. It is a prudent move, general."

"You are probably right. I say are there any Portuguese speakers with our chaps. We can't understand the locals."

"What is it that you want sir?"

"Well, I would prefer to sleep in a house rather than a tent. What do you think?"

"If you come with me, sir, I'll see what I can do." I led the general and two of his aides towards the village. I saw two men drinking outside a tiny bodega. They both assiduously ignored us. I asked them, in Portuguese, where the Prefeito was and their attitude changed. It turned out that one of them was the Prefeito. I explained that the Portuguese army was coming and asked if they had rooms for Sir Brent. They shook their heads until I took out a gold Louis. It changed their minds and loosened their tongues.

I turned to Sir Brent. "They have two rooms for you sir but the food will be extra,"

"I say, Matthews, you are a fine fellow to have around. Good show!"

"You are welcome sir and if you could arrange the defences."

"Of course, Major Matthews, my pleasure."

I was still awake when Sir Arthur returned. He looked angry but, as always with Sir Arthur, he kept his anger in check. His clipped sentences were the evidence that his interview had not gone well.

"That man, Major, will undo all the good work we have done."

There was little to say to that. "I have asked Sir Brent to place his troops on the western ridge."

"Facing south."

"Yes, sir."

"Good. I would have you scout again tomorrow."

"You wish me to find Junot?"

"We know where Junot is. I would have you find his dispositions."

"Some of the other troops have arrived, sir."

"Good. I need this battle fighting and winning. Soon I will not be in a position to decide on a battle plan. I will be fourth in command."

"Sir John seems to know what he is about, sir."

He nodded, "That may be but we have Dolly and Betty in command now!" I stifled a smile. "You have done well today, Major Matthews. Get some sleep for I want you out before dawn. Find me the French order of battle and we can win this war before nightfall."

Sharp was waiting by my tent with a mug of grog. "Here sir. I got this from the lads on the sloop."

I drank the hot and powerful drink. It would aid sleep. Not that I needed any help. I was exhausted. "We ride early in the morning Alan. You had better inform, Sergeant Smith. We will need ten of his chaps too."

"They all want to join the 11th sir. It seems they don't like their officers."

"Sharp!"

"Sorry, sir but I am just saying what they did. It seems Captain Goodwin was not unique. They have some new officers who have just bought in to the regiment. It was a warning sir, that we may find problems when they land."

"All I want, Alan, is to be back with the 11th. Life is simpler there."

It was still black when we left. There were two roads I could take. One led due south while the other went south-east towards Torres Vedras. I decided to head towards Torres Vedras and if I found nothing head across country and come back along the other road. Dawn was just breaking and we were only ten miles or so from Vimeiro when we saw the French advance guards. It was the Chasseurs.

I wheeled us around and took the patrol to a crossroads further north. There was a wooded knoll where we could hide. When we reached it, I scribbled a note. "Sergeant Smith, send this back to the general."

"Sir."

Once the rider was away, we waited. "Make sure your carbines and pistols are loaded." I heard Sergeant Smith chuckle, "I have amused you, sergeant?"

"Sorry sir, it's just that we have used more ball and powder in the last day or so than in the last six months."

I remembered Sharp's words. "Your officers don't like to waste powder and ball?"

"They prefer a sabre charge, sir." He shook his head. "Your ways are safer sir." He pointed towards Sharp's saddle. It must be handy having a pair of pistols instead of just the one."

I lifted my pelisse. "And three pistols are even better, sergeant. A word of advice instead of just looking for coins on the dead Frenchmen take their pistols. It is how Sharp and I acquired ours."

The sun had now risen above the hills to the east and we heard the hooves of the French as they came on. We would have to move soon or we would be trapped. When they reached the crossroads, some two hundred yards from our position, they halted. I saw the marshal and his staff as they rode to the head of the stationary column and consult a map. After a few moments, he pointed to the road which led north towards the village of Ventosa on the eastern ridge close to Vimeiro. Sir Arthur had no men on that ridge. I had not thought to defend it. Were we about to be outflanked?

A couple of squadrons of Dragoons led the nine battalions of light infantry north. The road, I knew, twisted and turned through the hills before emerging at the far end of the eastern ridge. They would arrive unseen.

I watched as the rest of the army took the road west towards the village of Vimeiro. Junot was going to divide his forces and outflank Sir Arthur. "Right boys, let's get back but I do not want them to know that we have spotted them."

Our circuitous but unseen route meant we did not reach the village until nine o'clock. I galloped hard for the last mile or so and hurled myself from my saddle. Generals Nightingale and Ferguson were with the colonels and poring over a map with Sir

Arthur. The general looked up eagerly when I entered the tent, "Yes, Major?"

"Junot is less than five miles away." I jabbed a finger at the western ridge. "He has sent a column of cavalry and infantry there to outflank you."

"Has he by God! Good work Major!" He turned to his two generals, "Take your brigades and Colonel Bowes too and defend the eastern ridge. Stop his flanking attack. Take a couple of guns too." They left quickly. Colonel Trant and General Crauford take your men north and outflank this column. Detach your cavalry for Major Matthews to command."

"Sir!"

He turned to me. "The rest of the 20th are being disembarked. They are, along with the handful of Portuguese, our only cavalry. "If what you say is true and there are over fifteen hundred cavalry then we will need them as a reserve. Order them to the north west of Vimeiro. Disguise them on the reverse slope."

"Sir!"

I left the tent. "Sergeant Smith, your regiment is being disembarked. Give them Sir Arthur's compliments and have them assemble to the north west of Vimeiro on the reverse slope."

"Sir!"

"Sharp, go and find Captain Moreno. I want the Portuguese cavalry in the same place. I will be there when you arrive."

I waved the detachment of Light Dragoons to follow me and I led them up the steep reverse slope to Vimeiro. Sir Arthur had been up early to spot the reverse slope. It was perfect. We would remain hidden behind the village and safe from the French artillery.

"You lads make a horse line here. Better mark it out for the rest of the regiment."

I left them to it. Dismounting I led my horse to the front of the village. The riflemen were already in position in the rocks beneath the village. I watched as Colonel Fane placed his line regiment, the 50th, behind his skirmishers. Any French attack would have to climb a steep slope with ball and bullets decimating them.

"Good position here, Matthews." I turned to see General Wellesley arrive.

"It is sir." I waved a hand around the narrow streets. "This is a killing zone; if they get through the rifles."

"It all depends on how badly he wants it. I want you to command the Portuguese cavalry today and stay here on the ridge with me. The 20th have a major who is in command. We will use them to follow up any success." He saw my look which displayed my disappointment. "The Portuguese have done more than enough and the 20th are fresh. This will be a long campaign for when I defeat these Johnnies here today, we will push on to Spain."

I went a little closer to him, "But what about General Burrard? Will he not wish to take command?"

Sir Arthur smiled, "He is staying on his ship until General Moore arrives." He adopted an innocent look. "If the French attack I shall have to defend eh?"

I returned to the horse lines. The troopers had done a good job. Captain Moreno and his half a dozen undersized troops were there. "Just have your men dismount. We will not be needed until the latter stages of the day. There is no point in tiring out the horses."

Just then I heard the clatter of hooves as the 20th arrived. Suddenly I heard a familiar voice, "Who in God's name has picked such a God-awful place for the horses?"

I turned to see the man who had made my life such a misery in the early days at the regiment. He had been a captain then but now he was a major, it was Major DeVere who commanded the 20th.

Chapter 12

"Actually Major, it was me, under orders from Sir Arthur Wellesley."

As soon as he recognised me, I could see the anger as it filled his face and he fought to control it. "Until Sir Harry Burrard comes ashore that is."

I pointed to the south where the first blue columns could be seen in the distance. "That will be after the battle then as he is still aboard his ship. The French, apparently do not wait upon Sir Harry!" Before he could retort I snapped, "And Sir Arthur has asked that your regiment prepares to follow up on any advantage which might present itself. If you would await my instructions here, I would be grateful."

I had deliberately avoided the use of the word order but I wanted him under no illusions. It was I who would tell him when he could advance. He turned to a cornet, "Cornet Welsh ride to Sir Harry and inform him that the French are about to attack and there will be a battle soon!"

I saw the triumphant look upon his face and I shook my head. He knew little of battles. By the time Sir Harry reached the battle it would all be over. As I recalled Major DeVere had yet to fight in anything other than a skirmish. His first battle might come as a shock.

I waved over Captain Moreno and gave him his orders. "Captain, if you would have your horse holders retire down the slope. The English horses are a little bigger and after weeks on a ship will need to relieve themselves. It could become rather smelly and slippery around here. Your men can take a position behind the walls which overlook the village." He laughed.

Major DeVere coloured. I suspect he thought he had been insulted by me in Portuguese. "And who is in charge of these damned foreigners?"

"Normally Colonel Trant but today they are seconded to me."

He laughed, "So you have found your level at last Matthews. Johnny foreigner is all that you are capable of leading."

I smiled, "Until your officers disobeyed Sir Arthur's orders, Major DeVere I commanded the 20th. Your troopers and sergeants are excellent. They are good enough to be in the 11th."

It was like waving a red rag at a bull. "Where are my officers?"

"Captain Goodwin died and Mr Hart lost an arm and has been invalided back to England. The squadron is being led by Sergeant Smith and he is a sound man. You are lucky to have him."

I saw DeVere flash an angry look in the direction of the sergeant who sat a little taller in the saddle. I had wasted enough time on him. "Captain Moreno, see if you can get some muskets and pistols for your men. I know we captured some from the French the other day. Position them behind these walls. We may not be charging today but I guarantee that we will be fighting."

"Yes, Colonel."

DeVere might not have understood much Portuguese but he recognised the word '*Colonel*'. "Did that man call you colonel?"

"As a matter of fact, he did. The Prince Regent appointed me a colonel in the Portuguese cavalry." I smiled thinly as I said it. I outranked him for the first time and I could see that he did not like it.

Lieutenant Brown hurried over to me, "Sir, Sir Arthur needs you."

"Right Sharp, if you stay here in case Captain Moreno needs a translator." I lowered my voice. "The Portuguese act under my orders only. Understand?"

He grinned, "Yes sir!"

When I reached Sir Arthur, he had just lowered his telescope. "Ah Matthews, the French are coming on. I shall need you as an aide today. No charging off for derring-do eh?"

He was in a better humour now that he was on the battlefield and the French were obliging him by marching towards us in a column forty men wide by thirty men deep. It was the classic French formation. The light infantry darted in front of them skirmishing and when they were close enough the column would deploy into a three-deep line. I had seen it work against Austrians, Italians and even Prussians but the British were a different matter. Even as we watched the 95th and 60th Rifles began to pepper the skirmishers. They had no answer to the Baker. They had to endure the fire without reply and gradually their numbers thinned to the point where they did not function as skirmishers any more. The rifles then began to pick off the officers and sergeants in the column. That proved crucial for there was no one to order them into line and they kept coming up the slope.

No one could doubt the bravery of these young conscripts. The guns were firing Colonel Shrapnel's new shell which exploded in the air above them. The pieces of metal scythed through the column; killing and maiming. As the 95th and 60th raced back to the protection of the village Sir Arthur shouted, "Colonel Fane whenever you are ready."

"Sir. West Kent Foot prepare your muskets!"

I heard the sergeants repeating the order down the line as one thousand men marched steadily towards the five hundred men of the 50th regiment. At one hundred yards I heard the order to fire and the column disappeared from sight as the smoke wafted across our front. The howitzers were still hurling their shells blindly above the column which was a target too big to miss. There was a thin ripple as the eighty muskets which could be brought to bear, fired at the 50th. Two hundred and fifty muskets replied and then the second rank's two hundred and fifty. By the time they had fired the front rank fired again. In a minute and a half two and a half thousand balls sliced through the blue column and it broke.

"Cease fire!"

As the smoke cleared, we saw the mangled and bloody blue bodies littering the field and the survivors running back to the protection of their army.

The soldiers cheered before Sir Arthur roared, "Colonel Fane, control your men."

As the sergeants regained order, I saw the rifles skipping down the slope to bring down some of the survivors.

"Sir Arthur, there is another column coming from the right."

Our right flank was less secure. The cannons could not fire in this direction and there were no rifles there. The 43rd were the skirmishers. They were as good as the rifles but their muskets did not have the range.

"Colonel Anstruther, whenever you are ready."

This time there were three regiments who were ready to receive the French. The twelve hundred men would have to endure the fire of over two thousand redcoats.

"Sir Arthur, they have brought cannon with them." I pointed to where seven cannons were being manhandled into position.

"That won't do. Major Matthews get some of your Portuguese fellows and be ready to capture those guns when Colonel Anstruther has dealt with the infantry."

I missed witnessing the slaughter as I ran the hundred yards to my horse but I knew that the result would be the same as the first attack. "Captain Moreno, mount a squadron. We are to capture some guns."

As he raced off Major DeVere was forced to be polite in order to discover what was going on. "What is happening Matthews?"

"The general has just seen off one attack and now he's going after another."

"What are these Portuguese chaps about?"

"Just going to stop some guns upsetting your horses Major!"

As I mounted, I saw some staff officers making their way up the slope. It looked as though Sir Harry Burrard had arrived. I had no time for that.

"Follow me!"

The French column, although they had not had to suffer the shrapnel, had had to endure five volleys from two thousand men. They were fleeing down the slope. The French gunners were trying to attach the traces to their horses and save their guns. There was no time for an order. We had to make our way down the slope. I could see why the general had asked for the Portuguese. Their horses were smaller and more sure-footed and we picked our way down the steep and rocky slope. As soon as the French saw us and heard the cheers from the Portuguese they fled down the slope, abandoning their guns. One officer and sergeant bravely tried to stand. My sword flicked out and the officer's sword flew from his grip. I held the point to his throat. "Surrender sir or die!" Behind me, I heard a pistol shot as Sergeant Sharp fired over the sergeant's head. He raised his arms. "Come, sir, your deaths can not save the guns. You have both fought bravely."

He nodded, reached down and handed me his sword hilt first. "Captain Moreno, take the guns back to the general."

There was a wall of cheering as we took back our seven prizes. The French had conveniently managed to attach the horses to the guns.

"Take the guns to the rear." They began to manhandle the guns to safety behind the village and General Hill's brigade.

I dismounted and handed my horse's reins to Sergeant Sharp.

"Well done, Matthews. That was smartly done."

"Thank you, Sir Arthur." I pointed down the hill to the west, "Sir I believe that Sir Harry is coming."

"Dammit! Who alerted him?"

"I believe it was Major DeVere." I did take some pleasure in informing on the major. He had deliberately informed Sir Harry to inconvenience and upset Sir Arthur. He was a fool; Sir Arthur was our only chance of winning the battle.

"Can't be helped but this is not over yet." He pointed down the slope where I could see another column forming. Even at this distance, I could see that they were grenadiers. These were the best that Junot had. They would not flee in the face of fierce musket fire. I had witnessed them being decimated before now and then charging home.

I could see that there were two columns approaching us. One was heading for Colonel Fane while the other was approaching Colonel Anstruther's position. This would be harder than repulsing the earlier attack. They were dividing our fire. The two columns were still forming up as Sir Harry appeared.

"What's going on Wellesley?"

"The French attacked us this morning, Sir Harry. We have repulsed them and captured some guns."

"Right, well carry on but no advance, mind. Sir Hew Dalrymple has just arrived and he needs time to assess the situation."

I could see the frustration on Sir Arthur's face. He gritted his teeth and said, "Yes sir. Now if you will excuse me, we have another attack to fend off."

Sir Harry looked down the slope. "Should we withdraw do you think?"

Every officer who heard those words could not believe them. "Er no, sir. We shall beat these fellows off but if you wish to retire a little."

"Er no, Wellesley. I shall stay here and watch for a while."

The grenadiers began their march up the slope. Their artillery fired in support at first but soon they had to stop to avoid hitting their own men. The rifles thinned them out again but it was our artillery and shrapnel which did the most damage.

"Matthews go and watch the other column. Let me know if they get too close."

"Sir." I joined Colonel Anstruther.

He nodded at me, "Smart work with those guns Matthews."

"Thank you, colonel. These chaps are a little more resolute than the others were."

"I know. Still, the lads will hold."

I could hear the fighting to my left as Fane's men came to grips with the attacking grenadiers. I saw the 43rd skirmishers as they pulled back and then Colonel Anstruther yelled, "Fire!"

The whole of the hillside was wreathed in smoke as volley after volley rang out. This time the resolute grenadiers were giving as good as they got and were aided by the slope. I heard a French voice ordering the charge.

"Colonel Anstruther, they are about to charge."

"Are they by God! Fix bayonets!"

I drew my pistol and my sword. Turning to Sharp, I said, "Ask Captain Moreno to bring his men up to the cemetery wall. They can add their fire to ours."

"Sir, you watch out for yourself now!"

"You sound like my mother, Sharp!"

Suddenly a huge grenadier launched himself from the smoke. I barely had time to pull the trigger on the pistol. The bayonet scored a line across my cheek as my ball, fired from no more than a foot took his head off. His body fell back and I slashed at his companion who was taken off balance by the dying body. My blade ripped across his nose and into his skull. As he put his hands to his face, I stabbed him in the stomach.

The 9th were being forced back into the narrow village. The grenadiers were bigger and stronger men and they had the advantage of numbers.

I heard Anstruther, "Hold them 9th! Hold them!"

I watched as men fought with bayonets and knives for they had no time to reload. Suddenly I heard a ripple of pistols and muskets. I turned and saw the Portuguese horsemen above the wall with Sharp and Moreno exhorting them to reload and fire. The extra firepower finally broke the grenadiers who began to slowly fall back.

"Push them back!" An officer stabbed at me with his sword. It was shorter than mine and I deflected it easily. I gave a riposte and then my blade flashed forward. It pierced his shoulder and he fell to the floor. I stepped over him and brought my blade in a wide arc to clear a space before me. A bayonet suddenly lunged at my middle and I grabbed the barrel and thrust it aside. I punched the grenadier hard in the face with the hilt of my sword and he collapsed in a heap at my feet. And then there was no-one before me. Before I could celebrate, Lieutenant Smith found me. "Sir Arthur asks you to order the 20th to pursue the French."

I nodded and turned. It was like walking through a charnel house. There were bodies in blue and red littering the narrow streets. Sir Harry Burrard was talking with Major DeVere.

"Major DeVere, General Wellesley asks you to take your squadron and harass the French."

He nodded and said, "Now you will see real soldiers at work." I was not certain if the comment was aimed at me or General Burrard. He raised his sword as though he was a knight in shining armour. "20th follow me. We ride to glory!"

The squadron was on the side of the village without obstructions and the two hundred and forty men thundered down the slope in straight lines. The grenadiers were no fools and they formed a square. Unfortunately for the brave men, they had not reloaded and the horses ploughed through the square. It broke and the 20th hurtled down the hill sabring all before them.

By the time I reached Sir Arthur they had almost completely destroyed the grenadier column and I expected them to sound the recall and return up the hill. To my horror, DeVere turned and began to charge the infantry who had earlier charged. They had reformed and also reloaded. Even worse there was a regiment of Dragoons close by and they were charging their flank.

"Captain Moreno, have your bugler sound recall!"

The strident notes echoed across the hills but it was too late. The French were inside the cavalry. With blown horses and outnumbered they stood no chance. The bugle had gone silent. Sir Arthur shouted, "Keep sounding the recall, damn it!"

"Keep sounding the recall!"

The bugler carried on and, thankfully, I saw knots of horsemen disengage from the disaster and make their way up the slope. I could see the bodies of the horses and troopers of the 20th littering the field.

"Fane, give the fools covering fire!"

The rifles discouraged the Dragoons and the one hundred and twenty survivors, led by Sergeant Smith rode into the village. Sir Arthur was incandescent with rage. "What a waste! It is not as though we have hundreds of horsemen to waste." He shook his head, "I should have sent you and the Portuguese, Major Matthews. You might have been tired but at least you know how to obey orders."

One of Fane's ensigns came up to the general. "Sir, there are about three thousand French and they are attacking the eastern ridge."

Sir Arthur turned to me, "Tell General Hill he is in command here until I return. Then follow me, we will see how General Nightingale fares."

Sir Harry Burrard did not look happy about being ignored but I obeyed orders. I had found that it was the best way to stay out of trouble. General Hill's men had not seen much action hitherto. "How is it going, Matthews?"

"We have repulsed their attacks, General. Sir Arthur is going to the eastern ridge for they are trying to flank us. Sir Arthur wishes you to command until his return."

'Daddy' Hill, as his men affectionately referred to him, took off his head and rubbed the sweat away. "Just stay put eh?"

"Yes General," I lowered my voice. "General Burrard is in the village."

"Ah. Thank you for the information. I will try to keep out of his way."

The other ridge was but a mile from the village and I soon caught the general. He did not acknowledge my presence as he hurried to the lower end of the ridge. We reached the centre of the ridge just as the attackers were driven off, leaving three guns there to be captured.

"Well done, Nightingale, well done."

In answer, the general pointed to the north eastern end of the ridge. "If you look there my lord you will see that General Ferguson is about to be flanked. Should we turn the line?"

He shook his head, "Major Matthews, ride to Crauford and Trant. Have them bring their fellows up and attack the column in the flank."

"Sir." I could see the reserve force not far from Ribamar, just half a mile away. Caitlin Crauford had the 91st and the 45th. Both were, as yet, untried but so far none of the regiments had let us down.

It was less than half a mile and we soon reached the Portuguese and Light Brigade. I saluted both Colonels. "Sir Arthur's compliments, Colonel Trant and General Crauford; he asked if you would be so good as to bring your brigades to support General Ferguson. His brigade is being attacked in the flank.

"About time too. "Come boys. Let's get into this war."

Colonel Trant barked out his orders and the Cacadores sprinted forward in pairs. So far, from what I had seen, the Cacadores were the equal, in this terrain, of any British Light infantry. As we approached, I saw that the French had recaptured two of their guns and were deploying three more which they had brought. I turned to Nicholas. "I am going with some of your Cacadores. We will see if we can stop them bringing those guns into action."

He nodded and waved his sabre. The Portuguese who had heard cheered.

I turned to Sharp, "Ride and tell the general that we are going to attack this column and stop the guns being fired."

As I neared the Cacadores who were running up the valley I shouted, "Follow me! We will attack the guns!"

I drew my sword and slowed my horse so that we were going at the same pace. I found out later, when he was captured, that the general leading this assault was Brennier. He must have thought that victory was almost within his grasp as the 71st and 82nd were pushed back. He did not see the approach of the two hundred Cacadores. Perhaps my blue uniform also fooled him.

We halted at a hundred yards and the Cacadores began to pick off the gunners. They were devastating and the gunners fell. I yelled, "On! On!"

I saw the Chasseurs charging towards us and I wanted to reach the safety of the guns before they did so. I arrived first and I leapt from my horse and, standing behind it aimed my pistol at the leading Chasseur. He raised his sword to split open the head of a Caçadore. My ball struck him in the shoulder and he tumbled from his horse. The Caçadore rolled underneath a four-pounder and began to reload his musket. Out of the corner of my eye, I was aware of the rest of the British and Portuguese Brigades as they double-timed to reach us.

I drew another pistol and fired at the next Chasseur. The rider ducked and missed. I pulled my last pistol and snap fired as he swung his sword at me. My ball caught him in the chest and threw him to the ground. General Brennier had sent light infantry to recapture the guns. There was a ripple of musket fire and my mount slumped dead at my feet. I lay down behind her and began to reload.

The French light were finding it hard to hit my Cacadores with volleys and the Portuguese were picking them off with impunity. The French infantry had turned to face this new threat and were forming a line three deep just a hundred yards away. This would get bloody soon.

I heard Crauford's voice behind me, "Prepare muskets! Fire!" The orders were repeated by the sergeants and a cloud of smoke enveloped me as a thousand muskets were discharged. Then Trant repeated the order in Portuguese and a thousand more muskets spoke. It was impossible to see anything and I just lay behind my dead horse.

After another four volleys, I heard the command, "Cease Fire!"

As I stood, I looked down and saw that a musket ball had scored a line along my boot. I had been lucky. I walked forward towards the body littered field. As the mist of war cleared, I saw the dead, dying and wounded Frenchmen. There was a huddle of officers near to a dead horse and a wounded man. As I approached, I saw that it was a general.

"Sir, you have lost. Your sword if you please and we will get you medical attention."

They looked in surprise at the perfect French. I recognised the general. I had seen him in Italy when he commanded a brigade. He would not recognise me.

He handed me his sword, "I am General Antoine-François Brennier de Montmorand. I surrender my sword." He smiled at me. "You are a reckless fellow. Are you Portuguese?"

"No sir, Major Matthews of the 11th Light Dragoons."

Sergeant Sharp galloped up. "The general is well happy, sir. I still think you take too many risks." I turned to the Cacadores. "Make a litter and take the general to the village. You six, escort the prisoners."

We had fought two battles within a week and won both of them. On that day, the 21st of August all the signs were hopeful that we would have a rapid victory and drive the French back over the Pyrenees. We were wrong.

Chapter 13

By the time I reached the village there was a furious row going on between the generals. Sir Arthur had returned from the eastern ridge and was having a fierce debate with Sir Harry. "But General, the road to Lisbon is open. We can drive the French south and free all of Portugal."

"You have done well, Sir Arthur, but Sir Hew Dalrymple is landing tomorrow and we will await the arrival of Sir John Moore. When he arrives, we will have thirty thousand men. Then we can advance."

They both seemed to notice me. Sir Harry seemed pleased with the distraction. "Yes, Major Matthews?"

"Sir, we have captured some generals. One or two have been wounded. I thought you should know." I added lamely.

"You see, Wellesley. A great victory, now don't go and spoil it."

I saw Sir Arthur gritting his teeth. He rolled his eyes at me, "Major Matthews, take some of the Light Dragoons and see to their fellows. You know what the locals are like with bodies on the battlefield."

"Yes, sir."

He was getting rid of me so that he could have a frank discussion. "And Matthews, well done for today."

I mounted the horse I had found wandering the field. It was a French Chasseur's. I led Sergeant Sharp to the horse lines. "Sergeant Smith, bring a troop of your men and see if you can find a cart. We need to recover your dead."

He mounted his men and we rode down to the scene of the reckless charge in a sombre silence. The foolish Major DeVere had gone well beyond the Toledo Brook. It had disrupted their lines and made them an easy target for the Dragoons. I could see the distress on the faces of the troopers as we collected the remains. The horses and their dead comrades had suffered horrific wounds. The musket balls had torn huge holes in the sides of the animals.

As we had approached the carrion had flown off to wait in nearby trees for our departure.

I found my old adversary dead amongst some of his officers and his bugler. He had been cut about so much that it was hard to recognise his body. He had died bravely but I could never forgive him for the dead troopers whose lives he had wasted. The 20th had sound troopers in its ranks. They had deserved to be better led.

Sergeant Smith and his men had found a cart. He shook his head, "It won't be big enough sir."

I nodded, "We will bury them here. Collect any personal items and we will send them to their families."

"We have no spades, sir."

Sergeant Sharp said, "I'll get some sir and I'll bring the rest of the squadron. They should be here for this."

It took the rest of the afternoon to identify the bodies and dig each grave. There was just one lieutenant and a cornet who had survived from the officers. They both looked to be in a state of shock. Only Sergeant Smith and two corporals remained from the non-commissioned officers. Sir Arthur would have to rebuild this squadron.

When they were in the ground, we made crude crosses from the muskets of the dead Frenchmen and the broken guidons. The survivors stood in a reverential circle.

As I began to speak, I was aware that I was speaking for the troopers rather than the fool who had led them to their death. I forced myself to remember that.

"These men died well and they died bravely. We have won a great victory today over the French and this is due in no small part to the courage of these troopers." I saw Sergeant Smith give me a grateful nod. "We will remember them and talk about their courage. We are soldiers and it is our lot in life to die. We can, at least, die well. These men died well. Lord, take their souls and welcome them. Amen."

"Amen."

Each trooper had his carbine and they all fired at the same time. The carrion, which had returned to the dead horses, scattered into the sky when the cracks sounded. Sergeant Sharp looked at them, roosting in the trees. "Sir, we can't leave the horses…"

"I know. Have the men gather some wood and we will burn them." I nodded up the hill to the village. "Some of the lads up there will make a feast of the dead horses otherwise."

It was a sad fact of life that the misery of the horsemen over dead horses was not shared by the infantry. They saw it as good food going to waste. We burned them and the air was filled with the smell of burning horseflesh, drifting across the battlefield. The troopers watched until all trace of their dead horses was gone and we made our way back up the hill.

I reached my tent on the beach after dark. Sir Arthur had not bothered using the village and he was in his tent. He shook his head as I entered. "What a waste! We are on the verge of victory and our two glorious leaders want peace."

"Sir Hew has landed?"

He nodded. "And you have your orders too. You are to find Junot and ask for his surrender." My mouth must have opened and closed for he shook his head again. "I know it is madness. I suspect the marshal will think it is a trap. You leave in the morning with a list of the prisoners we have."

"Sir, when that is done have I your permission to go to Lisbon and find Donna Maria?" He hesitated, "Sir John Moore has yet to arrive …"

He smiled, "Very well. You have earned it. I confess I will be sorry when you join Sir John. You have been invaluable to me; not least because you have such good language skills. More than that, however, you can keep your head and that is a rare thing in a cavalry officer as we discovered today."

"I served with DeVere."

"I guessed as much and…"

"I did not like him."

Sir Arthur did not seem surprised. "We cannot like all our brother officers but from his leadership, I am not surprised. Do not feel guilty about it."

"I don't but I wanted you to have an honest opinion."

"And that is the other thing I like about you; your honesty. You had better speak to the prisoners about where to find Junot although I do not think he will have gone far."

I sought Brennier. He was with the surgeon. As I walked in, he looked at my face which still had the scar from the bayonet. "This will not do Major Matthews. That will become infected." He had one of his assistants clean it up and then he wiped it with neat alcohol. "Do this each day until it heals over."

"The French General?"

"He is in the tent."

I found him heavily bandaged and speaking to a lieutenant who had also been wounded. "Are they looking after you?"

"Yes, Major. Thank you for your hospitality. You are most kind."

"We are all soldiers. I have been charged with finding your marshal and asking for the surrender of the army."

He smiled, "That is generous of you. I have seen your army you could capture him with just a battalion of your riflemen."

I shrugged, "None the less I need to speak with him."

"He will be at Torres Vedras."

"Not Lisbon?"

"Have you seen Lisbon?"

"Just once."

"Then you know it cannot be defended and besides your navy controls the seas. No, the Marshal will be at Torres Vedras." I nodded, "Tell me, Major, how you learnt to speak such good French?"

"My father was French."

"Then why do you not fight for France."

"I have no love for Bonaparte."

He nodded. "Some men love him and some hate him. It is a pity. You would have made a good soldier of France."

The next day Sharp and I left for Torres Vedras. Poor Sir Arthur was most unhappy. He now had two masters and he approved of neither.

We found the first of the stragglers almost immediately. There appeared to be little order to the retreat. It seemed to me more like a rout. The soldiers we encountered had no fight left in them. They heard the horses and almost resigned themselves to capture or death. There were hastily covered bodies showing where soldiers had succumbed to their wounds. It was not a pleasant sight.

The first organised soldiers I discovered were a half troop of Dragoons. As we trotted along the road they stopped and turned to aim their muskets at us.

I held up my hand. "I have been sent by General Wellesley to speak with Marshal Junot."

The Major was a grizzled old warrior who reminded me of Albert, my former commanding officer in the Chasseurs. He had been wounded and his arm was in a sling.

"Who are you?"

"Major Matthews of the 11th Light Dragoons."

"I saw you leading Portuguese."

I nodded, "My regiment has yet to land. I was lending a helping hand."

"You have courage and skill." He winced as he controlled his horse. "Is your army following?"

There was little point in lying. "They will be coming down the road soon but your men are not in danger of being ridden down and attacked."

He laughed, "You English fight a strange war. You would have had our sabres in your backs before now if our positions were reversed."

I shrugged, "The generals are gentlemen."

"They are fools but I will take their generosity." He nodded to a Brigadier, "Lafayette. Take the Englishmen to the Marshal."

"Thank you."

"I may see you again."

"I hope your wound is healed. I do not like to take advantage of an injured man."

The major laughed, "Do not worry Roast Beef, it is my left hand. I can still fight."

The presence of the Dragoon ensured a safe passage through the French army. We found Junot with the remnants of the Grenadiers who had been slaughtered on the ridge.

"Marshal Junot, I have been sent by Sir Harry Burrard to arrange surrender talks."

The shock and surprise were clearly in evidence on the face of both Junot and his staff. He dismounted and invited me to do the same. He led me away from the road to an olive tree which gave some shade from the sun. He spoke quietly.

"Is this a trick? Do you intend to attack us when our guard is down?"

I shook my head, "You have my word, sir, as an officer and gentleman, that this is neither a trick nor a trap."

"Did this general command at the battle?"

I shook my head, "No, sir. He arrived after the battle. Sir Arthur Wellesley was the general."

"And at Roliça?" I nodded. He smiled, "I am guessing that he does not approve of these talks of surrender." I kept a neutral expression on my face. "I know you cannot say." He appeared to consider the sky. "Tell your general, who seeks my surrender, that I will meet him at Sintra." I nodded, "It is just north of Lisbon."

"Why there, sir?"

He pointed to the hills around us. "The Portuguese would love us to camp here and wait for your generals. Half of my sentries would never see daylight. Cintra is closer to Lisbon and safer. We will wait there. I will send word to Lisbon. If you give me your word, we will not be attacked then I will tell my troops that hostilities have ceased."

"You have my word. Thank you, sir." I was about to go when I had a sudden thought. "Marshal Junot, may I ask a question of you?"

"Of course."

"A Portuguese lady, Donna Maria d'Alvarez was captured in Oporto and taken to Lisbon. She is a friend of mine and I would secure her release if I could."

His face saddened, "I am afraid that is nothing to do with me. I cannot help you. She was taken with other hostages by officers sent by Fouché." My face must have shown my recognition of the name of Bonaparte's spymaster and spy catcher. "I see you have heard of him. When we have discussed the surrender and I am back in Lisbon I will do what I can but... I should tell you that Colonel Laroche is a cruel man. I would not have him serve under me." He shrugged. "He is Fouché's man. They were being held at Queluz."

"The Royal Palace."

He nodded and it was his turn to look surprised. "You seem well informed. Your French and your knowledge tell me you are no ordinary soldier."

"I serve my country, that is all."

"As do I. Tell your general, I await him at Torre Vedras."

By the time I reached the army more troops had landed. We also heard that Sir John Moore was unloading the army at Oporto. I would soon be returned to my regiment. There was a massive contrast between the three generals. Sir Arthur was young and full of ideas. Sir Harry and Sir Hew looked like the old retired generals I had seen at Colonel Selkirk's club.

"Can we trust this fellow Junot, Major?"

"We can but his army is defeated, sir. There is no fight left in them. They have been beaten twice and taken heavy losses."

"You seem a useful sort of chap Major. Take a message to Lieutenant-General Moore. He should be in Oporto. Tell him to take command here."

I saw Sergeant Smith just before we boarded the fast sloop. "Good luck, Sergeant. When I have finished here, I dare say I will be rejoining my regiment. The 20th will not be alone for much longer."

"Good sir and if they are all half as good and you and Sharpie, I for one will not be unhappy." He saluted me.

"Watch over your lads, Sergeant, they are good soldiers."

"I know sir."

It took a day to reach Oporto and the army had yet to fully disembark. Sir John had taken over a tavern close by the harbour.

He was delighted to see me. He had heard of the victory at Roliça but not Vimeiro. "So, we have driven the French from Portugal."

"Not quite sir. Sir Harry and Sir Hew are discussing peace terms."

"What? But, from what you say we have them."

"Aye, sir. Sir Hew wants you at Torres Vedras with the rest of the army. They suggested you sail in the '*Crocodile*'."

"They might do but I have no intention of abandoning the army. They can wait. They do not need me to discuss peace terms for a battle I had no part in."

"Actually, sir, neither did they. It was all Sir Arthur."

He smiled, "You are a good fellow and very loyal. I admire that. We shall sail with the fleet and arrive together. However, I shall travel with you in the sloop. I am anxious to discover what our enemies are like."

"Of course, Sir John. Er if I might just visit with my squadron while the troops are embarking?"

"Of course."

Sergeant Sharp and I walked down to the harbour and hired a ferry to take us to the ship which had been identified as the one carrying the 11th. Once at the tumblehome I shouted, "Sir John Moore's aide seeking permission to board."

The Second Mate waved us up. "Come aboard sir."

Percy and William strode up to meet me. "Good to see you, sir. We have heard that Sir Arthur has had a great victory. Are we too late?"

"No Percy. We are to sail to join the rest of the army I just popped on board to see how things were. Did the horses travel well?"

Percy smiled, "Don't worry sir Sergeant Seymour looked after Badger. He is right as rain."

"And the men?"

"Fed up with being at sea and I dare say it will take some time for them to get their land legs again."

I turned to William, "How is the new officer working out?"

"Cornet Williams? Keen as mustard and he is desperate to meet you. Your troopers have been filling his head with the tales of your adventures."

I groaned. That was all that I needed, hero worship. "One thing you ought to know. The 20th were in action and their commanding officer, Major DeVere," the two officers recognised the name and looked at each other, "yes, the same. He charged too far and he and half of his squadron were killed; over a hundred and twenty men died uselessly. I tell you this for two reasons: one it cuts down the number of cavalry we have and it means that the rest of the army does not trust Light Dragoons. We need to behave impeccably. Understood?"

"Yes, sir."

"Well, I shall see you in Maceira Bay. I would suggest you find men who are good at swimming."

"Why sir?"

"It is a beach. There is no port!"

It was almost a leisurely cruise south as we sailed at the speed of the slowest transport. I was able to give him all the details of the action and the performance of the different branches of the army. Sir John was both pleased with the performance of the light infantry and rifles as he was appalled at the lack of control of the cavalry. He was also delighted that we had Portuguese allies who could be relied upon.

"It may well be, Major Matthews that I need you less as an aide and more as a commander of cavalry; although you seem to have been more than useful to Sir Arthur."

"I hope so sir although it took some time to get used to his ways."

He chuckled, "I have never met him but I have heard that he can be slightly abrasive."

I laughed, "Then those reports are accurate sir."

Chapter 14

We reached Maceira Bay on the 24th and it took three days to unload the ships. Fortunately, the seas were calmer for this landing and only a couple of soldiers were lost. Once again, I stripped to my overalls and swam Badger ashore. It was much easier with a horse that I knew. Sharp was reunited with Maria and he was happy again.

Generals Crauford and Hill took it upon themselves to tell Sir John of all that had happened including the peace which would allow Junot and his army to be repatriated in British ships. Sir John like the other two generals was appalled. Sir John, however, was a pragmatic man and he had said to the others, "We are soldiers and we obey orders. The responsibility lies with the senior generals. We must be ready to do all that we can. Where is the headquarters now?"

"The generals are at Torres Vedras."

"Then I think we begin to move the army there as soon as is practicable. Major Matthews tells me that it will take some days to reach there."

They both concurred and on the 28th we began the long slow journey south. I could have ridden there in one day on Badger but we ponderously snaked our way south. Sir John allowed me to travel with my squadron and I pointed out the graves at the side of the road marking the final resting places of many Frenchmen. It felt better to be with my men but I knew I still had unfinished business. The scar-faced henchman of Fouché, Colonel Laroche, had Donna Maria and other hostages. I knew that I could not rest until they were safe.

When we reached Torres Vedras on the 2nd of September, we discovered that the headquarters had moved to Cintra, just outside of Lisbon. Sir John was annoyed, "Major, you and I will go to headquarters once all of the army has arrived. We will take one of your troops with us as an escort. I know the French have surrendered but there may be those who have not heard the news yet."

It took another four days for the rest of the army to reach Torres Vedra and with the passing of time, I was increasingly worried about the hostages. Two weeks had passed since I had discovered their whereabouts. Who knew where they were? I used 7 Troop as an escort and left William and Cornet Williams with the others. It would do them both good to be without me looking over their shoulders all the time.

Sir John visited with Sir Hew by himself and we cooled our heels outside. When he emerged, he was less than happy. "I hate politics and it seems that we have nothing but politics here. I have been ordered to move the army to Lisbon." He shook his head, "The Portuguese are less than happy with this peace and when the politicians at home read of it then I suspect that all hell will break loose. Come, we will head back to the army."

"Sir, if I might be permitted."

"Carry on Major Matthews. Sir Hew and Sir Harry were more than pleased with your efforts in the battle. Your star is on the rise."

That did not interest me but I inclined my head at the compliment. "Sir, I am anxious about these Portuguese hostages held at Queluz."

"Surely they would have been released by now?"

"There are no British troops in Lisbon and the French army is not known for its mercy."

"But they surrendered."

"I heard that it was Bonaparte's secret police which held them, sir."

"Then you had better go. Take half of your troop. I would not wish you to come to harm."

"A sergeant and four men will do."

Joe Seymour handpicked the four troopers and the six of us rode to Lisbon. There was an ugly mood in the town. The local populace had been badly treated by the French and they could not understand this peace which allowed the French to wander around, free. Even worse was the news that some of the French generals were plundering the churches as well as stealing works of art. I would have much to report when I returned to Sir John.

It was quiet around the pretty pink palace of Queluz. However, I drew my pistol and turned to the others. "There may be French around. I have heard they are looting whatever they can to take back to France with them. Keep your weapons cocked."

The doors were ajar. The building had an empty feel to it. The last time we had visited it had been filled with courtiers and soldiers. There were signs of looting too. Cupboards and wardrobes were open and showed that they had been ransacked. The walls were devoid of paintings and the statues which had adorned it were all gone. I shouted, "Hello, anyone here?" There was no answer. The palace was empty.

"Search the palace. Sergeant Sharp, come with me. We will search the stables."

There was a coach house and a stable block. We made our way towards it. The gaping door was an indication that our search would be fruitless. However, as we neared it, I heard a whinny. We made our way into the stables and there were two horses remaining. Neither of them looked to be in the best of condition. If there were horses then there would be someone watching them.

I saw a movement from the hayloft. I raised my pistol and said, in French. "We are armed come out with your hands up."

There was no movement and I repeated it in Portuguese. A voice shouted, "I am coming, do not shoot me! I beg of you!"

An old groom clambered down. "Where are the rest of the servants?"

"The French took them last week when they fled."

"And the prisoners?"

He nodded, "They took them with them."

"And how did you avoid being taken with them?"

"I hid when they killed the others."

"Killed the others?"

He nodded and led us to the back of the stable. The smell from the bodies was already becoming unbearable. The male servants had been shot. It looked like a firing squad. I saw one freshly turned grave with a crude cross upon it.

"Why were they killed?"

"The man with the scar said he wanted no witnesses."

"You speak French?"

"He said it in Portuguese, sir. There were some traitors with him."

"And do you know where they were going?"

"I think they said Badajoz."

"Thank you. You have done well."

"Will you follow them, sir?"

"I will."

"Then kill them for that was my son." He pointed to the recently dug grave with fresh soil upon it.

Sergeant Seymour joined us. "Nothing in the house, sir."

I pointed to the bodies. "We will have to bury these before we go."

After we had buried them, I turned to the old man. "What will you do?"

He stood proudly, "I am the last of the servants. I will stay here until the royal family return."

Sadly, it would be many years before that happened.

When we reached camp, it was too late to report to Sir John but I found the other officers waiting up for me. Percy had served with me for years and he knew me well. There was a bottle of brandy waiting. "We thought you might need a drink, sir. How did it go?"

"They have been taken. It is a damned shame. We only missed them by a few days."

"The lads were talking with the 20th. They told us about the actions of their officers." I gave Percy a disapproving look. We did not discuss officers with the enlisted men. "I know, sir, but they were saying it wouldn't have happened if you had still been leading them."

"But I wasn't. There is no point in speculating about what might have been."

"No sir, but we were just saying that it was a lesson for us all. It is up to us to control our men."

"Lieutenant Austen, Captain Stafford until you are in a charge, do not presume to know if it is easy or not to control your men. I am not condoning Major DeVere but suppose he had not been attacked by dragoons and had broken their lines. What then? Would he not be a hero?" I could see them ruminating on my words.

I was remembering a time in Italy when we had charged in just such a situation. We had been lucky; we had broken the Austrians. There was a fine line between success and failure.

When I reported to Sir John the next day and told him of my news, he was worried. "We should have soldiers in Lisbon. I will have to speak with Sir Arthur."

"You have not seen him yet?"

"No, and that worries me. He knows what he is about. All the time we waste here the French across the border are getting stronger." He suddenly looked at me. "Matthews, did you say the hostages were being held at Badajoz?"

"Yes, sir. Why?"

"We can kill two birds with one stone but only if you think you can succeed."

I began to become excited. "Yes, sir!"

"Hear me out first."

I smiled, "Yes sir. Sorry."

"We need intelligence about the enemy. Could you take some horsemen to Badajoz and scout the French? If you could rescue the hostages then so much the better but I do not want you to take any risks! Both you and the cavalry are important. I would lose neither."

"Yes, sir. I could take ten of the 11th and eleven Portuguese. That would be a small enough force to scout and yet large enough for a rescue."

"Very well then. I will write out your orders."

"There is no need sir; a verbal order is good enough."

He shook his head, "Always get your orders in writing Major Matthews. It makes life much simpler."

I chose Captain Moreno and ten of his excellent horsemen. Joe Seymour handpicked the ten troopers and I chose Cornet Williams to accompany me. Poor Percy was distraught. "But sir, he is new and he has no experience."

"Then this will give him experience. The general will need you and Captain Stafford here. Besides I can get to know him a little better."

We took six of the captured French horses; they might become useful and they also carried the tents we would use. It was coming on to autumn and I had heard that, while it rarely rained, when it did it was a deluge. We also took some civilian clothes; I did not tell General Moore that we did so. He might not have understood the need. He was a soldier who obeyed the rules; I was not. We left Torres Vedras and headed east to the fortress of Badajoz. We were taking the war to Spain and the French invader.

Two of the Portuguese troopers had been chosen by Captain Moreno because they had grown up on the border. Antonio and Carlo also spoke Spanish. It was they who led the way and scouted for us. I made the troopers form the two different troops to pair up. I wanted the Portuguese to learn English and vice versa. Another part of me knew that it would make them closer as a fighting unit. I wanted them to become one force.

Luis was charmed by young Cornet Williams. He was barely seventeen. I had been a soldier at the same age but I am certain I never looked as young. I was not even certain if he had begun to shave yet. He was, however, a bright lad and soon began to pick up the language. The two of them got on well.

We were going to camp when Luis pointed out that there was a small village some way ahead. Coruche might have an inn was his plea. I balanced the thought of the men having drink with the thought of a warm night and reaching Badajoz sooner. We pushed on.

Arriving just after dark the large village appeared to be deserted. There were no lights. Had we been alone I would have carried on but Luis found the largest building. He dismounted, walked up to the door and rapped smartly on it. An ancient blunderbuss emerged until Luis began to speak. They were too far away for me to hear and I was beginning to regret not camping while we had daylight.

Then the door opened and a man emerged. Luis brought him over to me. "Sir, this is Senor Morello the Prefeito of Coruche. We are welcome to stay the night but he has a story to tell you first."

I dismounted and handed my reins to Sharp. "Cornet Williams, go with Sergeant Seymour and see that the men are safely billeted. I will not be long."

The old man took us into his living room. There was a fire but the room did not feel homely. He gestured to a seat and poured me a beaker of wine. It was a rough but honest brew.

"The captain tells me that you are a Colonel in the Portuguese Army."

I nodded, "But I serve in the British army."

"Yes, but it is important to me that you fight the French for Portugal." I could tell that he had something important to tell me and I had to be patient.

"The captain said that you seek a Frenchman with a scar and some Portuguese nobles." I was suddenly all ears and I leaned forward eagerly, nodding. "A week ago, French soldiers guarding two coaches came to the village." He shook his head, "You must understand that we are a peaceful village and we wanted no trouble. We watered their horses and we thought that they would be on their way. We heard a Portuguese lady telling us that these men were murderers. Some of the young men in the village..." He covered his face and shook. I let him compose himself. "It is my fault. I am the Prefeito and I should have controlled them but since my wife died, I have lost the will to make such decisions. The young men tried to rescue her and the French slaughtered them. The ones they did not shoot they hanged. They took the silver from the church and killed the priest when he tried to stop them. All the time I cowered in my home." He shook his head. "It is my fault."

"The lady you tried to rescue is a strong woman. Had she known what would have resulted from her call she would have remained silent. Had you intervened then you, too, would be dead and we would not know where they went."

"Is that true or are you trying to make an old man feel better about having lived too long?"

"No. I speak the truth. Now tell me where they say they were going?"

"I do not know for certain but I did hear one of the Portuguese drivers say that they had another two days of hard driving ahead of them," he spat into the fire. "They were traitors. If I see them again then they will die."

"Two days of hard driving would take them to ...?"

"Badajoz."

It was confirmation of the information I had gathered in Lisbon and I was pleased that I had taken Luis' advice and visited the village.

We found the same story the further east we went. It seemed the scar-faced Frenchman felt he could act with impunity and take whatever he wished. We found one small village where the bodies of the hanged men still swung beneath trees and the discarded bodies of the women and girls lay ravaged in their homes. My troopers were as grim-faced as the Portuguese when we buried them.

Poor Cornet Williams was pale as we laid the last stone on the graves. "Sir, how can soldiers do this to women and girls?"

"They are not soldiers, Cornet. They might wear a uniform but they are not soldiers." I had known too many like the scar-faced Frenchman, Colonel Laroche. They were not the Chasseurs like Jean, Pierre and Albert. These were politically connected and hid behind the Revolutionary and now Imperial doctrine. They would never stand in line and defend a flag. They would change their masters with each change of the wind.

Joe Seymour put the spade back in the house even though there were only ghosts in the village. He had overheard the Cornet. He spoke to him like a big brother. "You will soon learn the difference, sir. When the Major catches them then they will wish they had never been born."

As we went back to the tents the Cornet asked me, "Sir, the men said that you have killed many men." I nodded. "Were they all in battle?"

"No Cornet. In serving my country I have had to end the lives of many enemies of the king. When we catch these animals, they will receive justice. It is more than they deserve but we are not like them." He handed me a mug of sweetened brandy which Luis had concocted. "When you have to take a life do it swiftly and do not hold back. If it is someone else's life or yours then you will need to be ruthless. It is easier killing on a battlefield where you have no time to think but the men will look to you, Cornet. Do not let them down."

"I won't sir." He sipped his own brandy and coughed a little. I smiled. It was a potent drink. "Sir, why did you bring me? Lieutenant Austen has more experience."

"So that you can gain experience." I waved a hand around the troopers who were talking, haltingly, with the Portuguese. "You are young and inexperienced but before we return to England you will have to lead these men. You should know them and they should know you. This week will see you become part of the 11th Light Dragoons."

We camped just five miles from Badajoz. Our local troopers had told us that we had crossed the border but you would not have known it. The terrain was the same. We could see the river winding past the imposing border fortress. It lay on the southern bank and guarded the bridge over the river. There was a flag flying but we were too far away to see what colour.

We had our pairs of guards out as usual; one trooper and one Portuguese. I had the rest gathered around me. I told them of my plans. It was difficult for I had to do it in English and then Portuguese. I was gratified that each seemed to know some words of the other's language. The trip had borne fruit already.

"Tomorrow I will take Sergeant Seymour, Captain Moreno and six of the Portuguese soldiers into Badajoz. We will try to find out where the hostages are. Sergeant Sharp and Cornet Williams will scout the perimeter of Badajoz and find out what defences there are outside of the town. We will meet back here tomorrow night."

When I had explained all, they nodded. Alan did not look happy. I knew why. He hated letting me out of his sight but I needed someone who could speak Portuguese. Joe could speak a little but not enough to command the Portuguese. Cornet Williams asked, "What if some do not make it back to the rendezvous?"

I spoke slowly, "We assume that they are dead and return to the General." To make it clear I spelt it out. "If we are captured, Cornet, then you will be in command and you will return to Lisbon and report to Sir Moore. Is that clear?"

He looked pale, "Yes sir."

"Now get some rest. Tomorrow will be a busy day."

As I lay down in my blanket, I heard Sergeant Seymour say, "Don't worry Mr Williams. The major won't leave you behind. He doesn't want you risking your life for him. That's the way he is."

We changed into our civilian clothes and left two troopers at our camp to guard our tents and clothes. Sergeant Seymour and I rode French horses. We left Badger at the camp. The docked tail on Joe's horse was a sure sign that it was English and Badger, although he did not have a docked tail was such a striking horse that he would have stood out. We wished to be anonymous.

We rode in groups of twos and threes. The two local troopers had told us that there were a number of gates into the town and we each took a different one. Our rendezvous would be in the square close to the cathedral.

Two of the Portuguese rode in before us. I allowed a good gap to avoid any suspicion. There were two French guards at the gate. They gave a cursory look at the two troopers who were ahead of us and then allowed them to pass. "Let us dismount, Joe. They rode in and we will walk in. You are my Portuguese servant. The French will not know that you can barely speak the language."

"That's good then, sir because I am bloody awful at it."

"From now on speak only Portuguese even if it is just yes and no."

He nodded and we led our horses towards the gate. I had decided on a story already. I was a winemaker from northern Italy; close to Nice. It would explain why I could speak both Italian and French. Joe was my guide. I was visiting the region to buy some red wine to supplement the fine rose wine of that region. I had learned that if the story was in my head then even if I did not need to use it, I was more confident.

The Corporal put his hand against my chest. "Where are you going?"

He said it in French and I replied in the same language but I accented it slightly. "I am travelling through the region buying wines for my business."

He laughed. I noticed that both of them were a little overweight and a little old. These were not the front-line troops we had fought at Vimeiro. "When there is a war going on?"

I shrugged. "We saw no war in Lisbon. There were some unhappy people but no war."

He leaned in to me, "Well I would buy your wine quickly and get out because the war is coming." He stepped back and patted the walls of the fortress. "And I am happy to be behind these thick walls. Pass through and watch these Spaniards. They would steal the coins from a dead man's eyes."

And we were through. I saw the perspiration on the sergeant's brow. He could face an enemy charge without blinking but subterfuge was not in his nature.

We continued to lead our horses. It afforded a disguise. I was mindful of Sir John's mission and I examined every French soldier that we saw. There were not many. This was a scratch garrison drawn from the dregs of the army. The cathedral dominated the city and was easy to find. I saw the others there. I handed the reins to Joe and told him, in Portuguese, "Just walk around the square. I will come back to you. Smile at people and keep your eyes open."

We had decided that four of us would go into bars and see if we could find where the prisoners were being held. The two local troopers, Luis and I would try to blend in. I saw a lively looking place with a great deal of noise coming from within. I wandered in.

It was crowded and that was unusual for it was not lunchtime yet. I saw that a quarter of the clientele were French artillerymen. They appeared to be in the same sort of condition as the others we had seen. The rest of the customers were a mixture of working girls and traders. There appeared to be some sort of auction going on.

I made my way to the bar and managed to order a jug of wine. One sip told me that it was one step away from vinegar. It would be easy to nurse it. Two men cleared a space and, as they spoke, I realised that they were French. They shouted in poor Portuguese for silence. One of them then stood on a chair and held a cloth over an object. Like a magician, he whipped the cover from it and I saw that it was a fine painting. It was a fine painting I had seen before; it had been hanging in the Regent's chambers at the palace of Queluz. These were the men I sought.

They auctioned a number of items and they each went for a high price. Before the last one was sold, I left the bar and walked into the Cathedral Square. I saw Joe and I waved him over. I pretended to be looking at one of the hooves of my horse until the two men came out. The one who had been selling carried the large bag with the money while the other held a naked sword. They were taking no chances. I saw in which direction they were heading and we set off slowly. They soon overtook us; the one with the sword pushing me aside in the process. We carried on a little faster and followed them. When they came to a narrow street, I handed my reins to Joe and removed my hat and coat. I followed them through the street and they emerged into a smaller square. There was a large white building ahead and I stopped in a doorway to watch for there were two armed guards outside. As I watched a figure came out on to the balcony and waved at the two men from the auction. He had a long scar running down his cheek. I had found the hostages.

Waiting until all but the two sentries had gone in, I wandered across the small square. I did it purposefully as though I was going somewhere. I was watched every inch of the way by the two guards. I continued beyond the building. Fifty yards later I found myself in another small square and there was a stable. As there were no guards around, I opened the door and entered. There was a coach and ten horses. They were all fine animals and I knew that they came from the palace at Queluz. I quickly left. The road was wider and I followed it for another sixty yards until I reached the eastern gate. To my left rose the castle itself and the garrison. It was an imposing-looking fortress. The gate was still open and there were another two sentries there guarding the entrance.

Rather than retracing my steps and risking the scrutiny of the two sentries, I headed along a row of small shops and workshops which ran parallel to the wall of the fortress. I took a right as soon as I could and entered a maze of streets. Eventually, I found myself in the square in which I had left Joe. I could see him looking nervously around. I reached him. As he handed me the reins he said quietly, "The captain and his men have left the town. I think they are going to close the gates soon.

"Follow me." We mounted and I led him down the narrow street towards the house where the prisoners were being held. The two sentries had their weapons in their hands as we clattered through. We carried on without looking at them. When we reached the eastern gate, the sentry held up his hand.

"We are closing the gates soon, my friend. It is dangerous out there. There are Spanish Guerrillas who will slit your throat."

I held out my hands in apology. "My servant and I must get back to my home with medicine for my sick father."

"Be careful then and God speed."

The road turned south as soon as it left the fortress. There was a ford across the stream and then the road headed south. We were forced to follow it. I saw another small fort to the west and there was a track which ran alongside it. We had to get back to the west and the camp. I took the road. As we passed the fort, I could tell that it was deserted. It was light enough to see that the ramparts had no sentries. I stored that information. Eventually, the track joined the road down which we had travelled. I wondered why I had not noticed the fort when we had entered the city earlier that day.

As soon as we reached the road Joe began to chatter. "And Sharpie has done that sort of thing before sir?" I nodded. "He's has got bigger balls than me then, sir. When I was waiting for you, I was terrified."

"And you looked it. Listen, Sergeant, if you have to do something like that again, don't look as though you are on guard. Smoke a pipe. Smile at people as they pass. Fiddle on with the horse's saddle. Do anything so long as it doesn't look as though you are watching."

"But how do you watch then, sir?"

"Surreptitiously."

Luis and the others were watching anxiously when we reached the camp. They had bought some food in the city and brought it with them in terracotta pots. It was still warm and more than welcome. As we ate, he reported what they had seen.

"We did not see the hostages nor the man with the scar. My men searched but they could not find the coaches. I am sorry, Colonel."

"Do not worry I found both the hostages and the coach. How many sentries did you see?"

"We found four gates and there were two men on each gate. The exception was the northern gate at the bridge over the river. There were eight men there and the fort on the other side was manned too."

"Good, then I have my plan."

After we had eaten, I gathered them around me and, using the soil as a drawing board I gave them their instructions. "Sergeant you and the Cornet will wait at the deserted fort, as soon as it starts to get darker then you head towards the castle gate. We will have to risk you being seen. Perhaps the sentries will take the blue uniforms as their own. If we are pursued it is up to you to hold up the enemy." I turned to Luis, "You saw no cavalry?"

"We saw neither cavalry nor horses." He smiled, "Your eyes are sharper than mine Colonel."

"Perhaps I just knew where to look. Cornet you need to have two men with the spare horses. If we have to, we will ditch the tents. We can sleep rough if we have to."

The Cornet looked shocked, "But sir, you said one of the hostages was an elderly lady."

"She is Cornet and she is a tough one too. I want you to make sure that the men and horses get a good rest tomorrow during the day. I want to use the night to put as much distance between us and the French before dark. I want to reach Portugal before we rest."

They all seemed clear and I hoped that my plan was as cunning as I hoped it would be.

Chapter 15

We reached the unmanned fort before dawn. "Now I am assuming there will be no more than eight hostages."

Cornet Williams asked, "How do you know sir?"

"The coach could only hold a maximum of eight and it would have been crowded. We should have two spare horses at least. Remember Cornet, that you will need to be close enough to the gate before they close it. There are places for you to hide close to the wall. If you hear shots then get to the gate as soon as possible." I saw him biting his lip nervously. I leaned in and said quietly, "Trust Sergeant Seymour. He will not let you down."

I let the others head to the castle in dribs and drabs. I intended to have us arrive over the whole day to avoid suspicion. There would be thirteen of us this time. Sharp and I left in the middle of the day. It happened that when we reached the gate, they were in the process of changing the guard. The bell was tolling twelve. As luck would have it, it was the same pair we had met the previous night. We had to wait until the guard was changed.

"How is your father?"

I shook my head, "Not so good. I have come to get some stronger medicine."

"Why not ask for a doctor to visit?"

I pointed to the hills. "Until the guerrillas are dispersed there will be no doctor's visits." He waved his arm to let us pass.

"You have a different servant today."

"Yes, Jorge had too much wine last night. It is my fault I allowed him too long in the town." He nodded as though he understood the problems of servants. "You have a long shift ahead of you, my friend."

"No, I we will not be on as long today. Our shift finishes at the four o'clock bell. It is the others who will be on until eight." He smiled, "Perhaps I will have too much wine tonight."

I noted his words. They would help us to escape. The gate would be closed at eight. We needed to strike by seven.

The Portuguese were spread out in pairs around the perimeter of the building. Luis and the other troopers would be in the bar across from the cathedral. I walked past our watchers. Each gave me the barest of nods as I passed. There was nothing to report.

When I reached the square, I took out a cigar and went to the candle on Luis' table. I spoke so quietly that only he could hear. "We must be gone before eight."

He nodded. "No one has left yet."

I turned and walked out with Sharp. There was a fountain and water trough close by the cathedral and I sat there and smoked the cigar. Our horses drank. It looked natural. I began to tell Sharp my usual jokes. He had heard them all before but it looked more natural to passers-by. He dutifully laughed at the appropriate moments. The bell tolled for two o'clock and Sharp gripped my arm. It was the scar-faced man and two of his men. I took a drag on my cigar as they passed and listened.

Colonel Laroche pointed at a small shop. "Tell Gerard that he needs to buy some more cheese we are running out."

"Yes, colonel."

"Fool! Do not use my title."

They entered a small place which I knew served food. I stood and stretched. That was the signal and Luis and his men left the bar and collected their mounts. I handed the reins to Sharp. "Wait here for Luis. I will not be a moment."

I slipped inside the shop and bought a round of sheep's cheese. When I reached the others I said, "Luis you and Sharp come with me. Follow my lead. The others can follow with the horses in five minutes. If we are not inside within five minutes then we will have failed."

After the horses were collected, we walked down the narrow street. "You two walk a little way behind me. Sharp, tell Luis one of my jokes. Watch for my signal and have your knives ready."

As I entered the small square, I saw the two men looked at me suspiciously. I sauntered nonchalantly across the square as though I had all the time in the world. I heard Sharp's boots behind me but the focus of the two men was on me.

"Go away!"

I feigned outrage, "The man with the scar; the colonel he paid me to deliver this cheese to someone called Gerard." I shrugged, "If this is a mistake then I have a fine cheese and a silver coin for my trouble."

Their guard relaxed, one put his arm out while the other opened the door a little, "No, this is the place. Give me the cheese and be on your way."

Both men were looking at the cheese. I held it in my left hand and then dropped it. As I expected they both cursed and reached down for it. I reached down too but I reached for my stiletto. I pushed the nearest man back against the door which swung in and ripped my blade across his throat. Before the other sentry could utter a sound, Luis had him pinioned and Sharp had cut his throat.

The other troopers arrived with their horses. "Take the horses to the stable. Leave two men on guard and bring the rest in. Bring these bodies inside. No guns. Just knives."

Luis grinned, "That is how we like it, colonel."

It was a grand house. The door we had used led to a large vestibule. I drew my sword and slowly opened the door. I could rely on Sharp to cover me. The hall was empty. I stepped in and quickly examined the exits. There was a large double stairway leading to a balcony which ran around the entrance hall. It was obviously the place Colonel Laroche had watched his men the other day. There were three doors leading off on the ground floor. I nodded and pointed to Sharp who took the one on the far right. I took the one on the left. I opened it slowly and saw narrow steps leading downstairs. I could hear the sound of someone singing. That would be to the kitchens. I was guessing that Gerard was down there.

I turned to signal to Luis. I drew my finger across my throat and pointed downstairs. He nodded and tapped two of his men on the shoulders. I had worked out that there would probably be ten men in all. The old man in the village had estimated a dozen but there were only enough horses for ten. Two were dead and three were in the square. That left five. Assuming that there was at least one in the kitchen we could expect another four.

Sergeant Sharp shook his head. I moved towards the last door. I slowly opened it a fraction and I listened. I heard voices. I guessed it was two men. I turned and held up two fingers. Luis and Alan nodded. I pushed the door open and leapt into the room. Two men were sitting on chairs with their feet on footstools. They were smoking cigars and drinking brandy. They stared in shock as the three armed men ran into the room. I ran one through and Luis killed the second while Sergeant Sharp despatched the third. They had been relaxing and were taken totally by surprise.

As we entered the hall again the two men Luis had sent to the kitchen stood there. One held up one finger while the other clutched a bleeding arm. Luis went to the wounded man and fashioned a crude bandage around his arm then pointed him to the stables. He left. There were now four of us against two. I guessed that they were upstairs.

We slowly climbed the stairs. This was the difficult part of the escapade. If they came out, they would see us and raise the alarm. I guessed that the commander of the fortress was complicit in all of this. We could not afford the alarm to be raised. He might not want the hostages on public display but the scar-faced colonel would have alerted him to their presence. A gunshot would bring soldiers running and the game would be up.

There were four doors and another set of stairs leading up to the next floor. I went to the first door and listened. I heard no sounds from within. Luis, his trooper and Sharp went to the other three. Suddenly Luis' arm came up and he waved us to the far doorway.

I scurried across the landing. I could hear the buzz of conversation. This would be the hardest task so far. We had no idea what the hostages looked like. We would have to play this by ear. I put my hand on the door and eased it slowly open a fraction. The sounds of the voices became louder and I heard a French voice shout, "I hope that is lunch Gerard, we are starving!"

That was my cue. I flung open the door and leapt in. The voice had come from my left and I saw a soldier with a pistol in his belt.

He went to grab it. I knew that he was not a hostage. My sword slashed across him and his throat erupted in a fountain of blood. There was a scream. I turned and saw at least three women and some well-dressed men. It was like a tableau; they were frozen with shock. Luis was pulling his sword from the last guard.

One of the men dropped to his knees and began to splutter, "Please do not kill us! Please!"

I heard Donna Maria's exasperated voice, "Don Francisco, be a man and compose yourself. These are our saviours and not our killers."

She was seated in a large chair. I went to her. "Are you hurt Donna Maria?"

"Just a little tired." She held out her hand and I kissed it. "I know not how you managed it but I knew that you would come."

Suddenly we heard the bell tolling at three o'clock. "Are there any more guards?"

"How many have you seen, Robbie?"

"We have accounted for ten."

"Then you have them all. Three of them left a few days ago for Madrid." She chuckled, "Hopefully the guerrillas will have had them."

Our early rescue had caused problems. We could not get the hostages out until we had disposed of the guards at the gate. It was too risky to do before they changed. And then there was the problem of Colonel Laroche and his men. They would be returning soon.

"Luis, send a man to Cornet Williams. Tell him to move to the gate when they hear the bell toll four o'clock." He nodded and disappeared. "The rest of you get your things. We are escaping."

The man who had begged for his life, a man as old as Donna Maria asked, "How? We are in a French fortress."

"I have men outside. We will ride out of here."

The man shook his head. "I am too old to ride!"

"Then stay here and die!" Donna Maria covered her mouth to hide her smile at my command. I turned to face the hostages. "All of you listen to me. We have one chance to get out of here and that means all of you doing exactly as I say. I will not risk my men's lives for any of you if you disobey me." I looked at each face in turn. There were three young women and another who was middle-aged. There were two men; Don Francisco and a younger man who looked to be related for he had features which looked similar. They all nodded. "Good. It will take us three days to reach Lisbon. Get all the clothes that you can carry for it may be cold. You ladies had better split your skirts. We have no side saddles." They all looked equally shocked. "You men, get a sword and a pistol from the dead Frenchmen."

They were now too shocked to argue and they began to obey. Donna Maria helped the women to adjust their dresses. "Alan, you take them to the horses. Get them mounted and then wait. We escape after they have changed the guard." He nodded. "Luis, you and I will remain in the house with two others. We have the last three Frenchmen to deal with and I suspect they will be the hardest."

We got them downstairs and Luis ran to the narrow alley while they slipped out and went around to the stables at the rear. Even if something happened to us, they would, at least, have a chance of escape. The gate was open and they could ride down the two guards. I preferred a silent and unseen escape if I could manage it. Miraculously we managed to achieve our objective.

"Now, Luis, leave the front door open." As he did so I picked up one of the first two men we had slain. "Bring a chair from inside the room." The two men manhandled the chair and I put the man in it. I positioned him so that he looked as though he was asleep. "Do the same with the other two."

"I do not understand. What are you doing?"

"When they return to the house, they will see no guards and the door open. They will be suspicious and they will enter with drawn weapons. When they see their men asleep their leader will be angry but he will lower his guard, quite literally. That is when we strike." I pointed to the door. "Two of us on each side. Their attention will be on these two. Luis, you take the far side."

The men had finished with the bodies. I went into the room with the two dead men and brought out their cigars, still smoking, and the brandy. I jammed the cigars in their mouths and the brandy glasses in their stiffening fingers. A little bandy spilt out but when I looked back at them, they looked like two guards who had fallen asleep.

I had no idea of the time but knew it was getting close to four o'clock. If Laroche had not arrived by the time the cathedral bell was tolled then we would leave. It was unsatisfactory but my priority was the hostages.

Annoyingly we could not see who was approaching the door. Both of them were solid and there were no side windows. We had to wait for the bell to toll or the door to be thrust open. We all had swords drawn and I had my stiletto in my left hand. If this colonel worked for Fouché then he would be a tough customer.

I heard voices. "Jacques! If you are asleep, I will cut out your heart!"

Just then the bell began to toll and the door opened. I knew that we would have to wait until they entered before we could attack them; too early and they would flee and raise the alarm.

"Your drunken pair! Gerard! Get up here now you imbecile!"

Scarface came in last. As the two others strode over to what they thought were drunken friends, Luis and one trooper leapt out at them. I lunged forward too. A heartbeat ahead of me the trooper standing next to me slashed at Scarface. The colonel's sword flashed and arterial blood flooded from the throat of the dead Portuguese. I flicked the sword away. But Colonel Laroche was good. He used the riposte and lunged at me. I had been taught by the best and he did not catch me out.

His eyes narrowed as we faced each other. "Who are you? A bandit or an assassin?"

I did not answer. I had my hands full with him. The other guards were struggling on the floor with Luis and the Portuguese trooper. The colonel dropped his eyes and then swung his blade at head height. I just managed to step back and as the blade scraped across my shoulder, I quickly stabbed forwards and my blade grated off his kneecap. He suppressed a shout as blood dripped to the floor.

I watched as he gritted his teeth. "You have skill and I believe you are a soldier; what are you English, Spanish or Portuguese?"

Again, he used his words to try to unsettle me. He lunged forward again even as he was speaking but his wounded knee did not give him the support he needed and the blade fell woefully short. I feinted to his left and, as he moved his blade to defend against my blow, I stabbed him in the stomach. "Scottish actually!"

One of the guards was about to stab an unconscious Luis and I stabbed him in the back. There was just one Portuguese trooper left. "Get the captain to the horses and I will join you."

The dying colonel looked up at me. "Who are you?"

"Someone who hates Fouché and Bonaparte in equal measure. Go to God!" The man was dying and I ended his misery by piercing his throat. I reached down and prised the sword from his dead hand. I had a home for that weapon.

The square was empty. I had thought the noise of combat would have alerted someone but it was still as quiet as the graveyard it had become. Once I reached the stables, I made sure that Luis was tied securely on to his horse. "Come Sharp, let us try our acting again." I turned to Luis' sergeant. "Count to fifty and then bring out the hostages. Head to the right when you get out. My men will be there."

"Yes, colonel."

"Robbie, take care!"

"I will Donna Maria."

As we stepped out, I put my dagger in my left hand. "We are drunk. Try just to incapacitate them. We will sing a French song." Sharp's accent could be atrocious but when he sang it did not matter. We staggered towards the gate and the sentries shook their heads and began to laugh. The slurring of our words seemed to fit in with two drunks.

I held my dagger so that the hilt was in my palm and the blade was up my sleeve. I raised my arms as I approached them. "My friends! I have won ten Louis at dice. I am a rich man."

"You are a drunken man!"

I had my right fist closed as though it contained coins. I held it before me. "If you do not believe me see the money!"

As one of the soldiers leaned forward, I smashed down on his temple with my dagger. Sharp's sentry was made of sterner stuff and he stayed on his feet. I lifted the musket which the falling sentry had dropped to the floor and I hit him hard on the back of the head. He went down and stayed down. I emptied the powder from the pan and then rammed the barrel into the dirt. It would need cleaning before it could be fired. I whistled and the troopers arrived. I saw Luis had a bandage on his head but he was upright and riding his horse. I threw my leg over the saddle of the French horse and we galloped out of the fortress.

"Keep low in case anyone shoots from the ramparts."

We had only seen a few sentries on the walls which surrounded the city and I counted on their eyes being drawn further from the fortress than the bottom of the walls. I was the last to trot through the gate and out of Badajoz.

Chapter 16

It was almost an anti-climax when we met Cornet Williams and my men close to the ford. As I had expected the blue uniforms had deceived, albeit briefly, the French guards on the ramparts. We were halfway along the wall before the alarm was raised. A couple of muskets popped away at us but we were too far away for them to hit us. I had already decided that we would get over the border before we even thought about stopping. The French were no respecters of borders but they might worry about Anglo-Portuguese forces being present.

"Sharp, stay here and see if we are pursued."

"Sir."

Trooper Harrison led Badger. I would change to him as soon as I could and I would change into my uniform. Both acts would make me feel better.

The older man, Don Francisco, complained the whole way. The women, Donna Maria apart, were obviously terrified but they hung on gamely. Don Francisco kept shouting at us to stop and rest.

Eventually, I rode next to him and said, "If you do not shut up then I shall leave you here!"

"Do you know who I am?"

"No, and quite frankly I do not care. I came here to rescue Donna Maria. I do not know you nor am I bothered about you so shut up or stay here. That is your choice!"

The other man said, "He means it, uncle. Do as he says."

A mile or so down the road Sergeant Sharp galloped up. "No pursuit, sir. We are safe."

We rode on until it became dark. We had ridden for almost three hours. I saw a light ahead. It was a farm. I headed towards Sergeant Seymour at the front. "We'll try the farm ahead, Sergeant." I gestured at the hostages, "These have gone far enough. Have the lads form a skirmish line and check out the land. I want a perimeter of guards a hundred yards around the farm. I'll get the Portuguese troopers to put up the tents."

"Righto, sir."

Cornet Williams said as I rode with the two of them. "Sir, that was so exciting. I saw the blood on your clothes. Did you have to kill anyone?"

"Yes Cornet, and we lost a soldier too. War is not glorious. Men die. Remember that."

Luis joined me at the door of the farm, "How is the head, my friend?"

He put a hand up and removed the bandage. The blood had ceased to flow. "I feel stupid for allowing that animal to get the better of me."

"They were all experienced soldiers and they were killers. It could have gone worse for us all."

"And yet, you killed their leader." There was admiration in his voice.

"Let us just say that I have fought his kind many times and I know what kind of tricks they play."

Luis rapped on the door. "We are Portuguese soldiers on the business of the Queen and we seek assistance."

A voice drifted back, "How do we know you are who you say you are? You could be guerrillas."

"Because if we were not then you would now be dead."

The door opened a crack and a fearful face was framed in the doorway. He saw the assembled host. "Our house is too small, we cannot accommodate you."

"You do not need to. We will camp behind the house. Have you a barn?"

He stepped out and pointed to a roof with four posts holding it up. "I have that."

"Good. And water?"

He became eager now. "Oh yes, yes. I have good water."

I pointed to the women, "The women will need some privacy."

He looked confused. "Have you a wife?"

"Oh yes and two daughters."

"Then they will know what the women want."

Realisation dawned. "Oh yes, sir. We have an outhouse."

"And we will use your fire. We have our own food and my men will not be in the way but we will use your fire."

He nodded, now eager to please. "Oh yes, sir."

I left the Portuguese setting up the tents. Cornet Williams returned. "It appears to be safe sir."

"Good. Half the men stay on watch and the other half cook the food. You and the sergeant arrange the watches."

He seemed to grow with the responsibility, "Yes sir."

I found that the hostages had dismounted and were standing around, Donna Maria apart, looking lost. "We will stay here tonight. My men are putting up tents. If you do not wish to use the tent then you can sleep in the barn over there."

Don Francisco decided to try my patience once more. "Why cannot we stay on the farm? They are merely peasants."

I was about to reply when Donna Maria stood before him, "Don Francisco I have had weeks stuck with you and you are the most appalling man I have ever met. I nearly told the colonel here to leave you to the French. You deserve each other. We cannot throw these people out of their home and besides I suspect they all sleep in one room on one bed. Should we all share?"

The women all laughed. Don Francisco tried to dig himself out of his hole. "I was thinking of you, dear lady."

"Do not '*dear lady me*'! I will happily sleep in the barn. A few more days of hardship are worth it. We now have our freedom and you may not have noticed but a poor soldier bought that freedom with his life. So be grateful."

I left them to it and changed into my uniform. The men had made horse lines and saw to it that the horses had been fed. The farmer did not know it but his winter barley had fed the horses before the trooper in charge had realised. He moved them but they were better fed than in a long time.

Trooper Cole was a fine cook and he used the dried meat and some vegetables we had found to make a very palatable stew. He fed the women first and then me. I saw the looks he was throwing the way of Don Francisco and his nephew. "Feed them too, Cole."

"He doesn't deserve it."

"I know but feed him anyway." I tasted it as he was walking off. "This is excellent, Trooper."

When we had finished the meal Donna Maria took a flask out of her bag and swallowed a mouthful. She gave it to me. "Drink with me." I drank some. It was very expensive brandy. "You are very handsome in your uniform Robbie. You should be married."

"I am… to the army. Tell me, Donna Maria, what happened? Why were you taken hostage?"

She moved a little closer and spoke conspiratorially to me, "We are all here for different reasons. The ladies are all the wives and daughters of prominent men in Lisbon. They were taken to ensure that their husbands and fathers cooperated with the French. Don Francisco is the most important politician in Lisbon. He and his nephew were taken so that the Lisbon Council would do all that was asked of them. He is a rich and powerful man. Most of the council owe him money and favours."

"And you?"

She laughed, "I would not shut up! They called me an agent provocateur!" She laughed. "At my age!"

"Were you to be kept at Badajoz?"

"Until the Emperor arrived, yes."

That was news which would be valuable to Sir John. "The Emperor is coming?"

"Yes, that savage Laroche, the one with the scar, kept boasting of that. When your Sir Arthur won the two battles and we had to leave Lisbon he told us that soon the Emperor would come and destroy all the English generals as he had with the Russians, Prussians and Austrians." She took another sip of the brandy.

"Were you at the battles?"

"I was. Sir Arthur is a fine general and he defeated them easily."

"Good. Then there is hope."

"There is always hope but the Emperor has many times the soldiers we have."

She nodded, "I understood some French. The Emperor has defeated his other enemies in Europe. It seems his war is now with

Britain and the countries of Spain and Portugal. It is up to your Sir
Arthur and others like him to defeat Napoleon."

I pointed to Luis and his troopers. "Your soldiers are stout
fellows. They fight as we do."

She nodded, "But they are not as well led. When my husband
was a general then we had good leaders. The Spanish did not steal
our land when he was in command. But you are right they are fine
soldiers and this may be the start of the end."

I had everyone up before dawn and on the road as the first rays
peered over the eastern horizon. Don Francisco complained again
but he was now shunned by all. I think this lack of power was a
new experience for him and he did not like it. I suspected I would
have complaints made about me when we finally reached Lisbon.

"Luis, have two of your men trail us by a mile or so. They can
warn us of any pursuit."

"Yes, colonel."

"Harrison, Cole. You two are scouts today. Ride a mile ahead of
us and keep your carbines on your saddles and ready to fire."

"Sir."

Now that I had Badger, my own saddle and my carbine I felt
much better. It was silly for the horse and saddle I had had were
both adequate. The familiarity of the leather and the mane before
me seemed to make me a better soldier. I loaded the carbine and
fixed it to the sling.

We headed back towards Portugal.

Although in theory, this was the safer part of our journey I knew
that there were those who would choose to exploit a land without
order. The guerrillas who fought against the French were one thing
but there were those who fought against everyone and did so
ruthlessly. The women we accompanied were an enticement to
bandits.

We stopped at noon when we reached a bubbling stream. My
troopers distributed the little food we had so that all ate. It would
be short rations for all. I constantly checked on Donna Maria. "I
am fine, Robbie. Your consideration and attention are touching but
I am tougher than you think. This violation by the French has given

me a purpose in life. When they killed my husband, they created a monster. Me!"

She was indomitable and in direct contrast to Don Francisco. I had no doubt that he would emerge from this war a richer man with even more power. The poor Portuguese trooper who had died to save him would not even briefly figure in his thoughts. That was the way of the world.

Perhaps the thought that we had only one more night before we reached Lisbon made me complacent but the shots from ahead made me alert.

"Cornet Williams, take five men and protect the hostages. Luis, watch the rear. Sergeant Seymour, bring the rest with me." I unclipped the carbine as Badger's legs opened. There were more shots from ahead.

As we turned a corner, I saw a dead horse and troopers Cole and Harrison sheltering behind the other one. They were shooting up into the rocks. I led my men through the tumble and jumble of stones, rocks and spindly trees towards the smoke which was rising from the hillside. I clipped the carbine on the sling and drew my pistol. Badger was relishing the ride and we outstripped the sergeant and the others.

Suddenly I caught sight of a blue uniform. I fired and the head disappeared. I took out another and when the man rose again to fire at me, I fired at him. The range was less than thirty yards and he fell back clutching his face. The French light infantry realised that we were the greater threat and they turned to fire at us. That helped us for they had hidden from the men in the road and not those on the hillside.

I holstered my pistol and drew my sword. A soldier suddenly rose from a rock before me and I lifted Badger's head to soar above him. We barely made the climb. The man dropped his head and I swept my sword across his back. The edge sliced through the greatcoat and tunic. It came away red.

When we landed, I wheeled around and rode at a sergeant who was reloading his musket. I jabbed the point of my sword into his neck. "Surrender, Sergeant. I have ten more troopers I have yet to use." I could see that there were only a handful of French left. I wanted no more casualties amongst my men. "Come, you have fought well. There is no dishonour in this."

He lowered his musket and shouted, "Cease fire! We surrender!"

There were just six men left to surrender. Two of the six were wounded and the sergeant saw to them. "Giggs, fetch the column up. Make space on two of the spare horses for the wounded."

The sergeant looked up at me. "Have we your permission to bury our dead, sir?"

"Of course. Lend a hand lads."

Joe and I took the spare horses down the slope as the soldiers piled stones on top of the seven fallen Frenchmen. It was not much of a grave but it would prevent animals from digging them up. The column arrived. "You can dismount and rest for a while. The men are burying the French dead."

This time it was Don Francisco's nephew, Antonio who complained. "Why bother? They have killed my countrymen."

I saw Donna Maria about to speak but I snapped, "When you have fought in a battle then I might heed your words. These men may be our enemies but they were brave men. They were fighting for their country. I hope you fight as bravely."

I saw the look of disgust on Luis' face at his countryman's words. I had seen this in England and France. The ones who sent young men to war did no fighting themselves and yet they always had a view on how they should fight and die.

When they had finished the sergeant said, "Thank you sir."

"Put your wounded men on two of the horses. Your men can lead the horses."

He nodded and the four fit Frenchmen helped those with wounds on to the horses. "Cornet Williams; keep your section at the rear to watch the French although I do not think they will run." I had noticed that their shoes were almost through and their clothes were little more than rags. "Giggs and Cole, take the lead."

I rode next to the sergeant. I took my canteen and offered it to him. He drank gratefully. When I took it back, I said, "You were at Roliça and Vimeiro?"

"Vimeiro."

"You know your Marshal surrendered?"

He shrugged, "We did not relish a prison hulk and thought to return to Spain."

"Then I admire your courage. The guerrillas are not noted for their kindness towards Frenchmen that they capture."

"I know but me and the boys were willing to take that chance." He looked up at me. "You have the accent of someone from the north and yet you fight for the roast beefs."

"I spent my childhood at Breteuil but my mother was Scottish."

"You led the Portuguese at Vimeiro."

"I did."

"You fought well. We had been told that the Portuguese would run away as the Spanish had."

"Would you run away if you were defending France?"

"No, I suppose not. What will happen to us?"

"I do not know. Your comrades are being sent back to France." He looked surprise and I shrugged, "A strange decision, I agree. If we reach Lisbon in time then you will join them and if not; I do not know."

He smiled grimly, "Then we will need to make sure we get there." He turned to his men. "Voltigeurs; we will show these English how to march. Double time!"

The column moved much quicker than it had done before as the Frenchmen cooperated with us. I found it ironic that the two Portuguese hostages did everything they could to cause problems whilst our French prisoners helped us. We were just fifteen miles from Lisbon when it grew dark. "Sergeant Seymour, take two men and ride to Lisbon. Find whoever is in charge and say that we are on our way with French prisoners and the rescued hostages." I leaned forward, "Tell them I want them off my hands."

He grinned, "Yes sir."

We ate a frugal meal although one of the Portuguese managed to bag a brace of rabbits and the thin stew, we made did at least warm us a little. I could see how hungry the French were for they ate the bones from the pot; grinding them to extract all the goodness.

We were met on the road soon after we began our last march. There was a company of the 9th with a provost marshal with them. "Have the French sailed yet, Captain?"

"No sir, more's the pity. The locals are getting a little upset by their presence."

I nodded to the Frenchmen, "These are good chaps and they will cooperate." I turned to the sergeant. "Your double time worked sergeant. You will sail back to France and live to fight us again."

He helped his wounded men from the horses. "Thank you Major. You are a gentleman and I would happily have served under you had you chosen to fight for France." He smiled, "If I see you on the battlefield, I will try to make it a quick kill."

"Thank you sergeant and I will try to do the same for you."

He turned to his men, "Attention!" They all saluted me. "Right turn!" And they marched off between the surprised soldiers of the 9th.

Once we saw Lisbon, I breathed a sigh of relief. My charges would soon be gone. I would be able to return to the regiment and back to the campaign. I rode next to Donna Maria, "What should I do with the others?"

I saw the shocked look I received from Don Francisco. He was not used to being referred to as baggage. "Where are you taking me?"

"The palace at Queluz. It will need some cleaning but..."

"Then take us all there. You have done more than enough Robbie. I know you wish to be rid of us."

I leaned in, "Them, Donna Maria, not you!"

She laughed, "Oh to be twenty years younger Robbie."

When we reached the palace, we were in for a surprise. It was now the headquarters of the Army. I saw tents arrayed in the grounds. Donna Maria said, "It seems I may be homeless again."

Sergeant Seymour must have found the general for Sir John Moore came to greet us as we entered the courtyard. I helped Donna Maria down. I saw the angry looks given to me by the two Portuguese men but before they could say anything to the general Donna Maria d'Alvarez said, "You must be Sir John Moore. I would like to thank you for sending this brave officer to our assistance. I cannot praise him and his brave men highly enough." Sir John gave a slight bow and took her hand to kiss. As he did so she added, quietly, "that was despite two very uncooperative gentlemen."

He nodded, "Thank you, major. If you would like to take your troopers to their camp, I will receive your report this afternoon."

I saluted, "Thank you sir." Turning to the hostages I added, "Thank you ladies and gentlemen. I apologise for any inconvenience you may have suffered during the journey. I meant for the best at all times."

The ladies all applauded and Donna Anna said, "Thank you Colonel. Your behaviour and that of your men was exemplary." She flashed an angry look at the two men. "Some of my countrymen could learn much from you."

I led my men away. I was just relieved that we had suffered such few casualties. It had been nothing short of a miracle.

Chapter 17

Joe Seymour had found the rest of the squadron. Already the field smelled of fresh horse manure. I had forgotten what it was like. Percy and William waited patiently for me to see to Badger before I joined them in the large tent they were using as a mess tent.

"Everything fine?"

"Yes sir. We were called upon to control some boisterous crowds the other day. We needed your Portuguese, sir."

I smiled, "You could have used Georgie as Sharp and I did. Even Joe Seymour managed to talk with the Portuguese."

"How did he and the troopers do sir?"

"Excellent Captain Stafford. They were a credit to the regiment and we even managed to capture some French Voltigeurs."

While I drank the wine, they had procured I told them of our adventure. After I had finished, I asked, "What of Sir Arthur? I ask for I am to be interviewed later by Sir John and I would like to know which way the wind blows."

"It seems that Sir John is making all the decisions, sir. Sir Arthur, from all accounts, is unhappy about the peace settlement. There is a rumour of a letter being sent to Sir John."

I could almost hear the gossip as it tittle tattled around the camp. I sighed, that was all I needed, politics.

"And did you see the French sir?"

"Just a handful at Badajoz but I fear that Bonaparte is about to make a foray into Portugal." Their faces showed that they were excited about the prospect. "Do not get excited, gentlemen. If he comes then his best soldiers will be here also. That means the Imperial Guard. I have seen little in our army, at the moment, which could stand up to them."

"But sir, you are normally so confident about our enemies."

"I am, which should warn you of the abilities of the Imperial Guard."

When I joined Sir John, later in the afternoon, I was delighted that he was of the same opinion as I was. My intelligence was greeted with caution. "I would expect the Emperor to change things around. He cannot be happy with the performance of his marshals."

In that I knew he was right. Bonaparte, like Sir Arthur, had very high standards and he did not suffer fools gladly. "That was a good example of Portuguese and British soldiers working together. It looks like that may be the way we have to work in the future. By the by the Earl of Uxbridge has just arrived to take over the cavalry. I know you will want to get to know him and you have the most experience of any cavalryman in the Peninsular. He will need all the help you can give him. I know that Sir Arthur is most impressed with your performance thus far. He is most sorry to have to lose you to me."

"How is he, sir?"

"You can ask him yourself. I invited him to speak with me this afternoon. I am a little worried about him. I can speak openly with you for you were close to him and I would not wish to embarrass Sir Arthur in any way." He leaned forward, "I know that you can be discreet."

"Yes sir."

He went to a table and poured two glasses of port for us. He handed me one. "I know that you are not cut out for the diplomatic service. Don Francisco was keen to have your skin pinned to the harbour wall!" I began to speak and he held up his hand. "Sir, do not trouble yourself. Donna Maria has told me all. I might not have been so blunt but I can understand your reasoning. You are a man of action and I admire that."

"How is the lady?"

"You may ask her yourself later on. She is living in the Queen's apartments. She is concerned that the palace should not be left to us rough soldiers; not without a woman's touch."

There was a rap on the door. The sentry said, "Sir, Sir..."

He got no further for Sir Arthur strode in. "You wished to see me, Sir John?" He smiled when he saw me. "Ah Matthews, good to see you too. I hear you have had another damned adventure!"

"Glass of port, Wellesley?" Sir Arthur nodded and I went to pour it for him. Sir John continued. "I received your letter yesterday and I thought we ought to chat about it." I handed the port to Sir Arthur. "Any objection to Matthews staying?"

"Of course not. He is one of the better soldiers. No secrets between us eh Matthews?"

"No, Sir Arthur."

"Now Arthur," I smiled when I saw the look of distaste on Sir Arthur's face; he hated informality. "I think you should reconsider your decision to return to England. I need you here. You have beaten the French twice and you know the men."

"Very kind of you Sir John but I am being tarred with the same brush as Dowager Dalrymple and Betty Burrard! It won't do. Matthews here will tell you that I wanted to pursue and finally defeat Junot. I did not want to give him a trip back to France courtesy of the tax payer!" He looked at me. "Tell him Matthews; you were there."

"That is correct, Sir John."

"You are not on trial here Arthur and I believe you. That is why I beg you to stay. You will be vindicated at the hearing."

"No, Sir John, that is why I must return. I have to defend myself. My name and my honour are at stake."

Sir John finished his port and held his glass out to me. "I agree with you; the action taken by the two senior generals was the wrong one but they have been recalled to London anyway. Until we hear from London I command and you know that I will listen to you." I took the glass and refilled it.

"I am sorry Sir John. I wish you success in your appointment"

He took the glass I offered him and shook his head. "I wish I had never been given this appointment. It is like a poisoned chalice. But it is the business of Government to remove me if they think proper. I can enter into no intrigue."

"In these times, my dear General a man like you should not preclude himself from rendering the services of which he is capable, by an idle point of form."

"I will do my duty, Sir Arthur."

"And I wish you well but I shall return to England on the morrow and clear my name." He emptied his glass. He nodded to me, "You can trust this one. He may have little breeding but he is a damned fine soldier, honest and brave. They are rare. Oh, and the only Portuguese soldiers I would trust are those commanded by Trant." He stood, "And the Spanish are not to be trusted or relied upon at all!"

With that he left. That was the last time that he and Sir John met. I believe that they would have made a good combination had they served together but it was not meant to be. Sir Arthur took a fast ship home the following day.

Sir John was genuinely sad. "I shall need you even more from now on Matthews. Have you an effective deputy?"

"Yes sir. Captain Stafford is a good officer. My men are sound."

"And that is more than can be said for the rest of the army. Sir Arthur told me there are none better when fighting but the rest of the time they are drunk and belligerent." He shrugged, "Now we await orders." He smiled, "If you would care to go and see Donna Maria; I know she desires conference with you and then find the Earl of Uxbridge. It is time you two became acquainted."

I spent the rest of the afternoon with Donna Maria. She had engaged servants and was repairing some of the damage from the looting. It did me good to speak with her. She brought everything down to a simple level.

Before I left, I went to the stables. They were cleaner now and there were more horses within. The groom recognised me. I shook his hand. "Your son is avenged."

He began to weep and I waited until he had composed himself. "Thank you, sir. The man with the scar?"

"I killed him myself. It will not bring back your son but he can rest in peace now."

I saw the groom's eyes stray to the grave. I had not brought my sword for I had planned on this meeting with the groom. I unclipped the scabbard and handed Colonel Laroche's sword and its sheath to the groom. "It is small recompense for the loss of a son but this is the sword of the man with the scar. You could sell it or…"

He shook his head as he took it, "Thank you sir but I shall not sell it. I will bury this with my son. Thank you again, sir. If all Englishmen are like you then my country will be safe."

I headed back to camp wondering if we could save Portugal from the Emperor Napoleon. I had yet to see Sir John in action. I had been confident in Sir Arthur's skills. I knew just how tricky an enemy Bonaparte could be. Sir John would need to be his equal if we were to win.

I took Sergeant Sharp with me when I went to introduce myself to the Earl of Uxbridge. I knew he had been the colonel of the 7th Light Dragoons and that was about all that I knew of him. He was outside his tent smoking a cigar and studying some papers when I arrived.

"Major Matthews, sir. General Moore thought we should get to know one another."

I saw him appraising me. "Ah yes, the chap who rescued those hostages from the French. Fine show. Take a seat. I hear you were involved in the two battles too."

"Yes sir."

"Dashed useful. And you are with the 11th?"

"Yes sir."

"I know Colonel Fenton. He is a good officer."

"Yes sir, we like serving with him."

He waved a hand and a servant appeared with some wine. "None of your local stuff. This is a fine wine from Italy. I bought in London before I came out. I wanted to have a fine wine to drink."

I looked at the label. "Actually, sir my family makes this. I can get you a case next time we get to London."

"'Pon my word. You are a useful chap to have around. I daresay there is a story there."

"I am distantly related to the Alpini family and I help them to sell their wines in London. I introduced them to Mr Fortnum."

"Good gracious! Is there no end to your talents? And you speak languages?"

"A couple sir."

"I speak English and a little Frog and that is about it." He leaned over. "Is that how you became a colonel in the Portuguese army?"

"No sir, I just helped a friend of the Queen and the Regent rewarded me."

"Hmn. Tell me what do you think of this Trant fella?"

"A damned good officer sir. The Portuguese love him."

"Quite but he does like the odd drink or two."

I held up my glass, "Many soldiers do sir."

"Touché! Point taken. I was just wondering if you might not like to lead the Portuguese cavalry. You have the ability and it would help me. We haven't enough cavalry as it is."

"Sorry sir, Colonel Trant is a friend and besides I am the General's aide."

"A man of honour. I can understand that. Well in that case we'll say no more about it. But I think we need you to use your expertise as a scout." He tapped his nose, "A little bird told me that you are quite good at operating in difficult circumstances."

I sighed. "I have been behind lines once or twice."

"Well we don't need that but look here." He pulled the map so that we could both see it. "Here is Madrid. From what you told Sir John, Bonaparte will be there soon. Now if he comes here, which is likely, he will come the most direct route." He drew a line with his finger. "He will come this way; to the north of the Guadarramas Mountains, through Salamanca and through Ciudad Rodrigo." He circled his finger. "As far as I can tell there is bugger all here to tell us what the terrain is like. This map has no detail on it. I want you to take a troop and scout it out for us."

"Go into Spain, sir?"

"Good heavens no! Just to the border. I don't want to risk a troop of cavalry. We have precious few of them but we need to know how the land lies, literally!"

"And Sir John?"

He smiled as he finished his wine. "He suggested it!"

I wasted no time and rode to Queluz. Donna Maria d'Alvarez was in the gardens with her women picking up leaves. I shook my head; she was a force of nature. An hour of picking up leaves and talking with her gave me an insight into my plan for the next ten days or so.

Cornet Williams was the most disappointed when I told him that he would be staying with Captain Stafford whilst Percy bounced around like a puppy. I would take my lieutenant with us. We had to take spare horses but the ones we had liberated from the French colonel were sound animals and they would suffice.

We left on the 21st September and headed along the Tagus. I had an idea that both Sir John and the Earl of Uxbridge were using us to find a safe way into Spain.

However, we hit problems as soon as we reached Villa Velha. The gorge was deep and I could see that the artillery and the wagons we used would not be able to either cross the river there or climb the steep sides of the gorge. It became just as bad once we crossed the Tagus. Quite simply they were not roads they were tracks. Hauling the cannon would be impossible along these primitive routes.

What we did find, however, was a complete lack of French soldiers. It was as though there was no war in this part of the country. I could see why. The French liked their artillery and their scouts would have told them that this was not artillery country. We reached Salamanca by the last week in September. I spoke with the equivalent of the Prefeito and received the disturbing news that there had been some Chasseurs in the vicinity in the previous week. The French were also scouting the plains of Spain. Madrid was now just a couple of days march away. The last that we had heard Marshal Jourdan was north of the Ebro. So long as he stayed there then Sir John could manoeuvre the army freely.

We turned around. There were rains and storms as we travelled back. I came back by a different route in the hope that the roads there would be better. They were not. Portugal had been baking in

the summer but now that it was autumn it became more like
England. The roads became quagmires. The journey was not
pleasant and we wearily reached Lisbon on the 3rd of October. Two
of the horses we had taken were lame and would have to be put
down. It was an indication of the problems we could expect. I
immediately reported to Sir John.

"Ah Major, have you had a successful patrol?"

"That depends upon your definition of success Sir John. You
cannot use that road for your artillery."

I saw his face fall. "Not even by manhandling it?"

"No, sir. The wagons cannot use it either. In places there is no
road and the river crossing is hazardous. Even our horses struggled
along the tracks, for that is what they are. Two out of the fifty
horses we took are now lame. If you multiply that by the army then
we will lose ten percent of all our animals.

"When you used the road to Badajoz was that any better?"

"Yes sir. Artillery could use that. If the French haven't reinforced
the fortress then there would be no problem."

He went to his map. "Come Major. I will use you to think things
through." He used a letter opener to point at the map. "I am having
increasing pressure from our Spanish allies to go to the aid of
Madrid. The French are obliging by keeping their forces north of
the Ebro however Madrid is in the very centre of the country. We
would have to march across half of the land to reach it. The route
you took is the shortest and the quickest. If we cannot take the
artillery that way then we have to travel this way." He traced a
long loop first east and then north east through Badajoz towards
Madrid. "That would take too long. We may have to split the army.
I am loath to do so but we may have no choice."

He sat down, "We now await orders from London." He shook his
head. "This is a poisoned chalice Robert. I think that Sir Arthur is
well out of this."

Chapter 18

I was summoned again to the palace on the 6th of October. Sir John was in high spirits. He pointed to the orders on his desk. "Well Major Matthews, I am in sole command now! I will no longer need to look over my shoulder."

As Sir John poured us a glass of wine each, I read the letter.

'Sir, His Majesty having determined to employ a corps of his troops, of not less than 30,000 infantry and 5,000 cavalry, in the North of Spain, to cooperate with the Spanish armies in the expulsion of the French from that Kingdom, has been graciously pleased to entrust you the Command in Chief of this Force.'

"That is excellent news sir."

"Yes, but I have also had a communication from Lord Castlereagh telling me that General Baird will be landing in Coruna in the north of Spain. You are telling me that the artillery has to travel to the south to reach Madrid. That means we will have to split the army into three."

"And that isn't good sir."

"No, it is not. In addition, we are having problems in the camps. The soldiers are bored and drunk. Sir Arthur told me to keep them busy but that is difficult here."

"Yes sir." I was out of my depth. I was used to managing one squadron and they were all easy to control. Troop Sergeant Grant saw to that.

"I intend to move out sooner rather than later. Be so good as to inform the earl of Uxbridge that I shall need some cavalry to escort the artillery to Valladolid via Badajoz. He should be prepared to leave as soon as I can get more information from our Spanish allies and direction from London." He shook his head. "I may be in command of the army but I have to cooperate with the Spanish and await instructions from London."

"Can we rely on the Spanish sir?"

"We have not the manpower to defeat the French alone. The Spanish have five times the number of men over here that we do.

They must be used. However, their generals do not like to take advice."

The Earl of Uxbridge was equally unhappy with the state of affairs. "I mean Matthews I like a drink but the rank and file just drink to get drunk!"

Therein lay the difference between the French and the British. The British drank when they were bored and the French drank to celebrate a victory.

"And like Sir John I am suspicious of the quality and intent of our Spanish allies. Still that is all politics. We are soldiers. Now then, you know the cavalry regiments better than I do. Who should it be who is given the task of escorting the guns?"

"Well sir the only two regiments I know well are the 20th and my own squadron the 11th. The 20th have more men and they are sound troopers."

He laughed, "Diplomatically put, Matthews. Sir Arthur told me before he left of Major DeVere and his ridiculous foray. The whole family are like that! They think they are on some damned fox hunt. Very well if you inform their commanding officer that he is to accompany Sir John Hope." Just then we heard women's squeals. "And I hope General Moore leaves the women behind. The last thing we need in this country is to be trailing such baggage with us." Although there had been lots drawn to see which women could accompany the army many more had contrived to sail aboard the transports with their men. They numbered the muster of a regiment! They were a different breed to the women I had grown up with. They were however as tough as any soldier who fought for Sir John Moore.

After I had told Major Simmons, the commanding officer of the 20th, of his new duties I returned to the squadron. "Troop Sergeant Grant, make sure the farrier has shoed all the horses and that every trooper has enough equipment which is in working order."

"We off again sir?"

I knew that if I told the sergeant that we were heading to Spain then it would be around the whole camp like wildfire. "I can't really say Sergeant. Sir John and the Earl of Uxbridge seem to like us, George. There is only number 8 Troop which has not been in action. I think we should be ready to go off into the wild blue yonder sooner rather than later."

"Righto sir."

Of course, I did not need such discretion with my three officers. I could trust them completely. I told them to be ready to move in the next few days. "We cannot rely on accommodation each night. Have your servants check the tents and the blankets. Use the spare horses as pack animals."

"Why not use wagons sir?"

Percy answered Cornet Williams, "Because young Cornet Williams, where we are going wagons cannot pass!" He tapped his nose, "Our last patrol gave us an idea of where we will be going."

The orders were sent out to the army on the 9th of October. I was charged with delivering the copies to the commanders.

'The Troops under Lieutenant-General Sir John Moore will hold themselves in readiness at the shortest notice. All heavy baggage will be left in Lisbon. Directions will be given with respect to the sick. The Lieutenant-General sees with much concern the great number of this description and that it daily increases. The General assures all troops that it is owing to their own intemperance that so many of them are rendered incapable of marching against the enemy.

And in the course of the long march which the army is about to undertake, and where no carts will be allowed, the women would unavoidably be exposed to the greatest hardship and distress, commanding officers are therefore desired to use their endeavours to prevent as many as possible from following the army. Those who remain will be left with the heavy baggage.'

I knew that only six women to every hundred men had been allowed to travel but that still left many. There were many who would manage to hide amongst the soldiers. I was just pleased that we had brought none.

We were due to leave on the 11th and on the 10th I sought out Donna Maria. "We will be leaving in the morning. If you wish to come with us, I could have an escort take you to Oporto."

She had shaken her head, "God intended me to be here and to look after the palace. I will be as safe here as anywhere." She had placed her blue veined hand on my arm, "Tell me honestly Roberto, can you win?"

"If Napoleon does not come then yes, I believe we have a chance."

"But you know that the Emperor is coming do you not?" I nodded. "What will he do if he comes here?"

I saw fear, for the first time on her face. "I believe that, while he would be ruthless to soldiers, he will treat women honourably."

"Good." She pulled my head down so that she could plant a kiss on each cheek. "And you take care of yourself and the sergeant. I will still be here when you return."

And I said goodbye.

The army left the next morning, a solitary drumbeat announcing its departure. The 11th were appointed the guides along with Colonel Trant's Portuguese Brigade. Its numbers were down as there had been much sickness and some desertion. The delay in Lisbon had cost us dear. They would come as far as the border and then return to Lisbon.

We left a couple of days later, allowing us to gather valuable intelligence. It proved vital for we learned that both the French and Spanish were manoeuvring in Aragon. Even though the main French army was still north of the Ebro it threatened Sir John Hope's column. We had kept ten troopers from the 20th as messengers and General Moore sent one to General Hope telling him to avoid Madrid at all costs.

We finally left Lisbon on the 27th of October. The autumn rains had made the roads slippery. It was hard enough on a horse but on foot it would have been almost impossible. General Moore was worried about our lack of intelligence. "Major Matthews, as invaluable as you are to me here, I need to use your eyes and ears. Take your squadron and ride to Salamanca and Valladolid. I need to know what awaits us there."

There were just ninety other ranks and the officers and sergeants. We were not a large force. When I reported to the Earl of

Uxbridge, he was pleased that we would be the advanced guard but unhappy about spreading the cavalry so thin. "We are relying too much on the Spanish, Matthews and I do not like having to split our forces."

"I know that the General feels the same my lord. His hands are tied."

"Keep me informed eh Matthews?"

"Yes, my lord."

Once again, we were heading into foreign territory. The position of both our allies and our enemies was fluid. I knew that the British Ambassador, Hookham Frere, was still in Madrid and I took some consolation from that. We reached Ciudad Rodrigo quite quickly and found that there were Spanish troops there. There were just a handful and they seemed very nervous about the proximity of the French. We pushed on to Salamanca where there was an equal air of fear. I sent two troopers back with the news. It meant that our army would not meet an enemy; not yet anyway. If Salamanca was filled with worried Spanish then at Valladolid, they were positively terrified. French soldiers had been spotted less than a day's ride away. I sent two more troopers back and then headed south towards Madrid. I knew that I was exceeding my orders but the French had been seen in that area. Sir John's flank was vulnerable.

We headed up the Guadarammas mountain chain. The trails were rough. They twisted and turned as they wound their way south. We were nearing the crest when Cole and Giggs galloped in. "Sir, we saw some French ahead."

"Sergeant Seymour, bring the first ten troopers with me. Carbines at the ready." We followed my two troopers.

"Just over the rise sir. They look like they are sleeping. We couldn't see any sentries."

"Horse holders!"

I led the other six troopers and we approached the rise. I could see the blue uniforms and Cole was right. The Frenchmen appeared to be sleeping. They were slouched over rocks and lying on the ground. I waved my arms and the others spread out to the left and right of me. As we drew closer the smell told me that they were not sleeping. The guerrillas had found the twenty-man patrol. Some of them had died in the skirmish but as we entered what had been their camp, we saw that eight had been captured alive. Two of them had been emasculated. Four more had had their stomachs ripped open while the last two had had a fire lit on their living bodies. I heard one of the troopers vomiting.

There was an unpleasant task which had to be done. It would be down to me. "Sergeant Seymour, take the men back to the column and carry on south. I will catch you up."

Sergeant Sharp said, "I'll help you sir."

Sergeant Seymour asked, "Help with what Sharpie?"

"Searching the bodies, Joe. They might have information."

It was a grim but necessary job. We discovered the identity of the men and they had maps. Other than that, we learned nothing. Had we had time we would have buried them but such niceties were luxuries we could ill afford.

We never reached Madrid. The blue column flanked by Chasseurs told us all that we needed to know. There were French troops between us and Madrid. More importantly they were headed towards Salamanca. General Moore needed to know that.

I detailed two troopers to take the news to the General and we retraced our steps. Captain Stafford asked, "Valladolid or Salamanca?"

"The General had planned on meeting the other two columns at Valladolid. I know that he won't be there yet but we need to see how close the French are."

We were just five miles from Valladolid when darkness fell. I sent 8 Troop back to Salamanca with Captain Stafford and I took the smaller 7 troop to scout out the town.

"Percy, you stay here with the bulk of the men. Sharp, Seymour and Lightfoot you come with me."

The town looked quiet but I would take no chances. When we saw the first building loom up in the twilight, I took the patrol to the right. I was looking for a side street or alley. I took off my Tarleton helmet and signalled for the others to do the same. I saw a small street which ran parallel with the main road and I took it. As soon as I could I led them down an alley. I dismounted and handed the reins of my horse to Lightfoot. I went first towards the end of the alley where I could see some light.

I peered around the corner and I saw that the street was almost deserted. This was a quiet town. I decided to take a chance. I waved at the others to remain where they were and I stepped on to the street. I walked down it towards the main square which I could see in the distance. This was a busier part of the town. There were people in sight. I smiled and gave a half bow when I met anyone. I knew that they were surprised at my lack of headgear. I began to regret taking off my helmet although it marked me clearly as British.

Suddenly I heard French voices ahead. I looked around for somewhere to hide. There was nowhere and so I leaned against a wall and examined the sole of my boot. I hoped that the approaching Frenchmen, and I assumed they were soldiers, would pass me by. I did not look up but I did take out my knife and began to clean off some imaginary and invisible deposit from the sole.

One of them said, "Spain is a filthy country is it not?" I could smell the drink on his breath.

Without looking up I nodded and said, "It is worse than the left bank in Paris!"

They both laughed, "That is the Sorbonne! What can you expect from students?"

"A spell in the army is what they need, Jacques."

"You are right Antoine, good night, my friend."

"Good night."

I looked up as they carried on down the street. Soon they would realise that they had not recognised me. In such a small town, they would know everyone. I saw that they were Chasseurs. I had had a blue uniform but I could almost read their thoughts as they tried to work out which blue uniformed cavalry were in Valladolid. I walked after them. They began to slow and I hurried. I still had my stiletto in my hand. They were quite close to the alley where my companions waited. They stopped.

I took a chance, "Did either of you drop this gold Louis?"

I distracted them by holding my left hand with a closed fist. They both looked at it. Instead of opening it I slashed across the throat of one man with the stiletto blade and I punched the other with my fist. He fell backwards. "Sharp. Seymour." The two of them ran from the alley just as the man began to rise. I was on him in an instant and I punched him with the hilt of the knife. The two sergeants finished the job by hitting him on the head with the butt of a pistol. "Get him in the alley." I looked around. The street was empty still and I dragged the body of the other French horseman into the alley. I dumped him there.

"Put him over your horse Sharp. Let's get out of here. We can tell the General that there are French horsemen in Valladolid."

Percy was relieved to see us and he and the others formed a rear guard behind us to allow us to watch the prisoner closely. The Frenchman had shown signs of coming to but Sharp's dagger pricked into the side of his neck silenced him. There could be French vedettes out and we wanted no alarm sounding. When we reached Salamanca, we saw the camp fires of the cavalry. The rest of the vanguard had arrived. The nervous sentries asked for identification.

"Major Matthews of the 11th with the patrol. Where is the Earl?"

"The big tent in the middle of the camp, sir."

"Percy, you see to the men. Sharp come with me. I am sure that his lordship will wish to question this man."

His lordship had a camp table with a lit lamp upon it. The colonels from the cavalry regiments were gathered around him.

"I have a prisoner, your lordship."

"'Pon my word Matthews but you are a fine fellow. Bring him into the light." He saw the blood on my uniform. "Is that your blood, Matthews?"

"No sir, his companion."

Sharp had his hand on the Chasseur's shoulder in case he tried to run. We could see, clearly, that he was a Chasseurs à Cheval. His lordship asked, in French, "How many of you are there?" In answer he spat on his lordship's boots. "We'll get nothing from this fellow. Have him taken away."

I stepped forward. "Do you mind if I try, sir?"

The Earl nodded, "I will be interested to see if you manage to get anything from him."

I nodded. The man had not reacted to the earl's words and so I assumed he could not speak English. "Sergeant Sharp, have your stiletto handy in case we have to persuade him to cooperate."

"Yes sir."

The Earl asked, "Persuade him?"

I took out my own stiletto which made the Earl's eyes widen and I held it close to the Frenchman's crotch. "Persuade him." Lifting it to the man's face I ran my finger down the side of the glistening steel and I smiled, "Now then... Antoine is it?" He nodded. He was less confident now. "I am going to ask you some perfectly reasonable questions. If I do not get the answers, I like then my sergeant will begin to cut pieces from you."

"But you are English gentlemen, you wouldn't."

"I once met Fouché, you know. He is no gentleman. I also recently killed one of his thugs, a Colonel Laroche. You are just a trooper why should your pain worry me?" For the first time Antoine showed a little fear. "What is the name of your regiment?" I pointed to the uniform. "I do not understand why you and your friend have different facings." I tapped his collar and then his facings with the point of my knife. "These indicate that you should be the 1st Chasseurs but your friend was the 3rd. Are there two regiments in Valladolid?" He hesitated. "Come Antoine, what harm is there in that answer? You rode through our camp with us. We are not afraid of just two regiments."

"We are one regiment; the 1st Provisional Chasseurs."

I patted him on the back. "There, that was easy was it not?"

He smiled weakly.

"Of course, the picket duty in such a place must be annoying."

"It is."

"I bet your Brigadier makes you do all the work while he slopes off and has a good drink."

"He does. Is it not the same in the British cavalry?"

"Sometimes. I would not know I am an officer and do not do picket duty. So, there are neither infantry nor artillery in Valladolid."

He started to move and Sharp restrained him. "I didn't say that."

"No but you said you had to do picket duty. We both know that if there is either artillery or infantry around then cavalry are excused picket duty."

His face gave me the answer. I did not like deceiving him but I needed to get the information one way or another. At least I had not inflicted any pain in extracting the information.

"It looks like there is just a regiment cobbled together from the remnants of others."

The Earl laughed and shook his head. "'Pon my word you are a remarkable fellow. Still it means the French are in Valladolid and that scuppers the General's plans. Now the question is, do they have the little Emperor with them?"

The English and French for Emperor are similar enough that Antoine showed the recognition in his face. "Where is the Emperor then Antoine? Still hiding behind Josephine's skirts? Or perhaps he is playing with his turbaned Africans?"

I had deliberately angered him. He tried to get to me but Sharp held him firmly. "How dare you insult the Emperor! He is with his Guards and they are but four days from here. When he comes you will pay for your insults."

"Well there you are your lordship. He is four days away with the Imperial Guard." The Earl nodded, "The question is does he know that we are this close to him."

"You have done well, Major Matthews." He turned to his aide, "Delancey, take this fellow to the guard tent. The general may wish to question him when he arrives."

Sharp stepped back to allow the aide to escort him out and, as the young lieutenant stepped forward Antoine grabbed the officer's sword and lunged at his lordship. Even as the tip touched the Earl's pelisse, I slashed my stiletto across his throat. The blood sprayed the shocked lieutenant as the Chasseur fell dead. The Earl picked up the sword. "Thank you Major, I am much obliged."

Chapter 19

Sir John reached Salamanca on the 13th of November. The rest of the army was spread out along the road from Ciudad Rodrigo. Our news just added to the bad news he brought with him. Napoleon had reached Burgos on the 11th. He was far closer than we had thought. The Spanish general, Joachim Blake had been defeated at Zornosa and there were French reinforcements joining Bonaparte's already huge army. The Spanish army had fled to the hills. They would harass the French but they were no longer a fighting force. General Hope and the artillery were still to the south and Bonaparte was between us and General Baird.

He looked at the ceiling of the tent as though to get divine inspiration. "And as far as I know the only Spanish army is one made up of peasants. We will wait a few more days and see if General Castanos can reach us. Even a peasant army might give us the numbers we need to hold off Bonaparte."

He did not sound particularly confident and I did not blame him. If Bonaparte had his Imperial Guard with him then he could have an army of over one hundred thousand. Even when Sir John Hope joined us, we would have less than twenty thousand men. They were not good odds.

Until the bulk of the army reached us, I was back with Sir John. Lieutenant Stanhope had grown up during the campaign. Before we had left Lisbon, he had seemed like a typical young officer; he liked parading in the fine uniform and enjoying the Lisbon social life. The weeks on the road had reduced his bright red uniform to the same rusty colour as the rest of the army. It had run into his grey breeches making them a strange brown colour. His hair had grown and he was not as clean shaven. However, it was not in the outward appearance where the changes were most apparent. He had grown up and matured as an officer.

The army left Lisbon and began to make its way to Spain. It was ponderous and slow moving. Even though they had had a week's start we caught them in less than two days. When we caught up with the column, even in those early stages, we saw the women who had fallen during the march. They had stayed with their soldiers who had become ill and when the soldier had died, they had been left behind. Some of them had babies and children with them. It was a sad fact of life that they should have stayed in Lisbon and there was no-one to look after them. Now, as we waited in Salamanca and the rear of the column finally dragged itself into the town, we saw how few of the women and children had survived the rigours of the march. The ones who had were as tough as the soldiers they had chosen but it was hard to see them living to see England.

"Major Matthews, why do the fellows bring their women with them? It puts them in great danger."

I shrugged, "I am the wrong one to ask, Stanhope. I have never had female entanglements." I pointed to some of the other officers. "Perhaps you should ask Garrington-Jones there. His wife was left in Lisbon."

"That is what I mean sir, why did the men not leave them in Lisbon?"

"That one I can answer. They were afraid."

"Who, the women?"

"Both. The women were afraid that their husbands would die and they would be left alone in Lisbon and the men were afraid that they would lose their women."

"But the women who come with us, what if their husbands die? Won't they be alone?"

I shook my head, "No lieutenant, the women would find another in the platoon to take up with."

"Really sir?" I could see the shock on his face.

"Theirs is a different world to ours. When this war is over what will you do?"

"I will stay in. I like this life."

"And if the government cuts the size of the army, as they did after the Peace of Amiens in 1805, what then?"

"Then I shall go on half pay and wait at home until they need me again."

"And there is the difference; when the ordinary soldiers are cut from the books, they have nothing. They have to make a living back in England. What skills do they have?" He shrugged. "As soldiers they learned to fight, they can drink and they can live off the land. They end up in trouble and, at best gaol, and, at worst are hanged. They leave the army and they end up in trouble."

"I didn't know sir."

"Until you know your men then you can never lead them. They will fight to the last for an officer they believe cares for them. They love your uncle. No matter what happens in this ill-fated campaign they will fight for him."

"Ill-fated sir?"

"Unless a miracle happens and General Castanos reaches us then we will have to fight the best general in Europe with the largest and best equipped army. The odds will be four to one, at least, in his favour. The only thing in our favour is the land. If Fate allows, we retreat but if Sir John makes a mistake then we are trapped, surrounded, and we die."

"God sir, that is depressing."

"I know. Your uncle is making the best of a bad job. He was asked to support the Spanish. He has done so but we have put our head into the lion's mouth. The question is can we pull it out before he snaps shut his jaws? Your uncle has the lives of every soldier in his hands and we must help him to make the correct decision."

The end of November saw two messages which decided the mind of Lieutenant-General Sir John Moore. On the 26th we heard from General Baird, who was at Astorga, that the French were moving to come between us. Two days later, on the 28th General Hope informed that he was being threatened by French cavalry and that he might not be able to reach us. And, later that day, the final nail was driven into the coffin of the army when we discovered that General Castanos had suffered a total defeat at Tudela.

There were just four of us in his tent and it was late. "Well gentlemen we are in a bit of a pickle here. What do we do?"

The Earl of Uxbridge shook his head, "I am sorry, General but it seems to me that we have but one option; retreat."

"But in what direction? Do we retreat towards General Hope and head back to Lisbon? Or do we retreat north towards General Baird?"

His nephew said, "Doesn't it all depend upon what the French do?"

"We cannot just react to Bonaparte. That would be a disaster." He looked at me "You have fought the French more than anyone else here, Matthews, and you seem to know this fellow Bonaparte. Sir Arthur reckoned you had a clever mind. What do you say?"

"It is true we do not know where he is yet but there is a prize he will value, Madrid. That means he is close to us but he believes he and his men are faster than any army in the world. In Italy and Austria, he simply out marched bigger armies. I think he will believe that he can capture Madrid with all the pomp and ceremony of an Emperor and still catch us. If General Hope could reach us then we would have a better chance of fighting off Bonaparte. Without artillery we have no chance."

The Earl nodded, "And General Baird?"

"Send him back to Corunna. We could retreat north east. That would take us away from Bonaparte. I do not think he would be expecting it."

"But. Matthews. that would mean he could just waltz into Lisbon."

"I know your lordship but having taken Madrid he will want to defeat Sir John here at Salamanca and claim a great victory. So far, he has not fought in Spain. He likes to show everyone how good he is. Besides we left ten thousand men in Lisbon. They could hole up in Torres Vedras."

"You seem to know him rather well, Matthews."

"Let us say that I have studied him."

Sir John nodded, "Perhaps some of us should have done the same. I am decided. We will ask General Hope to fall back to Ciudad and General Baird to prepare to retire to Corunna. We can delay the command in case we are able to link up." He smiled, "A withdrawal is a gentler word than retreat eh?"

Although the messages were sent and the army prepared for retreat, we did not move. The British ambassador sent daily messages urging us to move towards Madrid. When the people rose in revolt, I knew that our general was considering going to their aid. General Hope's column reached Alba de Tormes just fifteen miles away from us and he began to think that we might go to help of the Madrid people who had risen in revolt.

On the 10th of December our fate was sealed. We heard that Madrid had finally fallen to the French and had confirmation that Emperor Napoleon Bonaparte had an army in excess of a hundred and forty thousand men available to him. The orders were given and the army slipped silently out of Salamanca. Our Spanish adventure had ended ignominiously. We skulked out with our tails between our legs.

Once again, my troop was used to scout ahead as we made our way north to Alaejos. We had at least combined with Sir John Hope's column. We now had some artillery and we were reunited with our cavalry.

Before we left the slow-moving column, I spoke with my sergeants and officers. "More than ever before, we will be spread out thinly. I want the men operating in fives under a sergeant or a corporal. Lieutenant Austen and I will monitor five sections each. If we keep a mile between each section, we should be able to see a large area and be hard to see ourselves."

I knew that there were horsemen in Valladolid, to the north east of us and I rode close to Sergeant White and his section. It was a chill wind which whipped from the east and chilled us to the bone. There was a temptation to hide in one's cape and keep warm. We had to do the opposite. It was fortunate that we did for a keen-eyed trooper shouted, "Sir, a rider!"

There, just a mile away was a despatch rider and he was heading north, towards Valladolid. "After him! Sergeant you and two of the lads cut off his retreat, I think Badger has the legs of him."

Badger was a fast horse but more than that he had the stamina to keep going for long distances. The despatch rider would be equally well mounted. I leaned forward in the saddle and urged Badger on. Inexorably I drew away from the others and slowly gained on the despatch rider. He kept glancing over his shoulder to see where I was. That was a mistake as it allowed me to close each time, he did that. I kept Badger going at a steady pace.

Eventually the rider realised his error and stopped looking behind him. He leaned forward in the saddle and whipped his horse on. I stopped gaining. I was just fifty yards away and I might as well have been five miles. I did not look around but I knew that my men would be spread out along the road. I decided to waste some ball and powder. I drew a pistol and cocked it. I had one chance in a hundred of hitting him but I held the pistol before me and aimed low. It was a good shot but it did not hit him. It must have zipped next to him and his horse. He whipped his horse harder. I drew a second pistol and fired with that. I had the same result but this time it must have been closer for he jerked the reins to one side to get away from the danger. His horse's hooves left the poorly maintained road and must have caught one of the many potholes at the side. Horse and rider cart wheeled and crashed down at the side of the road.

I could see, from the unnatural angle of his head, that the young despatch rider was dead. The horse was not dead but both forelegs were broken. I took out my last pistol and, while I stroked its mane, I put the brave beast out of its misery.

My troopers galloped up alongside me. "Search the rider." I undid the girth on the saddle and took it from the dead animal so that I could get at both saddlebags. As I had hoped they contained despatches. I quickly went through them. As soon as I saw Berthier's letter I knew where Bonaparte was; he was in Madrid. I saw that the letter was addressed to Soult which put him to the north of us. This was like gold.

"Sergeant, continue scouting. I will take these letters to the general."

"Sir!"

The column seemed to fill the horizon as I approached it. The Earl of Uxbridge was with Sir John Moore. I waved the letter as I approached. "Sir, I have despatches from Berthier to Soult!"

The General's staff pulled over to the side as the ponderous column continued north east towards a meeting with General Baird. I proffered the letter from Berthier. "Sir, this is a letter from Bonaparte to Soult!"

"Well read it, my dear fellow. Your French is better than mine."

I scanned it. "Sir, Bonaparte thinks that we are in full retreat towards Lisbon. He has no idea where we are. I have here the figures for Soult's army and their line of march. He has seventeen thousand foot, six thousand cavalry and forty guns. He is close to Burgos and marching towards the south west."

"Excellent work, Major Matthews. Uxbridge, we will head towards Toro. We have a great opportunity here, gentlemen. We can join up with General Baird. We will outnumber Soult. This is our chance to give battle and to ease our journey!"

There was a spring in our step as we headed for Toro. We were, to all intents and purposes, invisible. The French had no idea where we were but, thanks to the despatches, we knew precisely where they were. Each day took us further from Bonaparte and increased our chances of salvaging something from this campaign.

It was on the 18th that we finally reunited the whole army. The air of expectation permeated the whole of the camp and the village of Villalpando. The Earl of Uxbridge sent me out to find the enemy. I took my troopers who now had the best eyes in the army. We headed to Saldana. We knew that it was on the route which Soult would take. I avoided Sahagun and approached Saldana from the east. It was a wise move and we saw the whole of Soult's army. I could see that the numbers were roughly the ones we had expected. I took us back to our camp but this time I passed closer to Sahagun. I saw that there were some cavalrymen there. It looked to me to be two regiments. They would be the vedettes for the main army and would be protecting Soult's left flank.

It was late afternoon when we reached the camp and the men were exhausted. Sharp and I reported to the Earl of Uxbridge and the General. "By God sir, we have him!"

Sir John sat back in his canvas chair. "Have who, Uxbridge?"

"Soult. Let me take Matthews here and some troopers. We can get rid of the vedettes and the road to Saldana will be open."

"What do you think, Matthews?"

"I think it is a good plan sir. The French will not be expecting it but the troop I took out will be too tired to go out again."

"Your boys have done more than their fair share already Matthews. It is time we blooded some of the others. I will take the 10th and the 15th. You have better change your horse. We leave in an hour."

Neither Sharp nor I even considered leaving our horses behind. When you went into battle then you needed a beast you knew. Maria and Badger would be rested the next day.

We approached the darkened village from the east. "Their main camp is to the north west of the town. I can only see pickets on the main road sir."

"Good. General Slade, you attack the town with the 10th. Major Matthews and I will go around the village and attack their camp."

The General nodded, "What will be my signal sir?"

"You don't need a damned signal! When you see the buggers you attack, sir!"

I smiled. Uxbridge was a cavalryman right down to his boots. We rode around the village to reach the far side. We had heard nothing from General Slade and the Earl was not disposed to wait, for he heard noises in their camp. Even though we were outnumbered by four to one he drew his sword. "Right 15th; let us see what you are made of. Sound the charge!" There was a huge cheer from the two hundred Hussars and we galloped into the French camp.

The bugle had alerted the French to our charge. They were hurriedly saddling horses. We fell upon them and caught them as they were dressing, saddling or in some cases, just waking up. The Dragoons tried to fire their muskets at us and that was a mistake. It was too dark and it ruined their night vision when they did so. I hacked down at a Dragoon who had not even had time to don his helmet. My sword sliced down and split his skull. Sharp was screaming his own war cry next to me as he sabred a dragoon who was trying to draw his sword. And then we were amongst the Chasseurs. I could see from the different uniforms that this was the provisional regiment we had seen at Valladolid. They had neither esprit de corps nor leaders. It was not a battle it was a slaughter. I saw the remnants of the Dragoons, in the distance, as they fled the field. Had General Slade been on time we would have had them all. As it was, we killed over a hundred and fifty Chasseurs that night. The 1st Provisional Chasseurs à Cheval ceased to exist. We lost two men dead and twelve others wounded. It was the most one-sided fight I had ever participated in.

It had the most dramatic effect on the camp. It was a bigger celebration than when Sir Arthur had defeated Junot at Vimeiro. We made plans to attack Soult on the 23rd. By Christmas we hoped to have secured this part of Spain.

The Earl forbade me to lead the patrols on the 22nd. "My dear fellow, you have done enough. Let your subordinates carry some of the responsibility. They are fine fellows and do you credit. You cannot win the war single handedly."

The patrols were productive although the news they brought was less than welcome. We captured more despatches and learned that Bonaparte and Marshal Ney were racing north with the Imperial Guard. Even worse was the news that Soult had summoned reinforcements. He now outnumbered us.

Lieutenant-General Moore looked despondent when we received the news. All of the senior officers waited for his decision. He shook his head, sadly. "We will not be able to attack Soult tomorrow after all, gentlemen. The outcome would be in the balance and I do not intend to become the Christmas nut in the Emperor's crackers. We break camp and on Christmas Eve we will head for Corunna. I hope to embark the army before the Emperor arrives. I would save the army to fight another day."

Even the most belligerent of senior officers saw the wisdom in that but it was a hard order to give and so began the disastrous retreat to Corunna.

Chapter 20

Sergeant Sharp could not understand the delay in beginning the retreat. "It seems to me, sir, that if we have to retreat then the sooner, we start the better."

"I know how it looks Alan, but for once the generals have it right. We have to send the artillery first and then the wagons. If we do not then the road will become clogged. We move at the pace of the slowest. The cavalry will be at the rear. General Moore has to organise the regiments which will be the rearguard." I lowered my voice. "We both know there are some regiments who would not be the best choice for such a role."

"And what about us sir? Will we be the scouts again?"

"Not this time. We are to be with the Earl of Uxbridge with the cavalry and his brother General Paget will command the infantry. I, for one, am happy for it means we fight with the rifles and they are fine fellows."

The retreating column was filled with unhappy soldiers. We had little food and the British soldier always fought better on a full stomach; added to that the snow was falling heavily. Some soldiers had barely any shoes and the remaining women were all almost barefoot. It was a sorry army which headed towards the coast. The Earl of Uxbridge gathered his commanders together. There were just five of us. The 20th had ceased to be an effective force and they had been sent, along with other weakened regiments, to escort the heavy artillery to Vigo where they would be taken off. I wished that Colonel Trant and his Portuguese were still with us. He was a rascal but the man and the men he commanded knew how to fight.

"Gentlemen each regiment of horse will take it in turns to shadow the French. The burden will be spread. If the enemy come too close to us then it will be our task to slow them down and aid General Paget's rearguard. We all know what Black Bob and his men can do but we will play our part too." He paused. I knew why he made his next statement for he had already discussed this with me. "If any horse is unable to carry on then it must be killed. If the enemy is close by, then knives and hammers will be used to destroy the unfortunate animals." It was the hardest order to issue and the one which the troopers would find it difficult to obey.

The cavalry knew exactly where the French were. Every day the squadron at the rear skirmished with them. Every day we reported to General Moore of their proximity. We slept by our horses. There was no opportunity to erect tents. We ate whatever food we could gather or steal. We even pilfered from the dead both French and British. The packs of the dead men we found alongside the road were searched for any scrap of food. My priority was feeding Badger. Before we had left Lisbon Sharp had managed to obtain some grain for our two horses. We had not had to use it yet. It proved to be a godsend during the three-week retreat to Corunna.

It was the turn of 8 Troop to be rearguard when we crossed the last bridge over the Esla. The river was in flood. I had the troop a mile behind Black Bob Crauford and his light infantry. I knew that they would be preparing the bridge for demolition and we had to hold them up for as long as possible. The French Dragoons had come to respect us. My squadron was still the only one which regularly used their carbines. We had made sure that we were well supplied with both ball and powder. The twisting and treacherous roads were dangerous for attacker and defender alike. Sharp and I rode at the rear of the column and we had just turned a corner when I heard a cry from the rocks.

"Sir, I am injured. Can you help me?"

As soon as I stopped and dismounted, Sharp had his carbine out. I led Badger to the rocks and saw a rifleman. His leg was at a strange angle.

"I slipped, sir, and broke my leg."

I could not leave him there. "Come on then private. Give me your arm."

He put his arm around my shoulder whilst never letting go of his Baker Rifle. "And it is Rifleman sir, Rifleman Dawson."

"Right Dawson. Put your good leg in the stirrup." As I pushed him up, I heard him scream as he caught his broken leg on the saddle. "Sorry son." When he was on the saddle I said. "Take your foot out of the stirrup so that I can mount. Use one arm to hold on to me when I get up there."

In a perfect world I would have mounted first and pulled him up but he had needed help.

Sharp said. "Best get a move on sir. I can hear the dragoons."

I struggled to mount but I managed it. "Grab hold of me, Dawson." He was behind me and he wrapped his arms, still holding the rifle, around my waist.

Just then the first Dragoons appeared. Sharp fired. I drew two pistols and fired them both. Dawson must have had a ball in his rifle for he fired one-handed. The four shots cleared two saddles and the Dragoons retreated a little.

"Ride Sharp." As we galloped towards the bridge, I saw that Cornet Williams had organised a skirmish line. There was a flurry of shots from behind and I heard balls whizz above my head and by Badger's side. We were lucky and none struck either of us.

As we passed through the troopers Cornet Williams shouted, "Fire!"

The ragged volley appeared to have an effect for the Dragoons stopped firing. The bridge was just fifty yards ahead. I saw Black Bob; he was always an angry-looking man. He was shouting, "Damn your eyes, get over the bridge so that we can blow it!"

We thundered over the wooden bridge. As we reached the other side, I saw a Chosen Man and his partner run towards me. "Well Dawson, we made it."

As I reined Badger in, I felt Dawson's grip loosen and he fell into the arms of his two friends. A tendril of blood seeped from his mouth. He looked up at me. "Thank you, sir, but the damned Frogs have done for me." He closed his eyes and he was dead.

"How?"

One of his friends took his hand away from his back and it came away bloody. "He was shot in the back, sir." He stood. "Thank you for coming back for him. He was a good lad." He prised the rifle from his dead fingers. "Well, you won't need this old son." He made to throw it into the river.

"Do you mind if I have it, Chosen Man. I am not a bad shot and it seems a waste to hurl it into the river."

He handed it to me along with the powder horn and the cartridge pouch. "Good luck to you, sir. Use it to kill as many of the bastards as you can."

"Stand clear!" Black Bob's voice rang out and the whole of the bridge erupted as the powder ignited. They would not use this crossing. We followed the light infantry into Benevente. We had bought a little respite for the French would have to move along the other side of the river. Rifleman Dawson's death was not entirely a waste.

We managed to find some hay for the horses in Benevente and we even slept beneath a roof. When the snow turned to rain, we thought that our luck had changed. We were wrong.

The 3rd Dragoons, King's German Legion were at the bridge when the Chasseurs à Cheval of the Imperial Guard appeared. These were elite troops. In their red and green uniforms with the colpack, they were amongst the best horse regiments Bonaparte possessed. There were over six hundred of them. I rode down with my squadron to support the Germans. Our carbines soon discouraged them.

"Thank you, Major Matthews. Damned handy weapon."

"We find it useful, colonel."

He pointed across the river. The Chasseurs à Cheval of the Imperial Guard were heading upstream and had been replaced by some light infantry. "It looks like they are searching for another crossing. We'll move out of range if you would like to follow them eh?"

"Yes, sir. Trooper Cole, ride to his lordship and tell him that a regiment of Chasseurs à Cheval is heading upstream." We followed them by riding through the woods.

Sharp suddenly pointed, "Sir, up there. There is a ford!"

"Right boys ride!"

We had the advantage of high ground and we reached the river before the Chasseurs à Cheval. My men reloaded and I prepared the rifle. It was strange to think that I had served with this regiment when they were the Consular Guard in Egypt. Would I know any of them? It was probably better not to know.

"Prepare to fire but wait for my command." I knew that the rifle was accurate up to a distance of two hundred yards or more. The Chasseurs à Cheval of the Guard would probably advance to carbine range and then fire at us. I had just one hundred and ten carbines but the six hundred men who faced us could not bring all their guns to fire at the same time.

The Chasseurs à Cheval rode down to the river's edge and began to fire. I saw a major; he was about a hundred and fifty yards away. He was organising more troopers to move up. I aimed at his chest and fired. The rifle had a powerful kick but the major was flung from his saddle and I saw the other senior officers moving back and out of range.

The carbines on both sides were causing more smoke than casualties. Percy shouted, "They are coming across sir."

"Jones, sound retire." We moved back in good order and were joined by a troop of the Germans.

"His lordship sends his compliments. He wants us to draw them up into the woods. He has a trap laid."

"Delighted Captain. Reload." I turned to the captain, "When we have fired if you would like to charge and then retire, we can reload again and draw them on.

"Yes, sir."

"Fire!"

As the carbines barked, I heard the bugle sound the charge and the troop galloped down to the ford. I heard the clash of steel and then the recall.

"Ready." The Germans galloped past us and I shouted, "Fire!" It was hard to see casualties but I had to believe we had shot some of them. "Fall back."

Sharp and I were the last to turn and move after the rest of the troopers. I heard hooves coming from the smoke and as I turned, I saw a Chasseurs à Cheval of the Guard with his sabre held before him. I had no time to turn Badger and meet the attack with my sword. I drew my pistol and, as he swung the sword at my head, I fired beneath my arm. He was thrown from his horse. "Grab that mount!"

Good horses were hard to come by and this was a magnificent beast. I saw the 10th and 18th waiting by the side of the road. The Earl of Uxbridge waved at us to continue to retreat. We had gone a mere eighty yards when I heard the charge sounded and the trap was sprung. We turned our horses and charged too. We now outnumbered the French. They were good soldiers but they were surrounded. After a fierce fight, they fell back. I joined in the pursuit with some of my men. I saw a few troopers from the 10th and the 18th too. As we neared the ford, I thought they were going to make it across when one of the horses stopped and refused to enter the maelstrom of foaming, bloody water. I saw that it was the commanding officer; the general. He had lost his busby and was bleeding. I shouted to the trooper who was raising his sword to decapitate him. "Take him prisoner, trooper." He hesitated, "That is an order!"

The trooper grabbed the reins and led him back to us. "Well done Trooper...?"

"Grisdale sir, Trooper Grisdale of the 10th Hussars."

"Well, Trooper you have just captured the commanding officer of the Chasseurs à Cheval of the Imperial Guard. "

I turned to the General, "Your sword, General." I watched as a horse battery set up to cover the ford. The general shrugged and handed over his sword. "We had better get your head seen to General...?"

"General Lefebvre-Desnouettes. Thank you...?"

"Major Matthews of the 11th Light Dragoons."

We rode back through the battlefield. "Can I compliment you on your French sir? It is flawless." I nodded. "We were led to believe that English cavalry would not stand. We were wrong."

Sir John Moore was an old-fashioned gentleman. He insisted on having General Lefebvre-Desnouettes' wound dressed personally. He also loaned him a uniform to wear. Sergeant Sharp was sent, under a flag of truce, to fetch the general's baggage. He dined with us in a clean uniform. This was the civilised part of the war. It would not spread beyond the French and English cavalry.

At dinner, the general pointed to me, "That was a fine shot major. Do all Light Dragoons carry the Baker rifle?"

"No general, just me. I like to be as well-armed as I can."

He laughed, "The men in the mess talk of a soldier just like you who served with the Guard in Egypt. That was before my time of course. Marshal Bessières speaks fondly of him. He used to carry as many pistols as he could."

It felt as though someone was walking on my grave. "How interesting and what happened to him?"

He shrugged, "Apparently he was killed in Italy. At least that was the story."

I was then ignored as the others all asked for information and stories about Napoleon Bonaparte. I noticed Sir John watching me shrewdly as the, stories unfolded. When we left the table for brandy he came to my side. "Your knowledge of Bonaparte seems unerringly accurate Major. In fact, one would go as far as to say you know him better than anyone else save one who has served him."

"Put it down to a character defect. I need as much information and knowledge as I can get and I like to observe people, even from a distance."

I wondered just how much Sir John had deduced. However, he was an honourable man and never spoke of it again. Not that we had much chance for talking for the next day or, so. When we reached Bemibre the first regiments to reach the town found the vats of wine and broke into them. All discipline broke down. There were fights between men over wine which occasionally ended in violence and death but equally bad was the fact that many soldiers, already weakened by hunger simply succumbed to the drink and collapsed unconscious in the streets.

I was with the rearguard that day and the French, eager to make up for the loss of their cavalry leader were pushing hard. We no longer had the luxury of being able to chase off the eager scouts. We had to nurse and coax our tired horses. I would not want

Badger to be slain in Spain because I had ridden him too hard. We used our carbines and I used the rifle. I was now used to the kick and I was able to fire from a greater distance. Of course, it was hard to reload and frequently I would have just one shot from my rifle. But as I had my carbine and three pistols, we kept the enemy at bay. That day in Bemibre the French pushed on hard. It was no longer the Guard which pursued us but the Dragoons and they were keen to get to grips with us. We fired one last time and halted them, briefly, and we hurried through Bemibre.

It was the most horrific sight I had witnessed thus far. There were dozens of men and a handful of women who were lying, drunk in the streets. My troopers were appalled.

"Get up you fools! The French are right behind us!"

We either received laughter or belligerence for our troubles.

"Sir, can't we take the women with us? They will be sorely abused by the French."

Troop Sergeant Grant was the oldest man in the regiment and he had a wife and daughter back in England. This upset him. "I am sorry, George, we cannot risk the horses." There was a flurry of shots behind us as the French entered the town. "Ride on. We can do nothing for these."

It was heart-breaking to hear the screams and cries as the men were, slaughtered and the women taken. Neither army had the resources for prisoners. They were a luxury of a different type of war.

It did delay the French and we pushed on to catch up with the rear of the army. To my amazement, we found a square of men. In the middle two riflemen were stripped to the waist. It was a drumhead court-martial. I saw the glowering figure of Black Bob Crauford, "Sir, the French are coming!"

"These men, Major Matthews, were caught away from the brigade. They think because they are riflemen that they may do whatever they think proper. I will teach you different before I am done with you. One hundred lashes each!"

As the whips sliced across their backs one of their comrades muttered, "Damn his eyes!"

The unfortunate man was dragged before the General. "Three hundred lashes! Although I should obtain the goodwill of neither of the officers nor the men of the brigade here by so doing, I am resolved to punish these three men, even though the French are at our heels."

I turned and took my troop back down the road. I neither wanted to witness the punishment nor did I want them to be surprised. "Reload your weapons."

The men did so automatically. I am not certain any of them thought about the action any more. It was like breathing. It was something you did all the time.

Percy rode next to me. "Sir that is not right."

"Percy," I warned him, "He would have you flogged for such a comment. He is maintaining discipline." I pointed to the distant town. "Perhaps if their commander had been as strong then they would not now lie dead in Bemibre's streets."

The French, having finished with the stragglers, hurried on to catch us up. They found a wall of lead as they rode into forty guns. The ragged volley was enough to make them recoil and retreat. "Fall back!"

The punishment was over and I saw the wife of the man who had received three hundred lashes putting his tunic on his bloody and lacerated back. "Sir, the French are right behind us!"

"Thank you, Major. The Brigade will about-face and form two lines." He seemed as calm as if he was conducting a parade at Shorncliffe.

As we passed through them, I was amazed to see every soldier obey. There were two lines of muskets and rifles ready to greet the Dragoons who rode into them and were cut down. When the smoke had cleared and the road was empty General Crauford ordered his men to about-face and continued the retreat. The French did not follow. It was their last attack of the day and we trudged on through the snow.

Chapter 21

When we finally reached Villafranca we were able to get some
rest. We had bought time. The pursuing cavalry had had their noses
smacked by the rearguard and they retired back to Bemibre. No
doubt they would enjoy the wine without succumbing to it. Sir
John looked concerned when he saw me. "Major Matthews, I pray
that you take some rest."

"I will Sir John but our services are in constant demand." He
nodded. "I know, sir, that you may be disappointed in the
performance of some of the soldiers but the Light Brigade and the
cavalry are performing magnificently."

"I know." He gestured towards his aide, "my nephew here would
join you. I have told him that I need him close by me."

"Your uncle is right Stanhope. He holds the army together. We
just stop the dogs from snapping too closely at our heels."

"The next day it was the turn of the 15th to hold the rear. A
messenger galloped in, "Sir! The French are crossing the bridge at
Cacabelos! It is not just cavalry. There are infantry there too."

"Well, nephew you will get some action at last. Major Matthews
if you would be so good as to provide an escort we will go and see
what this is all about."

It was mid-afternoon and already regiments were foraging for
food. We passed a battery of Horse Artillery. "You fellows bring
your guns with us now." Sir John had a way of making an order
sound like a request.

It was six miles to the bridge and Sir John picked up the
stragglers from many regiments as we headed back to the crossing.
He encouraged them all, "Come along my good fellows. Let us
send the French back across this river eh?" The men all followed.
They would loot and drink when they could but they would always
fight; especially for Sir John Moore.

We reached the hill overlooking the bridge. The 15th were falling
back supported by the Light Brigade. Amazingly I could hear the
French bands playing music. They meant to force the bridge.

"Matthews, you are a sound fellow. Take these guns and these chaps and go into the town. We must extract those horsemen and hold them here. We do not want the rearguard to be wasted. General Crauford should retire. The guns should clear the bridge. I intended to pull back to Villafranca by dark."

"Yes, sir." I turned to my troop, "Lieutenant Austen, take command. Sharp come with me." I dismounted and handed Badger's reins to Trooper Cole. I did not want to risk my horse in such a confused skirmish. I turned to the Royal Horse Artillery. "Bring your guns and enfilade the bridge." I lifted my rifle. "Right boys let us show the French that they face Englishmen this day and not Spaniards. We will throw them back across the river!"

There was a cheer as the two hundred stragglers from many different regiments followed me down to the river. "Find cover in the houses and behind walls. Wait for my command." I ran to the edge of the bridge.

There was a captain there directing the fire of the squadron. He saluted, "Reinforcements sir?"

"No captain. Give them a volley and then retire. Where is General Crauford?"

He pointed to the bridge where Black Bob was directing the fire of his men. I dodged the hail of lead from the far side of the bridge, "General Crauford, the General is here. He intends to pull back to Villafranca."

He pointed to the advancing columns of infantry. "What about yon infantry?"

"I have a scratch battalion in the village. There is a horse battery about to fire as soon as we withdraw."

"Right Major." As I ran back to the shelter of the houses, I heard his Scottish tones ringing out, "The Light Brigade will withdraw and take a position in the village. Wait for it! On my command, retire!"

The light infantry had been trained by Sir John Moore and they were the best troops we had. They came back in pairs. One fired while one ran. Each covered his partner and the advancing French had to endure a constant fusillade as they tried to run them down. I slipped behind a wall and aimed my rifle. I heard the music and saw senior officers leading their men across the bridge. There were at least two generals. This was the most determined attack we had yet seen. The cannon cracked and cleared some of the men from the bridge but they were not large calibre guns. They did not do as much damage as we might have liked. I suspect most of the shrapnel had already been used. The Light Brigade hurled themselves behind our defences. I recognised the one next to me as being one of the companions of the dead rifleman whose gun I was using.

He grinned, "I see you are still using Archie's gun. He would be happy about that." He lifted his own weapon and shot a grenadier sergeant who was urging his men on.

I fired at a captain who was rallying some wavering soldiers. He plunged to the icy river below the bridge. The rifles were taking a toll on the sergeants and officers but there were simply too many Frenchmen. I laid down the rifle and drew my sword. "See if you can hit those generals, rifleman. It may dishearten them."

"Sir!"

"Right Sharp, let us get amongst them. Fix bayonets!" Lifting my sword, I led the improvised battalion to attack the infantry who had crossed the bridge. The cannon had now got the range and the numbers crossing were thinning. We just had to drive back the ones who had a toehold on our side of the bridge.

I drew my pistol and fired at the grenadier sergeant who raced towards me with his musket and bayonet. The double charge hit him in the chest and he fell backwards. I swung my sword overhand and sliced down on to the shoulder of the young lieutenant who was urging his men on. The spurting blood told me that he was dead. Sharp's pistol cracked next to me and I used my pistol to deflect the bayonet which was aimed at my side. I swung the sword and it ripped across the side of the soldier's head. It grated into the skull.

Suddenly I saw the general, leading the French, clutch his head and fall dead less than thirty feet from me. This was our chance, "Come on lads! Charge!" The General's aide fell to a second ball and I saw the doubt on the faces of the officers who remained. I clubbed one officer who was too slow to bring up his sword and I swung my sword wildly at head height. I am a tall man and the ones before me were light infantry; they were small. They ran. As they sped across the bridge the rifles and the cannon thinned them out. Behind me, I heard a cheer. We had won. I helped the officer I had clubbed to his feet and took his sword.

"You are my prisoner." He nodded, "Who is that general?"

"It is General Colbert and that is Colonel Maubourg."

"Sharp, take him to the general." The improvised battalion stood waiting for orders. "Well done men. Now fall back to the general!"

I retrieved my rifle. The rifleman said, "I have reloaded it for you, sir."

"Thank you. What is your name?"

"Thomas Plunet sir. A pleasure to serve with you."

"Well Rifleman, you have just shot General Colbert and perhaps saved the army this day so well done."

"It's a pleasure sir but why doesn't the General stop and fight?"

I waved my hand at the other side of the river. "We are severely outnumbered Plunet. The best that we can hope is to get out of this alive."

I passed Black Bob whose men were falling back in good order. "Well done Major! That was sound work."

"Hopefully they will take the time to lick their wounds and give us the opportunity to fall back."

When I reached the general, he had finished interviewing the prisoner. "Well, it seems that Bonaparte thinks we are beaten. He has gone back to Paris and left the pursuit to Soult and Ney. His lordship is bringing up the cavalry and they will deter the French. Well done, Matthews." He chuckled. "It was all that I could do to stop young Stanhope here from joining you."

We did not stop all night as we headed to Nogales. It was a pitch-black night. The terrain was treacherous. Great black chasms dropped precipitously on either side of the track and many an unwary and exhausted soldier fell to their deaths; unseen and unmourned during that long night march to safety. All the food had long gone and men were forced to suck on leather for some nourishment. Even worse, for the men I led, was the sight of many dead horses littering the side of the track. Some of them showed where starving infantrymen had hacked chunks from the still-warm horse. I could not blame them but it was upsetting to my troopers.

We were luckier than most. All of my men were mounted. We had brought with us the captured horses and were able to remount men. We had lost troopers; that was inevitable but none to desertion. Every man had fallen facing our enemies. The squadron could hold its head high. Cornet Williams had grown during the campaign. He was no longer the baby faced innocent. He had learned to lead and he had learned to kill. If he survived to return to England then he would be a good officer.

When dawn broke, we had outrun the enemy. The Earl of Uxbridge sent a message that the enemy had halted the night before. We stopped, exhausted, in Nogales for some rest. Men just fell to the floor and slept in the mud. They were all too weak to even search for food. Lieutenant-General Sir John Moore sent Stanhope to Corunna. "I want supplies laid in at Lugo."

"But sir, Lugo is still almost thirty miles away." Colborne was his Military Secretary and he was like a scarecrow. He was not used to such privations.

"And I am afraid, Mr Colborne, that we will have another thirty miles before we can eat."

It was the turn of my squadron to join the rearguard. From what I had heard the 15th had lost many men and horses. Soon they would cease to be an effective force of horse. As we trudged back along the road to the rearguard I saw the body of a young woman. She had frozen to death. I heard a noise. I dismounted and approached the woman. When I lifted her stiffening body, I discovered a new-born and mewling babe beneath. I grabbed my blanket and wrapped the baby in it. I looked around. This was not something I was familiar with.

I heard a voice, "Here sir, I'll take the bairn from you." I saw a ragged woman, barefoot with bleeding feet. She had two skeletons trudging with her. They were obviously her children. I handed her the baby. She shook her head, "Poor Mary Martin. I told her to stay with me. Well, she is with God now sir." She made the sign of the cross.

"Sharp!" Sergeant Sharp came over. "Give me your blanket." I took the blanket and placed it around the woman's shoulders. "What is your name?"

"Annie Macgregor, my husband was in the 92nd."

"Was?"

"He fell into one of those rivers. He is with God and I fear we shall join him soon enough."

I noticed that Sergeant Seymour and Sergeant Grant had put their blankets around the shoulders of the two children. If I had had food, I would have given it to her. I reached into my pocket and pulled out a handful of silver coins. "There may be food in Nogales but if you can reach Lugo then I promise you that you will find food. I will find you Annie Macgregor. Do not give up hope. There are ships awaiting us in Corunna. Baby Martin must survive to give some point to this slaughter and the loss of his parents."

She kissed my hand, "Thank you, Major, I will not forget you."

"Now hurry for the French are close."

As we rode towards the French, I determined that we would do all that we could to hold them up. Privates Martin and Macgregor had been wrong to bring their women from Lisbon but they had paid with their lives. If I could then I would see to it that the women and the children did not suffer the same fate.

The Earl of Uxbridge was with his brother General Edward Paget. They were smoking cigars. "A stroke of luck Matthews! We shot a French officer and he had these about him. Good eh? Want one?"

"No thank you sir. The General has ordered supplies to be at Lugo. We just need to hang on for another thirty miles or so."

"I am not certain that Soult and Ney will give us that time." He shook his head, "Your squadron will have to do the job of a regiment, Major. We have lost heavily during the night."

"We will do our duty sir."

"I know you will. And I shall see you in Lugo, brother."

"Don't worry about us, Henry. We have this lucky charm now."
He pointed to me. "The chaps think he brings good fortune. He
even rallied those stragglers."

As the Earl rode off, I said. "The rank and file just want to fight,
sir. Retreating without fighting does not sit well with them."

"I know but we have no choice now, do we?" He looked sadly at
the butt of his cigar and threw it to hiss in the snow. "Well major,
if you wait for the Frogs here, we will head up the road and prepare
to receive them."

"Right sir. We will buy you time."

The weary foot soldiers turned and marched up the road towards
Nogales. They would, at least, have something to defend there. I
had seen the last Horse Artillery battery being set up just outside
the town. Sir Edward just needed time to place his men.

"Captain Stafford, dismount half of your men and put them in the
rocks to the left of the road. Percy, do the same on this side. Horse
holders to the rear. The rest of you come with me."

I had twenty men with me. "Load your weapons. We will go and
entice the French on." We rode up the road. The pass was narrow
and we filled it in two ranks. I noticed that I had Sergeant Seymour
on one side and Sergeant Sharp on the other. We were in the
middle. Our human barrier would not run. The sleet, rain and snow
which were driving along the road made visibility poor. We would
be almost invisible to the French because we were not moving.
Men marching along a road tend to keep their heads down.

I heard the French as they sang. I said quietly, "Prepare your
weapons."

I was using my carbine. My new rifle was over my shoulder. One
of the horses whinnied and I heard the shout of alarm from the
French. I could not see them but I knew them to be there. "Open
fire!"

They were just eighty yards from us when we fired. We did not
do much damage but I saw a standard fall and knew that would
upset them. I drew my pistol and fired that. We had done enough.
"Withdraw!"

As we turned, I noticed that Trooper Smith lay dead. Corporal Jones, the bugler, grabbed the reins of his mount. We could not afford to lose a single beast. We went back at a trot. Even that was too much for some of the horses which could barely walk let alone trot. When we passed the ambush, we turned and dressed our ranks. "Reload." That was easier said than done with fingers frozen and stiff.

The French came on at a pace. This time they halted just fifty yards from us and formed three ranks. "Fire!" Our sixty guns barked before the order to fire could be given. I took a chance and yelled, in French, "Fall back! They have cannon!"

It was a crude trick but it worked and the column disappeared back up the road leaving a huddle of bodies bleeding in the snow.

"Jones, sound the recall." With everyone remounted we trotted down the road. They would soon learn the error of their ways and follow us. That trick would not work a second time but it had bought General Paget precious time to get to Nogales which was ten miles or so away.

We halted just a mile from the town. We had passed more stragglers who had fallen by the side. We made sure that they were dead; those that were not were put on our horses and taken with us. There were not many. The eight we had saved we urged to walk the last mile to safety. The brief rest on a horse had given them all a little energy. I hoped none were from the Light Brigade. It would not go well with them if they were. Black Bob had made his rules quite clear and there would be no exceptions.

"Sir?"

"Yes, Sergeant Grant?"

"We are down to ten balls each and the powder is running out."

"Sergeant Seymour. Take five men and see if any of the dead we have passed have either ball or powder." We had become master scavengers.

"Sir."

"And don't get caught eh, Joe?"

"No sir," he said cheerfully.

Despite the privations and the hardship, the 11th seemed to be handling the retreat better than most other regiments. There was a bond between them. We had all dismounted to save our horses. I took another handful of the precious grain we had saved and fed it to Badger. Every trooper cared for his own mount in different ways. Perhaps that was why we still had horses when many of the cavalry went afoot. I spied something reddish in the trees. I wandered over and saw that it was one last, gnarled apple which had survived the wind and the stragglers. Perhaps it was because it was too high for weary men to reach. I struggled up the tree and grabbed it. It was still sound.

"Here Badger, a little treat." My horse munched happily on the little piece of treasure I had found. It was ridiculous but I felt much better for having done that. Badger and Sharp were almost like family. If I had had a child, I would have done the same. It seemed unlikely that I would ever father a child. I never seemed to have either the opportunity or the time to meet any women.

I wondered how Baby Martin was faring. I took heart from the fact that I had not seen any of the family on the road. They would have made Nogales and that meant they would be with the other women. They were a close-knit bunch and the baby had more chance of survival amongst them. Of course, the prospects for all of them were not good. Even if they made it back to England, they would be destitute and forced to beg on the streets. Annie's best chance was for another soldier to take her on. With three children and emaciated as she was, I did not hold out much hope.

Suddenly I heard shots and Sergeant Seymour and his scavengers galloped in. "Chasseurs sir!"

"Mount and ready carbines."

I barely had time to draw a pistol before the first of the Chasseurs galloped down the road. They had seen the handful of troopers and thought they had easy victims. I pulled the trigger and drew a second pistol. Sheathing my first one I drew my sword. I kicked Badger on, "Go on Badger!"

I swung the sword at the head of the first Chasseur whilst firing obliquely at a second. I was wreathed in smoke. I holstered my pistol. A blade sliced down out of the fog. I jerked back on Badger's reins and his hooves came up as I blocked the blow. When he landed Badger caught the leg of the other horse and I heard an ugly crack as it broke and the horse and rider fell to the side.

I heard recall and turned Badger to trot back. Captain Stafford looked worried. "You disappeared in the smoke, sir! What happened?"

"Nothing. We just halted them. Fall back to Nogales."

I just hoped that the defences were ready. We had slowed down the advance and we made the two cannon which marked the edge of the defences. I leaned down to speak to the battery commander. "Chasseurs coming down the road, Captain."

"Right sir. We have loaded with all the bits of metal we could find. That should make a mess of them." He was making his cannon into a crude shotgun.

We were running out of everything. The next thirty miles were going to be trying for all of us. I reported to the Earl, Sir Edward Paget and Sir John Moore who were together poring over a map. "The French are right behind us. They are using cavalry again."

"I have ordered the army to dig in at Lugo. We will use the supplies there. I have asked Admiral Hood to bring up some ships to Corunna. I can only hope that they are there when we reach it." He looked at the three of us. "I am leaving now to prepare the defences at Lugo. Hold them for as long as you can and then make your way back as quickly as you can. Your rearguard, Sir Edward, has performed magnificently and the cavalry has done all that we could ask of them."

When he had left the Earl said, "There is little point in risking the rifles, Edward. Have your men give one volley each and then head for Lugo. We have the two guns and the cavalry; if we can bloody their noses, we might be able to escape."

"That is all we can do, brother."

The French advance guard had been reinforced by some Dragoons and they boldly rode down the road. I think they expected little opposition having cleared us from the road. The

Captain had disguised his guns and the Light Brigade was sheltering behind walls and in buildings. Sir Edward timed it to perfection. "Fire!"

The improvised grapeshot cleared the road and horses and men fell in heaps. The rifles and muskets scythed through the survivors. "Cease fire."

When the smoke had cleared, we could see only the dead and the dying. Without calls, Sir Edward led the Light Brigade at double-time down the road. The Captain reloaded his guns and Sergeant Seymour and his scavengers searched the bodies. They also managed to capture one horse. The rider had been cut in two but his horse had survived. We all had more ball and powder. The troopers were more cheerful with loaded weapons in their hands. Trooper Cole had also managed to find a whole cheese and some stale bread in one of the saddlebags of a dead horse. His section shared it between them. He offered some to Percy and me. "No thank you, Trooper Cole. To the victor go the spoils."

We had a short respite and then the French came again. This time they sent a light infantry screen and a horse battery. "Right boys, one volley and then get the hell out of here!" We watched as the French battery began to unlimber.

The Royal Horse Artillery needed no urging and they quickly double shotted the barrel with ball and grape. The double crack of the cannon and ripple of carbines sent a pall of smoke towards the French. The guns were limbered before the smoke had cleared. "Bugler, sound retreat!

As my men streamed down the road, I unslung my rifle and waited for the smoke to clear. The cannon had done their job well. One of the French guns had been knocked from its trail while the other had no wheels. The crews lay strewn across the road. I sighted on the colonel who began to urge his men forward. I breathed slowly and squeezed. At a hundred and fifty yards it was not a difficult shot and I watched the colonel tumble from his horse and lie clutching his shoulder. I turned and headed up the road as balls zipped around me.

Chapter 22

Lugo was the last stop before Corunna. I was the last soldier to arrive in the town on the 6th of January. Sir Edward shook me by the hand as I rode in. "Damned fine show sir!" He spread his arm. "There you are, sir! Food!"

I was less concerned for myself than for our horses. "Is there fodder for the horses, sir?"

Sir Edward looked at me as though I was speaking a foreign language. "Not sure what you mean sir."

"Never mind, Sir Edward. The French were bringing more guns up."

"Right, Major, we will get some defences prepared. You will find the town a little crowded, the whole of the army is here now."

I found the Earl of Uxbridge with Sir John and Lieutenant Stanhope in the small bar they had commandeered. Colborne was busily writing orders in the corner of the room.

The Earl looked up as I entered. "Damned fine show, Matthews. We may get out of this intact yet eh?"

"Sir, there is no fodder for the animals."

Sir John looked up, "I know Matthews. That is because I am embarking the cavalry. They are too valuable to lose and we are close enough to Corunna that we should not need them. From now on the Light Brigade and the Royal Horse Artillery can keep the French from snapping at our heels."

The Earl patted me on the shoulder, "Your chaps have done a damned fine job Matthews I will look after them and see that they get home safely."

"Yes sir."

Sir John jabbed a finger at the map. I intend to give the men a couple of days here to recover and then push on." He looked up at me. "I need to know how many men Soult has with him."

I nodded. I could see where this was going. "Yes sir, and you want me to find out."

"Precisely, now get a good night's sleep and leave before dawn. I shall stay here until the 9th. That will give the cavalry time to embark."

Lieutenant Stanhope chimed in, "That is, sir if the admiral has arrived."

"The Navy will not let us down, Stanhope. They will be there."

"By your leave sir. I'll just go and see to my chaps."

The exhausted troopers were busy attending to their horses. The infantry might be gorging themselves on salt fish and hardtack but my troopers and officers were fretting over animals which were close to exhaustion. "Sir, there is no fodder for the animals!"

"I know Troop Sergeant Grant. However, you are all leaving for the coast. You are to be embarked."

They all smiled at that but Percy suddenly said, "You said, you. Are you not coming with us, sir?"

"I am afraid not, Lieutenant. The General still requires my services. Sergeant Sharp and I will be staying."

The air of excitement evaporated like a morning mist. "Sir, that is not fair. You and Sharpie have already done so much. Can't someone else do it?"

"I am afraid, Sergeant Seymour, that it is our lot to be used like this; however, you can do me a favour."

He brightened, "Anything sir."

"I would exchange horses with you. You have the one we captured from the French. I would not risk Badger again and I know that you will look after him." The sergeant nodded. "And there is one more thing. You remember that baby we found by the road?"

"Baby Martin? Yes, sir."

I reached into my pocket and took out five gold pieces. "If you pass that family on the road then I want you to make sure they get on the ship with you. I don't know why but I want that baby and that family to survive. If you find them and they get back to England, pray ask Sergeant Major Jones to find the woman work in the laundry."

He took the money, "I will sir and we will find them! That is a promise." There was no doubt that he would do what I asked of him.

"Sir, you are coming back aren't you!" The Cornet looked almost terrified.

"Yes, Cornet Williams but... let us just say that a French horse will be more useful and... expendable."

I caught Sergeant Sharp's eye and he nodded, "Er Cornet Williams, you have a captured horse, I would like Maria saving too. She is a lovely horse." He grinned, "If you speak to her in French."

The cornet smiled, "It would be my honour Sergeant but, truth to tell, Sergeant, the one I have been riding is not the best horse. I suspect she is going a little lame."

"Then she will be perfect, sir. I am not certain that the ones the Major and I take will survive this little patrol."

As the sergeants left to inform the troopers of the new orders, I was left with the officers. "The Earl says he will look after the squadron, William, but I know they will be in good hands. You are a fine officer."

Percy had a look of pain upon his face. "Sir, this sounds like you are saying goodbye! What does the general have planned for you?"

"It is not goodbye but Sharp and I have to get close to Marshal Soult's army and ascertain numbers. You have seen the terrain. It may be that Sharp and I cannot carry out our orders and may be trapped behind the lines but I will return to England. It may take time but I will get back. We have lost many fine troopers in this retreat but the regiment can be proud of the way this squadron has carried out its duties. When others were losing their heads the 11th did its duty. I want those troopers to return to England with their most excellent officers. We will be coming back and Colonel Fenton will need both."

Captain Stafford said, "We will not let you down, sir."

Lieutenant Stanhope found us, "Sir, the Earl's compliments and the cavalry is leaving now."

"Thank you, Stanhope, the squadron will be along directly." I held out my hand, "Look after them, William."

"I will sir! And we will help Sergeant Seymour find that family. We all want them to survive. They are a symbol of this retreat."

Percy shook my hand firmly, "You watch out for yourself sir, I don't want to have to command the troop alone."

"You won't Percy. Cornet Williams here is now ready to become a First Lieutenant."

The cornet looked at me seriously as he shook my hand, "Thank you, sir. I have learned much riding with you."

"Good, and that bodes well, for the ones who were not willing to learn now lie dead in Portugal."

Alan came back leading the horses, "The Cornet was right sir, this one would not have reached the coast."

"Just so long as they can reach the French camp, that is all that we need. We can steal others. Well sergeant, one last time for King and Country eh?"

He shook his head, "We do it for the rest of the army, sir. King and Country are too far away here. It is the troop and the regiment who are more important. It is the likes of the rifles and the Light Brigade who make us do what we do."

We led our new horses towards the main square. Ahead of us, I noticed that the squadron had halted. I could hear a commotion at the front to the column. "Here, Sergeant, hold the reins while I see what the problem is."

As I got closer, I heard a maniacal voice shouting, "I am Sir John Moore. None of you buggers is getting past me!"

The soldier had a cocked musket and a fixed bayonet. I saw two of his comrades nearby. Poor Cornet Williams had no idea what to do. "What's the problem with him, Private?"

The soldier seemed to see me and he levelled his gun at me, "I told you! I am Sir John Moore and I command this army!"

One of the privates said, "Sir he ate raw salt fish and washed it down with rum. He has gone mad, sir."

"What is his name?"

"Private John McCain, sir."

I nodded and smiled, "Sir John, I have some urgent despatches for you." He looked puzzled. I held out my right hand as I stepped forward. I saw the bayonet dip as his attention wavered. I grabbed his musket, pulled him forward and punched him as hard as I could on the chin. He fell like a sack of potatoes.

"Take his gun from him and keep it from him until he is sober."

"Aren't you going to charge him, sir? Threatening an officer?"

"If we charged everyone who went mad, we would have no army to command. Carry on Cornet."

As I turned to walk away, I heard the Private say. "Is he a proper officer?"

Troop Sergeant Grant said, "He is the best officer you have ever met, sonny boy. Now get this idiot off the road before I run him down and shoot him myself."

It was just one of the many idiotic things men did on that catastrophic march to Corunna.

We slipped away before dawn. This would be the hardest mission we had ever attempted. These were the narrowest roads I had seen so far and it would be hard to get by unseen. I had a plan. When we saw the French fires, in the distance, we dismounted and took to the woods and defiles which lined the road. We were walking on virgin snow. Despite the cold, we took off our helmets and put them in our saddlebags. They marked us as British. Dismounting we led our horses through the thin woods which bordered the road.

The French had found a flatter part of the land in which to camp. I saw the glow of a pair of pipes ahead. We tied the two horses to a tree and, drawing our swords moved towards the two sentries who were huddled together. We were within ten yards before they turned.

"Who goes there?"

"Thank God we have found our camp. I feared it was the English."

"Stop there. Who are you?" I heard the musket being cocked.

I am Major Lejeune and I bring despatches from Marshal Berthier for Marshal Soult."

One of the muskets was lowered but the other man was still suspicious. "Where are your horses?"

"They went lame back there and we had to slit their throats. There were English cavalry nearby." I stepped closer and pointed behind me. Human nature dictates that eyes are drawn to pointing fingers. As they both looked behind us, we lunged forward with our swords. I struck the throat of one of them and he slid silently to the snow-covered ground. Sharp's sabre ripped upwards into the soft middle of the second sentry. The soldier fell with a groan.

"Quick get their capes and shakos." Once they were donned, we looked more like the French. "Grab his head." I held the feet of the man Sharp had killed. We walked over to the edge of a slope and hurled the body down. We repeated with the other. It was unlikely their bodies would ever be discovered. We recovered our horses and headed through the woods towards the camp. It was just coming to life.

We dismounted at the edge of the camp and walked in. I saw a huddle of men around a fire. I handed the reins of my horse to Sharp and wandered over. "Damned cold!" I said to no one in particular.

"What an awful country!" The officer who spoke had pieces of cloth wrapped around his shoes and he had a blanket with a hole cut in it for his head draped over his shoulders as an improvised cape. This was an army in as bad a shape as we were. He pointed to Sharp who stood with the horses. "I would keep an eye on those horses. Men have killed for scrawnier looking beasts."

I tapped my sword. "They would have to go through me first."

"That is a fine-looking blade. May I see it?"

"Of course." I handed it over and the officer examined it.

"A fine weapon, Austrian?"

"Yes. I captured it when we captured the Dutch fleet over ten years ago."

"You were amongst the cavalry at the Texel?"

"I was a Chasseur then!"

He took a leather skin from under his blanket. "Then have a drink with me, Captain Jacques Bréville, for my father was with the cavalry in those early days of glory."

I swallowed some of the rough brandy. "Thank you. What was his name?"

"Like me he was Jacques but he was just a sergeant."

"I do not remember the name. Where is he now?"

"He died in Egypt."

"Many good men fell in Egypt." I handed him back his skin. "And now I must leave you. I have despatches for the Marshal. Where is his headquarters?"

He pointed back up the road. "The farmhouse with the damaged roof; it is the warmest place he could find. It was good to have met you. What is your name? I should like to know in case I meet any of my father's old comrades."

"Pierre Boucher, I was a brigadier in those days. I have done well in this war."

"You have done well. Perhaps I will see you again when we have driven the roast beefs into the sea."

"Perhaps."

He waved farewell and began to talk to his comrades. When I rejoined Sharp we were not given a second glance. We had been seen talking to one of their own and we were dressed in French capes and shakos. We made our way through the camp and I saw that life was just as difficult for the French as it was for us. As we were passing the farmhouse, I heard a commotion and officers began to hurry from the building. Sharp began to examine his horse. It was showing signs of being lame. A major of artillery barged his way between us. "Out of the way. We are going to end the British retreat once and for all."

"I am sorry major. We have an injured horse."

"Then I would end its misery now and let the men eat some meat!" He laughed as he left.

I could see that the marshal must have held a briefing of some description. Officers were running hither and thither. We made our way to the far end of the camp so that we could see the forces at

Soult's disposal. We saw just one battery of guns but there were three regiments of cavalry, one Hussar, one Dragoon and one Chasseur. It was not a large force. I made a decision. "Sharp, take my horse and get back to the general. Tell him he is about to be attacked by one battery, three regiments of cavalry and I estimate, ten battalions of infantry."

He shook his head, "You go, sir! I'll make my own way back."

"Sergeant Sharp your French is adequate only. I can talk my way out of trouble and besides this is an order. Stay with the general and I will get back to you when I can." He opened his mouth to speak. "Alan, this is the best way and I will return. I was not born to die in a frozen Galicia."

He reluctantly mounted and joined the other soldiers heading towards the British lines. I had no doubt that he would be able to slip away and reach our lines before the French began their attack.

I led the lame horse through the French camp. The horse had become worse as we had progressed through the camp. I suspected that we had exacerbated and aggravated her lameness. She would have to be put down. I stroked her mane. "There, old girl; I am afraid this is as far as you go."

I did not notice the two men approaching me. One had an apron on. He said, "Sir, are you going to destroy that horse?"

I saw that is was a cook. "I am afraid I am; why?"

Well, sir, we could come to a deal. If you let us do it, I can provide the men with hot food. It would feed the men but I would not want you out of pocket. How about I give you a good hot meal and a bottle of wine?"

I was not worried about the payment but if I gave in too easily, he would be suspicious. "I am sure I could get more from the men if I offered her for sale."

He nodded, "I can give you a silver piece."

"Five."

"Two."

"Three and a bottle of brandy."

He grinned, "You drive a hard bargain!" He spat on his hand. "A deal."

After we had shaken, I said, "I will take off the saddle first."

"Isn't that included?"

I laughed, "I intend to ride into battle, sergeant and a saddle helps."

I let him lead the poor beast off. I heard the sound of the shot and felt sadness. I hated any animal being destroyed. I took the saddle into the canteen tent and put it in the corner. By the time I had sat down the cook had brought my bottle of brandy and my bowl of stew. There was also some bread. I had missed bread. The French army always had edible bread while the British army gave you hardtack. I wolfed down the food. The brandy I would save. It might come in handy.

The cook waved me over. "A little more? There is just a ladleful left. I am going to cook up your horse for the meal this evening when we have slaughtered the roast beefs."

"A good soldier never turns down food; especially on this march."

He put the food in my bowl and as I ate it, standing up he said, "Well you had better make the most of it. The word is that there are more regiments arriving tomorrow and you can bet they have no rations with them either."

"They never do." I handed him the empty bowl. "Thank you, my friend."

As I stepped out with the saddle over my shoulder, I just blended in with the milling mass of soldiers. My next task was to get a horse. I watched as the three regiments rode out followed by the artillery battery. The infantry had already marched out and the camp began to empty a little. I struck out for the smell of horse manure. If there were any horses which could be stolen then they would be where the cavalry had camped. It looked ominously empty. I saw that they had a blacksmith set up. I heard the farrier as he hammered a shoe.

"You have a warm job, my friend."

He laughed, "Only the cook is warmer. Come and get a warm, my friend." He saw my saddle. "I take it we eat meat tonight?"

"Yes. She was lame."

"There are too many lame horses."

"Is there any chance of a replacement? I need to deliver a message to Astorga."

"The only way is to get an order from Marshal Soult himself. We have lost too many for them to be given away." His eyes narrowed, "If this is an important message then the Duke will sanction it."

"It is not important. It is just a list of casualties. You know how Berthier is."

"He is a bookkeeper and not a soldier. You are welcome to wait here close the warm in case one turns up."

And so, I spent the afternoon with the farrier. It was productive. He knew the exact numbers of horses and guns. I would be able to flesh out Sharp's report; if I could ever get back to our own lines. It was getting on towards dark when I heard the sound of hooves coming from the south. It was reinforcements for Soult. The troopers had stiffened white uniforms. The high passes must have been horrific. Even as they stooped two troopers fell from their saddles. Their comrades quickly grabbed them and brought them over to the fire.

The Brigadier began to rub the hands of one of them. "They are frozen! They will die."

I took out the bottle of brandy and poured a little down the throat of the younger of the two troopers. He was blue with the cold. "Cover him with your blankets!" I had seen enough men on the point of freezing to death and knew what to do. The second trooper was a little older. I poured some brandy down his throat. The first one was a little less blue. I risked another mouthful of brandy. Too much could kill him. Thankfully he coughed. His comrades continued to cover him with blankets although the fire was having a beneficial effect. A second shot of brandy made the life of the other more certain.

Eventually, they opened their eyes. The Brigadier shook me by the hand. "I think…"

"Major, Major Colbert…"

"I think, Major Colbert, that you have just saved their lives. My men owe you." He seemed to notice the saddle. It was still the same one we had taken from the despatch rider. It had the panniers for despatches. "A despatch rider without a horse eh?"

"Have you got one you could loan me?"

He chuckled, "As it happens, we have a spare one. Poor Antoine fell from his mount and into a gorge but I cannot simply give it to you."

"It is army business and I will be returning."

"But who knows where we shall be or if you will return. The guerrillas do like to ambush despatch riders such as you, major."

I knew he was getting somewhere and I smiled, "What do you suggest, Brigadier?"

"We do owe you so perhaps the brandy..."

"Done."

"And that pistol looks to be a fine weapon."

"You would leave me defenceless?"

He tapped my saddle. "I see you have another one there, Major."

He was sharp. Luckily my rifle was hidden by my French cape else he might have wanted that. I held out my hand, "A deal," I leaned in, "and a little tip Brigadier, get to the canteen early tonight. There is horse stew on the menu."

"Then it is a deal. Come and we will get the horse. He has not been ridden since yesterday, he should be fresh. And thank you for the information about the food. There are ten infantry regiments and twenty guns heading up this road. The food will soon run out!"

The horse was a magnificent one. He was jet black. He helped me to saddle him.

"What is his name?" I put my foot in the stirrup and hauled myself up.

"Killer." He laughed, "It is our little joke for poor Antoine was the only one who could ride him. All his other riders were thrown. Who knows, he might have thrown Antoine into the gorge. Perhaps you may have better luck."

He and the troopers laughed at the joke. I did not mind. My first horse had been called Killer and he had saved my life. This was fate and I waved at the Chasseurs. I was forced to head south, away from the army but I was mounted and I was still at liberty. Where there was life there was hope.

Chapter 23

I rode south-east acutely aware that I needed another route. There had been a wooden signpost on the road. I saw the broken trunk in the ground. Obviously, the post itself had been used for firewood but it told me that there would be a road either on the left or the right. I found a wide cart track and it led to the left. I pulled the reins around. It was now dark and the snow had returned but I had eaten well. I had rested and I had a relatively fresh mount. I would ride all night if necessary.

The road was fairly straight and it took me over a small hill. The direction appeared to be to the north. I would need to turn west but that would be dictated by the appearance of a road. I decided that I risked death if I continue to play the Frenchman and I discarded the shako and donned my helmet once more. After a couple of hours of riding, I stopped to check the girths. There was a puddle of melting snow which Killer lapped up and I loaded my last pistol.

Once back in the saddle I realised we were slowly descending. Ahead of me, I saw the lights of a small village. I wondered how the Spaniards would view me. I decided not to risk an encounter. From the lights, I saw that the village was laid out in a cross. That meant roads coming from four points of the compass. I took a chance and I headed across a field to what I hoped would be a road to Lugo. The weather must have been warming slightly for the ground was turning to a slushy brown mess. I wondered if I had miscalculated when I saw a gate. I did not know the horse well enough to risk a jump and so I opened the gate and let myself through. The road did, indeed, head north-west. I could see, some way in the distance, the bivouac fires burning. I headed along the track which looked to be the way the people of the village walked into Lugo. That gave me hope for it meant that Lugo would not be too far away.

I must have been travelling longer than I had thought for dawn began to break when I was still some way from my destination. I heard the crack and thunder of cannon. It was a heavy sound and I knew that it must be the French eight pounders. Their attack was underway.

I urged my horse on. I had to find a way into the town without getting shot by both sides! The weather came to my aid. It had become slightly warmer and it began to rain. It was driving sleet. Although not very pleasant to ride through I hoped that I would avoid detection by the French as I was coming through their lines. I halted and loaded my rifle. I would need the firepower as I only had one pistol.

It was now daylight. It was a damp and grey sunless day and I felt chilled to the bone. The track joined a larger road coming from the east. Ahead of me, I saw blue uniforms and the smoke from cannon and muskets. I took shelter from both the rain and the eyes of the French in a stand of trees. There was no way that I could break through the lines here. There was heavy skirmishing and the crack of French cannon. Occasionally one of the small horse guns would fire in return but I knew they would do little damage. The British did have the advantage that they could shelter and fire from behind buildings and walls.

The terrain meant that cavalry were useless and if I tried to cross I would stand out like a sore thumb. I was forced to wait for a lull in the fighting. I knew there would be one. Cannon and muskets, especially the French, became clogged and blocked by the poor-quality black powder. I waited patiently for them to stop firing. As soon as I saw men relieving themselves down the barrels of their guns, I knew that the firing had ceased; at least for a while. I took off my helmet and hid it beneath my cape. I nudged Killer forward. I approached the French lines and the guns slowly.

When I neared the French guns the captain of the first piece said. "Are the cavalry coming to watch now?"

There was no love lost between the French cavalry and the artillery. I decided to use that to my advantage, "I could break through their lines on my own!" I feigned a drunken voice.

The whole gun crew fell about laughing. They all knew about the glory of hunting cavalrymen.

I drew my sword. "You do not believe me? I will show you how a cavalryman fights! On Killer! We ride to glory!" I galloped across the open ground towards the British lines. I had deceived the French who stood and watched in amazement as this lunatic charged the whole of the British army. I quickly sheathed my sword and donned my helmet. I felt ball from the British lines zip past me. I yelled, "British officer coming in! British officer!"

The balls still flew until I heard a voice shout, "Stop firing lads. It's that mad major!"

The firing ceased and I hurtled through the green jackets. I saw a familiar face, "Rifleman Plunet! Thank God you recognised me."

"I didn't really sir but I recognised the uniform and knew that there was only one mad bugger daft enough to do that."

"Where is headquarters?"

The general is close to the bridge over the river, sir, Black Bob is putting powder under it in case we have to blow it."

I made my way through congested streets. They were all filled with infantry who were filtering down to the front lines. I saw a despondent looking Sharp slumped outside a building with a Union Flag hanging from the balcony. I knew it must be the headquarters.

"Now then Sergeant Sharp, why are you so miserable?"

Joy lit up his face. "I was worried you had been caught, sir."

"You know me, Sharp. Always land on my feet. Watch my horse, he is called Killer."

Lieutenant Stanhope and the generals were all in what had been the dining room of the house they had commandeered. "Ah, Matthews! Well done. You have made it. Your Sergeant Sharp brought us news of the attack and we were well prepared."

"This is just the advance guard sir. Last night he received reinforcements. He has another cavalry regiment but even worse is the news that he has ten infantry regiments and twenty guns which just arrived in his camp."

"That is serious news. It means he will launch a major attack tomorrow."

"That would be my guess, sir."

"Then we disengage tonight. When the firing ceases I want the bivouac fires lit and we will leave quietly."

General Paget asked, "And when do we blow the bridge, sir?"

"We do not General, that would tell them that we had left. We will try to push on to Corunna. The cavalry should be there now and hopefully so will Admiral Hood. Have your rifles cover the retreat. I think that the Light Brigade has done enough. Keep one company of the rifles and General Crauford can take the rest over the mountains to Vigo. I would have them safe and I hope we will not need them again this campaign."

General Paget and the other generals left. There were just the three of us in the room. "Well Major what can you tell me of the French?"

"They are suffering just as much as we are, sir."

"Are they indeed? Would it surprise you to know, Major Matthews that we have lost over four thousand men so far and only five hundred of them in combat? It is an appalling waste. I am happy that I sent the artillery and the cavalry away. We shall need them before too long. I would be surprised if the French have lost so many."

"Many men returned today, uncle when we turned to face the French."

"And that is good but it does not excuse their behaviour on the road." He smiled at me. "You had better get some rest, Major. I wish you to ride to Betzanos. It is only twelve miles from Corunna. We may need to find somewhere to face Soult if we are to embark the rest of the men without loss."

"Yes, sir."

I was, in truth, exhausted. I was no longer the young French Chasseur. I was almost thirty-two. I felt sixty-two. I was cheered by Sharp who was keen to know how I come to obtain such a fine horse. "Let us find somewhere to snatch an hour or so of sleep and then I will tell you."

We were woken, by Lieutenant Stanhope, at nine. "The army will leave in an hour, Major Matthews."

"Thank you, Stanhope. Just one more ride and this nightmare should be over eh?"

"I have seen some glory too sir, along with the horrors. I have learned much but I would serve in a fighting regiment. It has not sat well with me to merely fetch and carry while others have fought and died."

"I too was an aide."

He laughed, "With respect sir, you were more of an advisor than an aide. You have seen more action during this campaign than any man alive. I know my uncle appreciates all that you have done for him and the army."

We rode hard and passed through Quitterez just after dawn. We paused only to speak with the Commissary officers who were organising the supplies for the army. Sir John knew that his men would have to fight a battle to enable us to leave. He wanted a better-fed army.

Betzanos was disappointing. It would not suit a defence. We arrived in the late afternoon and so I decided to wait until the following morning to make a judgement. The war had not touched Betzanos yet and we found both rooms and food. We ate and slept better than for some time.

Daylight confirmed my view. "Sergeant Sharp, find the General and tell him that Betzanos is unsuitable. I shall push on and see if there is not something better in Corunna."

I saw the defensive site the moment I approached the town. The river ran to my right and in front of me towered two hills, one higher than the other. The one close to the small village looked perfect. There were rocks and bushes to afford shelter to the riflemen. This would be the perfect place to halt the French. I stopped in the village to water my horse. I had a couple of words in Spanish and I learned that the village was called Elvina and the hill Monte Mero. I thanked the man and returned to the road which ran between the village and the river. As I descended into Corunna, I saw that it was barely two miles from the port. It afforded the best opportunity for embarkation.

I saw a small flotilla of ships in the harbour. There looked to be about four transports, a couple of battleships and some frigates. It was secure but there were not enough ships to take off the whole of the army.

By the time I reached the harbour, it was noon and I watched as a boat pulled away from the flagship. I waited patiently for its arrival. It was a flag lieutenant. He looked to be even younger than Lieutenant Stanhope. "Are you one of the Admiral's aides?"

"Yes, sir."

"I am Major Matthews, the aide to Lieutenant-General Sir John Moore. The army is less than two days away and we will need to embark as quickly as possible for the French are hard on our heels." I waved a hand at the transports. "We will need more ships than this."

"The Admiral knows sir. The rest of the transports should be here by this evening or tomorrow at the latest. They are only coming from Vigo. They should have picked up General Crauford and his men." I felt relieved. "Would you care to come aboard and speak with the admiral yourself?"

I knew that would delay me by some hours. I was keen to return to the army. "No, thank you, Lieutenant, I must report the good news to the general."

He hesitated, "Sir is it true we have been soundly whipped by the French?"

I saw the boat's crew listening intently. "Listen, young man, I have been with this army since we landed in August with Sir Arthur Wellesley. We have defeated the French every time we have fought them. Had our Spanish allies done what they promised then you would not have to embark us here for we would have held Madrid. The army you take off may be ragged and hurt but they hold their heads high. They have defeated everything the French sent their way including Bonaparte's vaunted Guards so remember that!"

The young officer recoiled, "Sir, I am sorry, and I meant no disrespect but the newspapers at home said…"

"Do not believe newspapers Lieutenant. They are written by men sitting safely behind desks in London who are reading reports of casualties. They are not at the battlefront. I would have liked to have newspapers on this retreat."

"Why sir?"

"They keep your feet warm and burn well! They are the only use I have for such things."

I saw the grins on the boat crews. I saluted, mounted Killer and rode back through the town. As I did so I passed through the market which was just about to close up. I saw some apples left and I haggled for them with the owner. He was grateful for the three copper coins I gave him. I put most of them in my bags but I gave four to Killer. He had deserved it for he had not put a foot wrong since I had bought him.

I reached the town of Betzanos just before the first of the army. I took rooms in the only inn in the town. It was tiny but it would accommodate the general, at least. I was able to watch the weary warriors dragging themselves along the road. The advance regiments of Sir John Hope's Division still marched but they looked like an army of bandits rather than the smart redcoats who had left England all those months ago. I saluted the general. Sir, I have taken a room for Sir John."

"Good fellow. He is with the main column." He dismounted wearily and approached me quietly, "Well Matthews, is it far?"

"Twelve miles sir. We can do it in one day."

"Thank God. And the ships?"

I shook my head, "They are expected, sir, in a day or so."

"By God, I hope you are right. I am not certain if these fellows have any fight left in them."

"I believe they will fight sir. It is retreating they have little stomach for."

He laughed, "You are probably right." He seemed to notice Killer. "That is a fine-looking horse, French is it?" I nodded, "How did you get him?"

"I swapped a Frenchman a pistol and a bottle of brandy for him."

He laughed so loudly that his men all stared at him. "By God Matthews but you are a rum fellow! I shall miss you when I get back to England. Never know just what you are going to do and say eh?"

I put Killer in the stable of the inn and sat outside watching the troops as they marched in. They had all been fed in the last day and were not as hungry as in previous marches but they all that sullen look on their faces. They resented running from the Duke of Damnation as Soult had been dubbed. Sergeant Sharp rode alongside Lieutenant Stanhope and they followed a tired-looking General Moore.

He dismounted when he saw me. "I have a room for you General."

"Good fellow and I see what you mean about Betzanos. How far is it to Corunna?"

"Just twelve miles but I have to report there are only four transports in the harbour as yet. The Admiral expected them at any time."

He put his hand on my back, "Tell me more but tell me when we are inside. I am chilled to the bone. And I wish to be away from prying ears. Morale is not high."

The innkeeper, at my behest, had built up the fire and it felt quite cosy. It became even more so when Stanhope and Secretary Colborne joined us. Sir John rubbed his hands and then turned his back to the fire. Well, Matthews if the ships are not ready can we defend against the French? We have outrun 'em but they will catch us up of that I am certain."

The innkeeper had brought in some bread, wine and cheese for us. I broke the bread into two lumps. I placed the bottle of wine behind the two lumps of bread. "The port is here and the road has to cross these two hills. The first one is higher but the second, the one closer to Corunna, the Monte Mero, is the easiest to protect. The river means you cannot be outflanked on that side. I think we can hold them and it is less than two miles to the port."

"Good, you have done well. If God and the Duke of Dalmatia allow, we may yet pull off this miracle and embark the army."

He poured us all a glass of wine. "Here's to my little band. You have all done remarkably well."

We nodded and drank the rough red wine. "And now Major Matthews I have one more task for you and the redoubtable Sergeant Sharp. I wish you to ascertain the numbers of Soult's advance guard and, if you can, the number of his guns."

"Yes, sir."   .

"But if you cannot then return without risk to yourself. If I have to fight him without knowing numbers then so be it."

"I will do my best sir."

Once outside I gave half of the apples I had bought to Sharp. "We had better feed up the horses, we are going out again."

Sharp was sanguine about the whole thing. "Well, sir we shan't have to do this much more."

"No, but we had better load up now. We know not when we will be able to do so again." I loaded my two pistols, carbine and rifle. The rifle was so handy that I knew we had to get one for Sharp. It could keep an enemy at bay. We rode through the army. The ones we passed were the stragglers. We saw the last of the women and the children. There were just a handful now and I hoped that my squadron had found Baby Martin and the Macgregors.

One limping private of the 82nd held up his hand and leaned on his musket. "How much farther sir, I am almost done in."

"Less than a mile to Betzanos and shelter. Then just twelve miles and we shall all be on ships for England."

He shook his head, "I'd rather fight the Frogs sir. Why doesn't the General fight them? We can beat them!"

"I know you can but Sir John knows we cannot win this campaign. Do not worry we shall come back. Keep up your spirits."

We offered encouragement to the stragglers as we made our way through them. Then there was a gap and we met the reserve division. Sir Edward had halted them and was talking to the two Generals, Anstruther and Disney. "Ah Matthews, are the ships here yet?"

"Not enough for the whole army but we are promised them."

He nodded philosophically. "And you?"

"Sir John wishes to now the dispositions of the enemy and their numbers."

"I could tell him that, my dear fellow; far too many of them. It's the guns you see. They seem to have an inexhaustible supply of them."

"That is what he needs to know my lord. If you could mention to your chaps that I will be out there, I would appreciate it. I don't fancy a musket ball between the eyes from one of our own fellows."

"I will pass the word but they all seem to know you. You have become a bit of a legend, Matthews; the ghost who vanishes behind the lines."

"Just so long we don't become real ghosts." I heard the pop of muskets ahead. "It seems the French are probing again, my lord. We will see if we can sneak behind their lines."

To the north of the road, there were thick woods. I knew that further away was the river. It meant we had a chance to climb through the woods and be able to spy down upon them. In normal circumstances, the woods would have been filled with light infantry but they were pressing hard after General Paget. I hoped that the woods be empty. It was our only chance.

The slippery snow made the going treacherous but I felt more confident that we would not trip over French vedettes. We climbed, twisting and turning through the trees which soon soaked us through. The sound of the muskets was fading as we headed further up the slope. We had travelled about half a mile or so when we came upon a clearing. We halted. We both knew better than to move into the open without first ensuring that we were unseen. Sharp pointed, "Look, sir, we have a good view down the road from here."

He was right. Although the visibility was not the best, we were able to see the blue snake of men marching from the east. I took out the telescope I had acquired and scanned the column. I could see that, while they were mainly light infantry there were grenadiers and fusiliers amongst them. I looked ahead and saw three batteries of eight pounders. That was the answer the General was seeking. I moved the telescope to view the rear of the column and I saw there the Dragoons and Chasseurs. It was fortunate that the battlefield would not suit cavalry. I was about to put the telescope away when Sharp shouted a warning. "Sir, Hussars!"

At the other side of the clearing, some one hundred and fifty yards away were six Hussars. They saw us and urged their mounts up the slope. "Carbine, Sharp!"

I took out the rifle and sighted on the lead rider. The gun bucked as I fired. One of the Hussars fell clutching his shoulder. I took out my carbine and fired at the same time as Sharp. Sharp's shot threw a second Hussar from his horse while mine hit a horse which threw its rider to the ground. Drawing our pistols, we both fired and another rider fell. "At them!"

There were only two unwounded troopers and we had the slope in our favour. We galloped towards them. I holstered my pistol and drew my sword. The French sabre had not changed since I had been in the Chasseurs. It was a slashing weapon. It worked best in a melee but in a sword fight my longer straighter blade had the edge. The keen hussar leaned forward in his saddle as he aimed his horse at me. I pulled my arm back and, as he slashed across, I stabbed him in the chest. I kept my arm stiff. Had I had a blunt lump of iron he would have been knocked from the saddle. As it was, he was dead when the blade pierced his chest and struck his heart. He was thrown from the saddle. I wheeled Killer around and he responded magnificently. It was a sergeant who was fighting Sharp and the Frenchman was having the better of it. War is, despite what poets say, not honourable and I brought my sword around to sever his spine and almost slice him in two. I carried on up the hill. "Let's get out of here, Sharp!"

I had no doubt that there would be pursuit but I wanted the luxury of a head start. We did not return the way we had come. I headed directly over the hill and down to the Mandeo River. We followed it down. It was a steep slope and a jumble of rocks. It would slow any pursuit. After a mile and with no sound of anyone following us, I headed south and we climbed to reach the tiny village of Armea. There was a track of sorts and eventually, we came out on the Betzanos road. We managed to enter the town unseen.

Sir Edward was surprised when we walked into the inn being used by the staff. "How did you get by my guards? I left word that I wanted to be notified when you were seen."

"Then you might want to place some sentries along the road to Armea. We came that way and saw no uniforms neither blue nor red."

He waved over an aide and rattled off his orders.

Sir John said, "Well?"

"There are at least three batteries of eight pounders and there are regular as well as light infantry."

"Then he will seek battle."

"They were still a couple of miles from the outskirts. If will probably be the morning before he reaches us."

Sir John seemed almost distracted. "We will embark all but three guns and the last of the cavalry when we reach Corunna. If Major Matthews is correct then we can hold Soult with just infantry and three guns."

As I retired for the night, I reflected that there was a great deal of pressure on me. Sir John was making decisions based purely on my views.

Chapter 24

When we reached Corunna, the transport had yet to arrive. The unpleasant weather we had endured had driven the fleet out to sea. Luckily there were shoes, weapons, ammunition and most important of all, hot food. The camp followers were sent to the harbour to board the transports which were already there. Sir John embarked all but a handful of light guns. When they had been kitted out and fed General Hope and General Baird led their men to the Monte Mero where they dug in on the slope facing the French. During the night of the 12th of January, the only bridge over the Mero was destroyed and we had one secure flank. If Soult was wily enough, he could attempt to turn our right flank. To do so he would have to best the two battalions of Guards who were our right bastion. Along with the Light Brigade, the Guards' discipline had been superb during the retreat. They were the steadiest troops we had.

I rode Killer down to the harbour when the transports began to arrive on the morning of the 13th. Boats ferried out the wounded and the cavalrymen. Only horses which were fit were to be embarked. I watched as one trooper from the 15th bade farewell to his horse and was rowed out to the transport. There were tears in his eyes. I could understand his feelings. Amazingly the horse jumped into the water and tried to swim out to the ship. It was a mark of the bond between horse and rider. I, for one, would not have left Badger behind. I was just grateful that the cavalry had departed some days earlier.

We now had a much smaller army. Six thousand men had fallen or been lost during the retreat. The wounded, the cavalry and the artillery had all left for England but the ones who remained were all keen to finally get to grips with the Duke of Damnation. All the frustration of the last month had come to a head. These soldiers would not slip away into the night; they would fight for the general who had brought them from a seeming trap to the edge of a miracle. I felt quite proud to have been part of it. There was no glory but there had been a bond between soldiers and officers which was rare to see. That had been down to Lieutenant-General Sir John Moore. He had not had the victories of Sir Arthur but, in my view, he had achieved far more. I was hopeful that when he returned to Portugal, he would make a real difference.

The loading of the ships seemed to take as long as the unloading had all those months ago at Montego Bay. We could not load the whole army so long as Soult still threatened us. There was no need for a scouting expedition. We could see the French as they brought up regiment after regiment; gun after gun. We had nowhere to go and Soult was in no hurry. He wanted a victory having chased us all the way across Galicia.

Sir John was in good spirits on the 16th of January 1809. We went to visit with Sir Edward first. Sir Edward had the reserve; it was made up of the rearguard regiments who remained. They had been the steadiest of troops during the retreat and the ones who had borne the brunt of the fighting. "Sir Edward, I know not when the attack will start but I wish you and your fellows to take advantage. Attack when you deem it appropriate. I trust your judgement."

"Thank you, Sir John. We will not let you down."

As we rode to join Generals Hope and Baird Lieutenant-General Moore said to me, "I want you and your sergeant to ginger up any of the regiments who look to be in trouble."

"Me, Sir John?"

He laughed, "You and Sharp are the ghosts of Galicia. That is the name the chaps have given you. There are all sorts of ludicrous stories about you dining with Soult; stealing Bonaparte's horse and the like. All nonsense, of course, but the rank and file believe it. You are a good luck charm and I will make a covenant with the devil himself to escape this trap."

"Very well, Sir John."

We reached the crest of the ridge. The other aides dismounted and set up the table with the maps. Sir John took the telescope from Lieutenant Stanhope and surveyed the scene. "Well Baird, they are about to come on and if I am not mistaken it seems that your division is their target."

Sir John Baird had the exposed right flank. "Then they shall have to endure the fire of the Foot Guards and they have been itching to have a go at the Frogs!" He saluted, "I shall see that they get a warm reception."

There were three French columns heading towards our lines. Voltigeurs, swarming like insects, flitted before them and the eight pounders began to fire at our defences. The Voltigeurs were, however, facing the company of rifles we had retained and were struggling. The sound of the drums and the shouts of, '*En Avant! Tue!*' filled the air. The British waited stoically. Such noise and bravado might make other soldiers quake but the red coats were made of sterner stuff and they waited for the blue columns to reach them.

The sheer weight of numbers began to throw some of the picquets back. Not so the Guards who stood steadfastly. "Come with me gentlemen, let us ginger them up eh? We have watched for long enough."

I drew my carbine and nodded to Sharp to do the same as we descended to the point of the attack. The French had almost gained the village of Elvina. As soon as the men saw the general there was a huge cheer. "Come on my fine fellows; let us be about these Frenchmen eh?"

There was a second cheer and the line surged forward. I saw a Voltigeurs raise his musket to shoot at the general. I had my carbine up and I fired in an instant. It was a lucky shot for it took the man in the head and flung him down the slope.

Sir John Moore nodded approvingly, "Fine shot Matthews. You must come hunting with me when we are back in England. You have the eye for it."

The French also had their eye in and cannonballs began to whizz around us. I saw one of the West Kent privates as a ball took off his head. Suddenly Sir John's horse began to rear and, as he was controlling it, a second ball took the leg from another fusilier. He began to roll in the mud screaming and clutching at his stump. I could see that some of the other West Kent men were looking nervously towards the French. With his horse under control, Sir

John said, "This is nothing, my lads. Keep your ranks. Take that man away. My good fellow, don't make such a noise; we must bear these things better."

Miraculously the man stopped shouting and the line steadied. Such was the effect of Sir John Moore. The King's Own were in danger of being encircled. "Matthews, go and order the 42nd to realign to the right."

"Sir."

I rode down to the Highlanders. "Who is in command here?"

A captain stepped forward. "I am, Major, the colonel and the major have been taken to the dressing station."

"Very well. 42nd dress your ranks!" The lines became straighter. "Sergeant Major I want the whole line to support the King's Own."

"Yes, sir."

With remarkable calmness and efficiency, the whole line turned by thirty degrees.

"Open fire!"

The rippling volleys began to strike the side of the French column which found itself facing not only the King's Own but the Highlanders too.

A French Voltigeurs officer, not more than twenty yards away aimed a pistol at me. I did two things at once: I drew my pistol and I moved my head. The ball scored a line through the fur of my helmet. I raised the pistol and shot the man dead. The 42nd cheered and a voice shouted, "Another victim of the Ghost of Galicia!"

"Carry on, captain."

"Thank you, Major."

I rejoined Sir John. He patted me on the back, "That is exactly how it should be done."

I nodded. As I had ridden back, I had seen the transports still being loaded and the troops watching from their decks. They had a grandstand view of proceedings.

Sir John rubbed his hands as the 42nd and the 50th began to retake the village; driving the French down the slope. The 4th began to edge into the village too. Suddenly the 42nd, probably thinking they had been relieved, began to pull back. "Come along gentlemen. Let us straighten the line." We reached the 42nd which were falling back. "My brave 42nd, rejoin your comrades."

They all about-faced and rejoined the battle. It was at that moment when I heard the bugles and trumpets as Sir Edward chose his moment well and launched the attack with his rearguard.

"Bravely done Paget!" shouted Sir John as they marched towards the enemy. They say that it is darkest before the dawn. I am afraid that the darkness came after dawn. General Baird came to report that the attack on the right flank had been repulsed when he was thrown from his horse. His right arm hung in tatters. He had been hit by grapeshot. "Take the general to the rear!" Aides quickly helped the barely conscious general back to the surgeon.

There was another crack and this time it was Sir John Moore who was thrown from his horse. I dismounted. Suddenly I felt myself being thrown to the ground as another cannonball struck. I was fortunate. The ball struck Killer who died instantly. Had I not dismounted I would have been dead along with him. His shattered body lay bleeding on that mountain in Galicia. I struggled to my feet, aided by Sharp. Stanhope knelt by his uncle.

"Get a surgeon now!"

I knelt on the other side of Sir John. He looked to be at peace and he smiled. I looked for the wound. He had been struck by grapeshot and his uniform had been driven into his shattered shoulder. His left arm was attached merely by a piece of skin. His ribs had been smashed and stuck out at angles and his chest muscles had been torn by the impact.

The surgeon reached us within moments. He took one look and muttered, "Hopeless."

Sir John heard and just nodded his head. I turned to the aides, "Get a blanket and we will take him away from the battle."

Surprisingly enough he seemed at peace and was watching the 42nd as they drove the French from Elvina. The aides brought the blanket and we eased the battered and broken general on to it. As he was being lifted on to it the hilt of his sword jammed into the open wound. Lieutenant Stanhope began to unbuckle the offending object.

Sir John restrained him, "I had rather it go out of the field with me."

His nephew nodded.

"Sharp, give us a hand. Each of you, pick up the blanket together." Eight of us held the blanket holding the battered and broken body of the great leader. "Now together by the right."

As we walked from the field we did so in silence. Sir John, who miraculously was still conscious, kept speaking all the way down. "I fear I shall be a long time in dying." Stanhope looked at me and I nodded encouragingly. He needed to hold it together for his uncle. "It is a great uneasiness. It is great pain."

I leaned in as we walked, "Should I get you some brandy, Sir John?"

He shook his head, "I have always wished to die this way."

As we reached the headquarters I wondered if I should be so calm when my time came. We gently laid him down and he nodded his head. He closed his eyes and I wondered if the end had come.

Every time anyone entered the room he said, "Are the French beat yet?"

Finally, as dawn began to break Sir Edward came in and said, "Sir John, the battle is won. You have a great victory and the French are defeated."

He nodded and, looking at his nephew said, "I hope the people of England will be satisfied."

I said, "They will Sir John, they will." Those were the last words he said although he tried to take off his sword. I reached down and unbuckled it. He was so close to the end that he could not speak but his eyes went to his nephew. I handed the sword to him and Sir Moore nodded. A few minutes later, just before eight o'clock, Lieutenant-General Sir John Moore died. I have no shame in telling you that all of us wept for he was a great man and a kind man.

We carried his body out of the headquarters building and found a piece of earth close to the Corunna bastion. There we dug his grave and, wrapping his body in his cloak, buried Sir John Moore. As the French cannon began to fire at the fleet we hurried to our ships and left Corunna. As I stood on the quarter deck of the transport with Sir Edward and the general's nephew, I knew that we would return. Sir John had saved the army and his legacy would be that we returned and freed Iberia.

Epilogue

They were five sad days onboard the ship. We had much to reflect upon. The authorities refused to allow us to land in daylight. It was bad enough that we had lost a popular general. The last thing the government wanted was for people to see the pitiful condition of its army. We were landed at Ramsgate. I took my leave of Lieutenant Stanhope first as Sir Edward oversaw Sir John's papers and belongings.

"Sir, I want to thank you for all that you have taught me. I believe I will be a better officer." He clutched at his uncle's sword. "And I will do honour by this weapon."

"Your uncle was a great man, Lieutenant, you have much to live up to."

"I know." He saluted and left.

Sharp gathered our belongings and led his horse from the ship. She had been one of the few horses we had saved. Sharp would not have left Maria and I could not see him leaving this one either. "I will go and hire you a horse, sir."

"Thank you, Sergeant Sharp."

Sir Edward came down the gangplank. He held out his hand. "It has been a pleasure to serve with you, Major. My brother spoke highly of you and I can see why. I would deem it an honour if you would serve as an aide to me when I am given my next command."

"And that in itself is an honour, my lord, but I am a cavalryman. If this campaign has taught me nothing else it has taught me that we are lucky in this country; we lead the bravest soldiers in Europe and I would continue to do so."

He nodded, "That is a good answer but I hope to serve with you again, Major Matthews."

"And you too General Paget."

We rode into the barracks at ten o'clock. The sentries snapped to attention as we entered. Perhaps word had been sent ahead of our arrival, I do not know, but the troopers who had served with me and left a week earlier all stood with their horses and saluted.

Colonel Fenton and the Major walked up to me and shook my hand.

"Major Matthews, you are a credit to this regiment and to the army."

"Thank you, sir. Sir John was a great man."

"He was and now that Sir Arthur has been exonerated, perhaps he can take Sir John's place."

"Perhaps. And now sir, if you don't mind, I would like to change. I have worn these clothes for almost three weeks and even I cannot stand my own smell."

"Of course."

As Sharp and I turned to head to my quarters I saw a huddle of civilians. Annie Macgregor stood there with her two children. They were clean, smartly dressed and had some flesh on their bones. In her arms was Baby Martin.

I smiled as I walked up to her. She looked like a new woman. I could now see that she was barely twenty years old. "I am glad to see you well Annie."

"And it is down to you sir. Joe told me what you said and did and I am much beholden to you. I have a job in the laundry!"

She seemed excited.

"And I am pleased that you look well and how is Baby Martin?"

"He is healthy and well but he is no longer Baby Martin, sir. We had him baptised and he is Robert Matthew Martin, by your leave."

She looked at me as though I might be offended. I smiled and stroked the baby's head. "I am honoured and you will always have a home here."

"Thank you, sir."

As I walked to my quarters, I reflected that life went on. Sir John had died and this young child was being raised in an army barracks. Who knew just what he might achieve? My mind was eased a little but that night, when alone in my room, I drank a toast and shed a tear in memory of Lieutenant-General Sir John Moore, the saviour of our army.

The End

Glossary

Fictional characters are in italics

Cesar Alpini- Robbie's cousin and the head of the Sicilian branch of the family

Sergeant Alan Sharp- Robbie's servant

Cacadores- Portuguese light infantry

Captain Robbie (Macgregor) Matthews-illegitimate son of the *Count of Breteuil*

Colonel James Selkirk- War department

Colpack-fur hat worn by the guards and elite companies

Crack- from the Irish 'craich', good fun, enjoyable

Joe Seymour- Corporal and then Sergeant 11th Light Dragoons

Joseph Fouché- Napoleon's Chief of Police and Spy catcher

Lieutenant Jonathan Teer- Commander of the Black Prince

Middy- Midshipman (slang)

musketoon- Cavalry musket

Paget Carbine- Light Cavalry weapon

pichet- a small jug for wine in France

Pierre Boucher-Ex-Trooper/Brigadier 17th Chasseurs

Pompey- naval slang for Portsmouth

Prefeito – Portuguese official

Roast Beef- French slang for British soldiers

Rooking- cheating a customer

Snotty- naval slang for a raw lieutenant

Tarleton Helmet- Headgear worn by Light cavalry until 1812

Windage- the gap between the ball and the wall of the cannon which means the ball does not fire true.

Maps

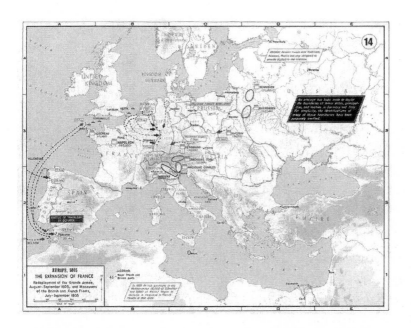

This work is in the United States because it is a work prepared by an officer or employee of the United States Government as part of that person's official duties under the terms of Title 17, Chapter 1, Section 105 of the US Code.

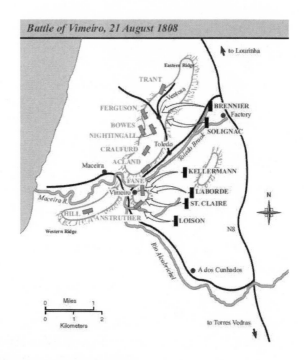

Battle of Vimeiro, 21 August 1808

Battle of Roliça August 1808
British losses- 441 killed wounded or captured including 190 dead from the 1st/29th
French losses- 600 killed wounded or captured, 3 guns

Battle of Vimeiro August 1808
British losses- 134 killed, 534 wounded, 51 missing (the majority of those killed came from the 20th Light Dragoons)
French losses- 1,500 killed and wounded. 300 captured including 4 French generals and 12 guns

Battle of Corunna January 1809
British losses-137 killed 497 wounded
French losses- 1,400 killed and wounded, 163 captured

Historical note

The 11th Light Dragoons were a real regiment. However, I have used them in a fictitious manner. They act and fight as real Light Dragoons. The battles in which they fight were real battles with real Light Dragoons present- just not the 11th.
The books I used for reference were:

- Napoleon's Line Chasseurs- Bukhari/MacBride
- Napoleon's War in Spain- Lachouque, Tranie, Carmigniani
- The Napoleonic Source Book- Philip Haythornthwaite,
- Wellington's Military Machine- Philip J Haythornthwaite
- The Peninsular War- Roger Parkinson
- Military Dress of the Peninsular War 1808-1814
- The History of the Napoleonic Wars-Richard Holmes,
- The Greenhill Napoleonic Wars Data book- Digby Smith,
- The Napoleonic Wars Vol 1 & 2- Liliane and Fred Funcken
- The Napoleonic Wars- Michael Glover
- Wellington's Regiments- Ian Fletcher.
- Wellington's Light Cavalry- Bryan Fosten
- Wellington's Heavy Cavalry- Bryan Fosten

The buying and selling of commissions were, unless there was a war, the only way to gain promotion. It explains the quotation that 'the Battle of Waterloo was won on the playing fields of Eton'. The officers all came from a moneyed background. The expression cashiered meant that an officer had had to sell his commission. Promoted sergeants were rare and had to have to done something which in modern times would have resulted in a Victoria Cross or a grave!

Colonel Selkirk is based on a real spy James Robertson who was responsible for getting Pedro Caro, 3rd Marquis of la Romana to defect to Britain from France with 8000 of his men. They were taken by British ships to Santander where they landed in August 1808. They then went onto harry Napoleon's forces. The Spanish Army had one success: Baylen 1808. Both Generals proved to be incompetent; the Spanish were less so. Nonetheless, it did have the effect of drawing away possible reinforcements for Junot.

The Braganza Royal family did flee Portugal when Junot invaded in 1807. The British urged them to go and provided an escort. The Queen had to be carried screaming to the ship as she was a little paranoid.

The fort at Coimbra was captured by students from the local university which allowed Wellesley to land his forces unmolested. The logistics of landing a fleet from Cork to coordinate and meet up with a force marching from Gibraltar in the days before radios etc is mind-blowing.

The quotation about Colonel Trant did come from Wellington. Colonel Lake did lose most of the 29th in a wild charge. He disobeyed Wellesley's orders. Had he not done so then the British would have lost a mere handful of men. As far as I know, the 20th did not scout at this battle and find the French; it was the 95th. However, the battle itself normally receives scant attention. The later battle of Vimeiro is seen as far more important for lots of reasons. However, I use Major Matthews and the 20th to assist the 95th. It is an invention of the author. The 20th did break a square at Vimeiro but their colonel, Colonel Taylor led them too far and they were attacked by dragoons. Colonel Taylor and half of his men perished at the battle. I have used DeVere instead of Taylor.

The Cintra Convention proved to be a scandal from which Burrard and Dalrymple never recovered. Both the British and Portuguese people were outraged that Junot and his army were repatriated to France on British ships. It was exacerbated by the looting of palaces and churches by the French. Sir Arthur was exonerated. One wonders what might have happened had he commanded along with Sir John Moore. Would the British Army have had the disaster of Corunna? Or perhaps it was like Dunkirk, 150 years later, the spur which would lead the British and her allies to victory.

The exchanges between Moore and Wellesley at Queluz were as reported. It implies that someone else was there as Moore died a few months later. I have used Major Matthews as the witness. The orders were as written as was Moore's instructions to the troops.

The manoeuvring in December was exactly as described and vital despatches were captured. The information was as Major Matthews reported.

Sahagun and Benevente were two of the best examples of the skill of the Earl of Uxbridge. Trooper Grisdale did, indeed, capture the general. The cavalry of the Imperial Guard was the best in Europe at that time and for them to be beaten by a retreating and dispirited army was nothing short of miraculous. Sadly because of a family disagreement, the Earl would not serve again until the Waterloo campaign. Who knows what might have ensued in the Peninsula had he led the cavalry?

The incident with the new-born baby actually happened and it was a follower from the 92nd who looked after the child. Many babies were born, and died, during the retreat. Some women were seen crawling along after the retreating army; it must have been a pitiful and dispiriting sight. One officer did pick up a child and wrap it in his coat swearing to have it looked after in England. Robbie's gesture was not unusual.

The berserk soldier holding up the retreat really happened. He had eaten raw salt fish washed down with rum. In reality, he was ridden down and trampled to death by the cavalry.

Wherever possible I have tried to use the words actually used by Wellesley and Moore. All the words used by Sir John Moore at the battle and until he died were spoken by him. I have used author's licence to add the dialogue of the others. He was a great general. Who knows if he was the equal of Wellington? However, one thing is certain; he was the only general who could have saved the army in 1808.

Major Matthews will continue to fight Napoleon and to serve Colonel Selkirk. The Napoleonic wars have barely begun and will only end on a ridge in Belgium in 1815. Robbie will be back to the same place he fought his first battles as a young trooper.

Griff Hosker November 2014

Other books
by
Griff Hosker

If you enjoyed reading this book, then why not read another one by the author?

Ancient History

The Sword of Cartimandua Series (Germania and Britannia 50 A.D. – 128 A.D.)
Ulpius Felix- Roman Warrior (prequel)
Book 1 The Sword of Cartimandua
Book 2 The Horse Warriors
Book 3 Invasion Caledonia
Book 4 Roman Retreat
Book 5 Revolt of the Red Witch
Book 6 Druid's Gold
Book 7 Trajan's Hunters
Book 8 The Last Frontier
Book 9 Hero of Rome
Book 10 Roman Hawk
Book 11 Roman Treachery
Book 12 Roman Wall
Book 13 Roman Courage

The Aelfraed Series
(Britain and Byzantium 1050 A.D. - 1085 A.D.)
Book 1 Housecarl
Book 2 Outlaw
Book 3 Varangian

The Wolf Warrior series
(Britain in the late 6th Century)
Book 1 Saxon Dawn
Book 2 Saxon Revenge

Book 3 Saxon England
Book 4 Saxon Blood
Book 5 Saxon Slayer
Book 6 Saxon Slaughter
Book 7 Saxon Bane
Book 8 Saxon Fall: Rise of the Warlord
Book 9 Saxon Throne
Book 10 Saxon Sword

The Dragon Heart Series
Book 1 Viking Slave
Book 2 Viking Warrior
Book 3 Viking Jarl
Book 4 Viking Kingdom
Book 5 Viking Wolf
Book 6 Viking War
Book 7 Viking Sword
Book 8 Viking Wrath
Book 9 Viking Raid
Book 10 Viking Legend
Book 11 Viking Vengeance
Book 12 Viking Dragon
Book 13 Viking Treasure
Book 14 Viking Enemy
Book 15 Viking Witch
Book 16 Viking Blood
Book 17 Viking Weregeld
Book 18 Viking Storm
Book 19 Viking Warband
Book 20 Viking Shadow
Book 21 Viking Legacy
Book 22 Viking Clan
Book 23 Viking Bravery

The Norman Genesis Series
Hrolf the Viking

Horseman
The Battle for a Home
Revenge of the Franks
The Land of the Northmen
Ragnvald Hrolfsson
Brothers in Blood
Lord of Rouen
Drekar in the Seine
Duke of Normandy
The Duke and the King

New World Series
Blood on the Blade
Across the Seas

**The Anarchy Series England
1120-1180**
English Knight
Knight of the Empress
Northern Knight
Baron of the North
Earl
King Henry's Champion
The King is Dead
Warlord of the North
Enemy at the Gate
The Fallen Crown
Warlord's War
Kingmaker
Henry II
Crusader
The Welsh Marches
Irish War
Poisonous Plots
The Princes' Revolt
Earl Marshal

Border Knight
1182-1300
Sword for Hire
Return of the Knight
Baron's War
Magna Carta
Welsh Wars
Henry III
The Bloody Border

Lord Edward's Archer
Lord Edward's Archer

Struggle for a Crown
1360- 1485
Blood on the Crown
To Murder A King
The Throne
King Henry IV

Modern History

The Napoleonic Horseman Series
Book 1 Chasseur a Cheval
Book 2 Napoleon's Guard
Book 3 British Light Dragoon
Book 4 Soldier Spy
Book 5 1808: The Road to Coruña
Book 6 Talavera
Waterloo

The Lucky Jack American Civil War series
Rebel Raiders
Confederate Rangers
The Road to Gettysburg

The British Ace Series
1914
1915 Fokker Scourge
1916 Angels over the Somme
1917 Eagles Fall
1918 We will remember them
From Arctic Snow to Desert Sand
Wings over Persia

Combined Operations series
1940-1945
Commando
Raider
Behind Enemy Lines
Dieppe
Toehold in Europe
Sword Beach
Breakout
The Battle for Antwerp
King Tiger
Beyond the Rhine
Korea
Korean Winter

Other Books
Carnage at Cannes (a thriller)
Great Granny's Ghost (Aimed at 9-14-year-old young people)
Adventure at 63-Backpacking to Istanbul

For more information on all of the books then please visit the author's web site at www.griffhosker.com where there is a link to contact him.

Made in the USA
Columbia, SC
27 May 2022

61015904R00157